'[Jonathan Carroll] has the magic. He'll lend you his eyes; and you will never see the world in quite the same way ever again'   Neil Gaiman

'On the level of sheer sentence construction and his pellucid prose Jonathan Carroll is among the most purely pleasing writers of the decade. Yet his elegant, entrancing novels have real depth'   *Independent*

'Carroll orchestrates this smartly layered narrative with skill, and does force you to turn the pages. File under "beachwear" and use accordingly'   *The Times*

'Imagine the sheer fun and imaginative sweep of something like *Twin Peaks* undergirded by an unwavering narrative touch and a very realistic concern with moral issues and characters'   *USA Today*

'Jonathan Carroll's books are sometimes pigeon-holed as fantasy, twentieth-century horror, literary fiction or even crime thriller. But most of all, he is a master storyteller'
                                                    Oxford Times

'Deeply layered and highly intelligent . . . [a] gripping storyline combined with a beautiful and precise use of language'   *Birmingham Post*

Jonathan Carroll was educated in the United States, but has lived in Vienna for two decades. His prize-winning novels have been translated into seventeen languages. The *Independent* has called him one of the 'most purely pleasing writers of the decade'. His most recent novel, *The Marriage of Sticks*, is also published in Indigo paperback.

By the same author

The Land of Laughs

Voice of Our Shadow

Bones of the Moon

Sleeping in Flame

A Child Across the Sky

Outside the Dog Museum

After Silence

From the Teeth of Angels

The Panic Hand

The Marriage of Sticks

JONATHAN CARROLL

Kissing the Beehive

INDIGO

An Indigo paperback
First published in Great Britain by Victor Gollancz in 1998
This paperback edition published in 1999 by Indigo,
an imprint of Orion Books Ltd,
Orion House, 5 Upper St Martin's Lane, London WC2H 9EA

Reissued 2000

A CIP catalogue record for this book is available from the
British Library.

ISBN 0 575 40291 1

Printed in Great Britain by
The Guernsey Press Co. Ltd, Guernsey, C.I.

TO

Pat Conroy

Stephen King

Michael Moorcock

Paul West

If you don't know the kind of person I am
And I don't know the kind of person you are
A pattern that others made may prevail in the world
And following the wrong god home we may miss our star

from 'A Ritual to Read to Each Other' by William Stafford

PART ONE

I do not like to eat alone and that is one of the reasons why I became famous. There is something both pathetic and unattractive about a person eating by themselves in public. Better to stay at home, drinking orange soup from a can with a handful of dry white crackers in front of the TV, than be seen sitting by yourself waiting for that forlorn single meal to be served.

I was having lunch with my agent, Patricia Chase, when I made this observation. Patricia is a big beautiful woman with balls of titanium. She looked at me as she has so often over the twenty years we've known each other – her unique mixture of amusement, exasperation and scowl.

'Where do you come up with these ideas, Sam? There's nothing *nicer* than having a meal by yourself! You bring along a book or your favorite magazine, you don't have to talk or be the life of the party, you eat at your own speed . . . I love eating by myself.'

I ignored her. 'On the other hand, the greatest thing in life is having dinner in a restaurant with a new woman. You order, and then you really get to talk with her for the first time. Everything till then has just been chatter. There's something magical about sitting with that new being in your life in a nice restaurant . . .'

She smiled and took a roll from the basket. 'Well, my boy, you've had your share of meals with new women over the years. What's the latest report on Irene?'

'She calls and taunts me with the fact she's hired one of the best divorce lawyers in the city. Then she cackles when she says how much she's going to ask for in court.'

'But you had that pre-nuptial agreement thing.'

'Those sound good when you're getting married, but somehow they go up in smoke when you're getting divorced.'

'Irene was your third wife. My God, that's a lot.'

'Just because you're mad at the fleas, doesn't mean you burn the blanket. Whoever said optimism was a good thing?'

'Seems to me that with all the money you're paying the other two, you should take Irene as strike three and just have girlfriends from now on. And speaking of money, what's up with your new novel?'

I cleared my throat because I didn't want the next sentence to come out either a peep or a squeak. 'Nothing, Patricia. Zilch. The cupboard is bare. I'm word dead.'

'This is not good news. Parma called and asked what was going on with you. He's used to chatting. He thinks you're hiding from him.'

'I am. Besides, Parma's spoiled. I gave him five books in eight years and made him a lot of money. What else does he want from me?'

She shook her head. 'It doesn't work like that. He gave you a big advance for a new book and has a right to know what's going on. Look at it from his side.'

'I can't. I have enough to look at in my own life. Everything in the book is goo. All the characters are stuck in suspended animation. The story is going nowhere.'

'The synopsis looked good.'

I shrugged. 'It's easy writing a synopsis. Ten pages of snap, crackle and pop.'

'So what are you going to do?'

'Maybe I should get married again. Take my mind off things a while.'

She sat back and had a good laugh. It was nice to see because I hadn't made anyone laugh for a long time. Especially myself.

The rest of the meal was a wrestling match between my glum and glib sides. Patricia knew me as well as anyone and could tell when I was faking it. I assumed her conversation with my editor, Aurelio Parma, had been a bad one because I was rarely summoned for a business lunch with her. Usually we spoke on the phone once or twice a month and then had a celebratory dinner whenever I handed in a new manuscript.

'How far have you gotten?'

'The man's left his wife and is with the girl.'

'That was on the first page of the synopsis, Sam!'

'I *know*, Patricia. That's what I was just telling you.'

'Well, what about . . .' She tapped her finger on the table.

'Forget it – I've thought through all the "what abouts", believe me. I started a short story but it was so dreary that even my pen threw up. I'm telling you, it's bad. It's not writer's block, it's writer's *drought*. My brain's Ethiopia these days.'

'You're lucky it hasn't happened before. You've published nine books. That's quite a few. Sounds like you're just written out.'

'Bad time for that to happen. Especially with Irene out there, sharpening her knives.'

We talked about other things, but the subject of my big silence hung over the rest of the meal like Mexico City smog. When we were finished and getting up to leave, she suggested I take a vacation.

'I hate vacations! When I was married to Michelle we went to Europe, but all I wanted to do was stay in the hotel room and watch CNN.'

'I liked Michelle.'

'I did too until I married her. She thought I could be a

great writer if I only tried harder. What did she think I was doing at that desk all day, making sushi?'

Patricia gave me one of her wise old owl looks. 'What would you rather do, write great books or ones that sell?'

'I gave up trying to astonish people a long time ago. There's a Russian proverb: "The truth is like a bee – it goes right for the eyes." One of the few truths I know about myself is I write books that are entertaining, but they'll never be great. I can live with that. I'm one of the few people I know who are genuinely grateful for what they've been given. I was in an airport one day and saw three people reading my books. I can't tell you how happy that made me.'

I thought the subject was finished, but Patricia said, 'Need makes you cry, sing or spring.'

'Huh?'

'I know those Russian proverbs too, Sam. I gave you the book, Dumbbell! It's all right to be satisfied with what you're doing if you go to bed at night feeling good. But *you* don't anymore.

'You wrote thrillers, they were successful, you were happy. Now you can't write, you're empty and sad. Maybe it's time to try and write a great book. See what happens. Maybe it'll get you out of your rut.'

There was a long pause while our eyeballs dueled.

'I can't figure out if you're a bitch or a guru for saying that.'

'A bitch. A bitch who wants you to get back to work so you can feed all your ex-wives.'

The ironic thing was the day was originally intended to be a celebration. My latest, *The Magician's Breakfast*, had just been published in paperback and I was in New York to do a signing at my friend Hans Lachner's bookstore, Cover Up.

I always like book-signings. It is one of the few times

when you are face to face with the people who have shared the most important part of your life with you – the time when you are telling them stories. Sure, you get a screwball now and then who wants you to autograph a towel, or someone you wouldn't dare sit next to on the subway, but all in all they're nice events and hearing compliments about your work doesn't hurt either. At first they scared me because I was convinced no one would show up. I will never forget the feeling of walking into that first signing session and seeing a horde of people waiting around for me to arrive. Rapture.

Hans Lachner had worked as an editor for a few years at a famous publishing house but got fed up with the politics and intrigue. When his parents died, he took his inheritance and turned it into Cover Up. It was a small store but beautifully designed, intimate, and his taste in books was impeccable. I once dropped in and saw him deep in conversation with Gabriel García Márquez. Later when I told him I didn't know he spoke Spanish, Hans said, 'I don't. But I learned *that* day.'

He had recommended my third novel, *The Tattooed City*, to a Hollywood producer he knew who bought it and eventually turned it into a film. I owed him a great deal and did whatever I could to repay him.

After my lunch with Patricia, I must have walked into his store looking like Peter Lorre in *M*, because Hans came right over and said I looked like shit.

'Dog or human? There's a big difference.'

'What's the matter?'

'I just had lunch with my agent and she fricasseed me.'

'Mr Bayer?'

I turned around wearing an instantaneous big smile and was greeted by a camera flash square in the puss. When the suns burned on to my retina faded, I made out a chubby woman wearing a Timberland sweatshirt and large silver-frame glasses.

11

'Would you mind, Hans?' She pushed her camera into his hand and came right up next to me. She took my arm. Hans counted to three and flashed my eyes back into blindness.

'I'm Tanya. When you sign my books, remember I'm Tanya.'

'Okay.'

She took her camera back and bustled off.

Hans put his arm around my shoulder and steered me toward the back of the store where a table and chair were waiting. 'Tanya always buys two copies of your books. Gives the second to her sister.'

'God bless her.'

I sat down and the first people came up hesitantly, as if they were afraid to disturb me. I tried to be as nice as possible, always asking for their names and then signing something personal so they could have a smile when they looked at the inscription. 'Breakfast with Charles. Thanks for sharing this meal with me.' 'This Magician says hello to Jennifer.' 'To Tanya who always buys two and deserves a double thank you for her support.' Time passed as I signed and smiled and made small talk.

'My name is Veronica. I have a whole bunch, so it's fine if you just sign them and ... well, you know, just sign them.'

Hans was handing me a Coke when she came to the table so I didn't look when she spoke. I put the glass down and saw the book on top of her pile; the German edition of my first novel.

'Jeez, where'd you get this?' I smiled, looked up at her and froze. She was a California blond with great waves of platinum hair down to her shoulders. Skin so radiant and fine that if you hung around her too long you'd have to sit on your hands or else end up in trouble. Her eyes were large, green and friendly but with a depth and intelligence to them that sized you up while welcoming you at the same time. The lips were heavy and almost purple, although it was clear she wore no lipstick. It was a decadent mouth, much too decadent for the sunniness of the rest of the face. It was a contradiction I didn't know if I liked. It turned me *on*, but I didn't know if I liked it.

'I bought it in Germany when I was there. I'm trying to collect all editions of your work, but it's difficult.'

'Are you a collector?'

'Not really. I just love your books.'

I opened the cover and turned to the title page. 'And your name is—'

'Veronica. Veronica Lake.'

My pen stopped. *'What?'*

She laughed and it was as deep as a man's. 'Yup, that's the name. I guess my mother was kind of a sadist.'

'And you look so much like her! That's like naming your son Clark Gable.'

'Well, in South America they name their kids Jesus.'

'Yeah, so when they die they can go to heaven. When *you* die, you're going to Hollywood, Veronica.'

I signed the book and reached for the next. The Japanese edition. Then came the Spanish. Outside my own shelves, I'd never seen such a collection.

'You write the kind of books I would, if I could write. I understand them.'

'Will you marry me?'

She pouted sweetly. 'You're already married.'

I went back to signing. 'Not for long.'

Before we could say anything else, I felt a hand on my shoulder and smelled the memorable cologne of my memorable editor, Aurelio Parma. 'Sam the Sham. Where are the Pharaohs?'

Instantly on guard, I tensed and said, 'The *sham*? Are you telling me something, Aurelio?'

'Nope. I just came down to watch you.' Aurelio turned to Veronica. 'I'm his editor,' he said condescendingly in his best 'L'état, c'est moi' voice. Then he flashed his dazzling Italian smile at her.

'I'm his fan.' She didn't smile back.

'She's got you there, boss.'

Aurelio doesn't like being one-upped. He shot her a glare that would melt parmesan, but she looked back at him as if he were an asterisk on a page. She won and he walked away.

'So Veronica, you're in the diplomatic corps?'

'I came here to see you, Mr Bayer. I want my five minutes. He gets to be with you all the time.'

'Not if I can help it,' I mumbled and picked up my pen again.

'I know this isn't the place to do business, but I'm a documentary film maker. I would really like to do something on you. Here's my card. If you're interested, please call me. Even if you don't want to be filmed, I'd love you to call me anyway.'

'I'm flattered.' I was finished with her books.

She scooped them up and bent down toward me. 'And I'm serious.'

She looked as good going as she did coming. Her directness was a little scary, but thrilling at the same time. The next person put a book down on the table and huffed, 'It's about time!'

'Sorry about that. Tell me your name.'

Chatting with Veronica had slowed things way down, so I worked fast and tried to keep my mind on what I was doing. It wasn't till a half hour later that I looked at the card she had handed me. Another big jolt.

In my novel *The Tattooed City*, the most important moment in the story comes when the bad guy takes off his shirt and the heroine sees his back for the first time. In Russian prisons, convicts who have done a lot of time have their backs tattooed with the most elaborate and Byzantine

14

designs imaginable. The work is done with a combination of razor blades, needles, and inks made from urine and burned shoe heels. The illustration is the convict's autobiography – what crimes he has committed, whether he is addicted to drugs, where he stands in the prison hierarchy. Each image is symbolic – a diamond meant he's spent half his life in jail, a spider that he specialized in burglary, and so on. On my villain, angels, the Russian church, bridges, dragons, clouds, trees . . . take up almost every inch of his back so that it looks like a kind of naive painting of the City of God.

Somehow Veronica Lake had gotten hold of the same photograph that inspired me years ago and used it for her calling card. The exact same picture, only with her name and telephone number embossed in silver letters over it. The picture, the memory of how I had worked it into my story, Veronica's boldness . . . all of them combined to send a big shiver up my spine. I hadn't been so intrigued by a woman since meeting my last wife.

But the day wasn't finished playing tricks on me. After the signing was over and I had bullshitted my way past Aurelio with a Mormon's zeal about the new book, assuring him everything was hunky-dory and boy, wait till you see it, I hurried out the door. I took a cab uptown to the garage where I'd parked my car, hoping to beat the rush hour traffic out of the city.

The drive to my house in Connecticut took a good two hours if there was no hold up, but gridlock hit as soon as I got on to the West Side Highway. If you have to be held up anywhere, this road was bearable because of its beautiful view of the Hudson River and the boats of all sizes moving up and down it. I plugged in a tape of a current bestseller and listened to two chapters of someone else's words before the cars started moving again. Things got better once we passed the George Washington Bridge. I sped up, reveling in the knowledge this day of forced smiles and false promises was over for me.

However, the more I thought, the more I realized no matter how far or fast I drove up the turnpike, my life would still be waiting for me at home. What the hell *was* I going to do about this stillborn novel that sat so lifeless on my desk? For the first time in my writing career, I had discovered that a novel could be like a love affair that starts off with long kisses and dancing in fountains, but then turns into your sixth grade teacher before you're even aware of what's happening. It had reached the point where I didn't even like to go into my study because I'd take one look at that pile of pages and desperately want to beam up to another planet. Any planet, so long as there were no books, deadlines or Italian editors there. Evil Irene had said it best.

'All the rats are jumping ship, Sam. Even your best friend in the world – your imagination.'

That was what astonished me most. Until recently it had been so simple. Every couple of years I would sit down with a couple of characters in mind and start typing. As I got to know them, got to know their habits and the way they saw the world, their story would walk out of the fog and right on to the page. I think it had also been easy because I was nice to them. I never forced them to do anything. Not all of these characters were my heroes, but I respected all of them and allowed them to follow whatever course they chose. Some writer said in every book he wrote, there comes a point where the characters take over and you just let them do what they want. For me that happened on the first page.

What was most disturbing about this new one was how embarrassingly flat it was. Characters said and did things but you didn't believe any of it because I hadn't been able to put any blood in their veins or a beating heart into their fates. I felt like Dr Frankenstein who had sort of succeeded at creating life, but not really. Like the doctor's monster, I could see how patched together and badly stitched my creation was. I knew it was going to go awry if it ever got up enough energy to stagger up off the operating table and walk into the world.

I was hungry. Hungry and tired and worried. I was going home to a house that was too big for just me and my dog, Louie. I'd bought the place when a house in the country with wonderful new wife Irene, a white puppy, and a big room to work in sounded like the best things on earth. Now the house was haunted, the dog was a misanthrope, and my study had turned into 'Room 101' from *1984*.

With these cheerful thoughts marching through my head as I entered Westchester County, I suddenly had an inspiration: I was going to go home. Home to Crane's View, New York, where I'd spent the first fifteen years of my life.

Although I passed near the town every time I drove to New York, I hadn't been back there for at least a decade. I'd never been very nostalgic and spent almost no time thinking about my old days. My second wife Michelle once said she'd never known anyone who spoke less about their past. I thought about that, then said I was frankly suspicious of people who went to too many class reunions or pored over photo albums and high school yearbooks. It seemed to me something was wrong there – as if they had left something essential behind, or were realizing life was never better than back whenever. So I skipped all of my reunions, lost the few yearbooks I'd kept, and indifferently shrugged at who I had been growing up.

The last time I'd been to Crane's View was when Michelle and I were married and she insisted I take her on a guided tour. She was a fanatical romantic and wanted to see everything. We visited the high school, had lunch at Charlie's Pizza, and walked up and down Main Street until even she grew bored of what little there was to see. But those were the days when I was happy and didn't need a history to sail on into my wonderful future.

It was already seven o'clock when I drove off at the exit but since it was high summer, the sky had the golden light of fresh baked bread. The winding road to town went past beautiful trees and large estates hidden behind high stone walls. When we were young, my parents used to take my sister and me on Sunday drives. How many times had we ridden past these impressive houses and heard my father proudly announce the names of the people who owned them as if he knew them personally.

And whatever happened to *that* nice institution; getting into the family car and just taking a drive? Sometimes you'd be out for hours, the parents talking quietly in the front seat, the kids swapping punches or whispers in the back, all of you delighted to be out together for the day in the big old black Ford or gold Dodge station wagon. Sometimes you'd stop for an ice cream or even better, at the miniature golf course three towns over where other families out for *their* ride had stopped too.

Memories like slow-moving tropical fish swam through my mind as I rolled towards Crane's View. That's the corner where Dave Hughes fell off his bike, Woody Barr's house, St Jude's Church where all my Catholic friends crossed themselves whenever we walked by. As expected, everything seemed smaller and gave off the faint aroma of a cologne you once used but not for years.

It struck me I didn't think much about my childhood because I had had a good one, albeit nothing special. A wholesome meal that filled me but didn't stand out in any way. My father worked for Shell Oil all his life and liked nothing more than to pad around our house in sneakers and khakis, smoking his pipe and fixing things that didn't always need to be fixed. My mother was a homemaker in the days when that wasn't a dirty word. They married straight out of college and enjoyed each other's company for thirty-four years.

We spent our summers in a small house in a town called Sea Girt on the New Jersey shore. We had a dachshund named Eli (my father had gone to Yale), a series of station wagons; we ate dinner together in front of the television set watching either Walter Cronkite or Perry Mason. For dessert we'd have Breyer's vanilla ice cream covered with Bosco chocolate sauce. Television was black and white, your hair was a crewcut, girls wore dresses. What could be simpler?

Just past the high school, Scrappy's Diner was my first stop of the evening. Decent food, the closest pay telephone to the school, and the patient good humor of its owners made it one of the two important places for kids in Crane's View. The other was Charlie's Pizza, but it was so small all you could do there was buy your slices of pizza and hang around outside on the street while you ate.

The diner, on the other hand, was large, air conditioned and full of comfortable screaming-turquoise naugahyde booths. There was music and a menu we could afford. It was ours. Kids own nothing – everything is either promised, borrowed, longed for or exaggerated. Scrappy's gave us a place to plan, dream and re-group. The way it broke down, if you needed to meet on your way to somewhere else, see you in front of Charlie's. If you needed to talk, it was Scrappy's.

The place was almost empty when I entered. I stood a moment in the doorway and let a quazillion memories hit me square in the brain. Every corner and booth was full of my life. Just seeing the room and smelling the familiar aroma of Bunn-O-Mat coffee, frying meat, body odor, floor cleaner and wiped tables reminded me so vividly of another now that had once been as important as today's. I sat at the counter and turned the revolving seat left and right.

A young waitress wearing too much lipstick and too little energy came over. Everything about her emanated that slumping spirit that comes from being on your feet too long or just being eighteen years old and life weighing too much for you.

'What'll you have?'

'A menu, please.'

She opened he mouth to say something but stopped and closed it. Instead she slowly reached under the counter and came up with a long red menu. 'Today's specials are turkey pot pie and meat loaf,' she sighed.

'Do you still make the California burger?'

'Sure! You want one?' To my surprise, her eyes brightened and she let loose a very friendly smile. Watching her, I saw that this young woman had only so much energy in her and would consume it all by the time she was only thirty-five or forty. After that, her life would be sighs and tired gestures but enough intelligence to realize she'd used up her share long before she should have. The thought crossed my mind like a shooting star and then was gone. I looked at the name plate over her breast. 'Donna.'

'Donna? I know a woman named Donna. She has two birds. Two cockatiels.'

'Yeah? *And*?'

'Annnd, well, I guess I'll have that California burger, Donna.'

As she turned to go, I put up a finger. 'Wait a sec. Do you go to the high school?'

She made a face. 'Unfortunately.'

'Does Mrs Muzroll still teach there?'

'She don't teach, mister, she *naps*. That's where you do your homework, in Mrs Muzroll's class. You went to Crane's View?' She threw a thumb over her shoulder in its direction.

'A long time ago.'

She smiled again. 'I wish I went there a long time ago!'

'Still bad, huh?'

'Naah, not so bad. I just like complaining. I'll get your burger.'

I watched her walk away, then checked out who else was there. A moving van was parked outside and I assumed the two giants down the counter eating meat loaf belonged to it.

I stared too long at a teenage couple in a booth who were having fun shooting paper wrappers off straws at each other. I remembered sitting in that same booth with Louise Hamlin one night after we'd had a heavy make out session behind the school. We drank cherry Cokes and stared at each other with the delight and gratitude that comes only after hours of monumental fourteen-year-old kissing. Something deep in my chest tightened at the thought of that night, and of Louise Hamlin with her strawberry blond hair.

'Here you go. Something to look at while you're waiting.' Donna put a book down in front of me. It was the *Periauger*, the Crane's View high school yearbook. 'It's from last year. I thought you might like to see what it's like there now.'

'Wow, Donna, that's really sweet! Thank you so much.'

'I've been keeping it in the back. You can see if Mrs Muzroll looks any different.'

'I doubt it. Thanks again.'

It was the perfect yellow brick road back into my old hometown. So much was familiar, so much wasn't. I knew none of the kids but the faces in any yearbook always look the same. Same unnatural smiles, straight posture, tough guys, geeks, future poets and fools. Only the size of the hair and the styles change but the faces were the same everywhere.

The school had built a new gymnasium and knocked down the old auditorium. Mr Pupel (known and hated far and wide as Mr Poodle) still taught French and looked as gay as ever. Mrs Bartel still had the biggest tits in the world and Coach Ater still looked like a warthog thirty years on. All these things heartened me and I pored over the yearbook, even after my good cheeseburger with all the trimmings had arrived.

'See anyone you know?' Donna leaned over the counter and looked at the book upside down. Her long brown hair was luminous and thick. Up this close, I could smell her perfume. It was smoke and lemon at once.

'Lots! It's hard to believe some of these people are still at the school. Pupel used to make the best-looking boys in class sit in the front rows. He once tried that with Frannie McCabe, but Frannie knew what *he* was up to and sneered "What, so you can look up my dress?"'

Hearing the name of the infamous McCabe, Donna reared back and put her hands on her hips. 'Frannie McCabe is my *uncle!*'

'Really? He's still in town?'

'Sure! What's your name? I'll tell him I saw you. You were in his class?'

'Yes. My name is Samuel Bayer. Sam. We were great friends. He was the toughest guy I ever met. What does he do now?'

'He's a cop.'

'A *cop*? Donna, there's no way on earth Frannie McCabe could be a cop.'

'Yeah well, he is. He was bad when he was a kid, huh?' The pleased look in her eye said she'd heard her share of stories about Uncle Frannie.

'The worst! Donna, when I was a kid, if there was one person I knew who'd end up on Death Row, it was your uncle. I do not believe he's a *cop*.'

'He's good too. He's chief.'

I slapped my forehead in astonishment. 'When we were kids if I'd said he was going to be Chief of Police here one day, he would have been insulted.'

'Hey Donna, how 'bout some coffee down here?'

She looked at the moving men and nodded. 'You should go to the station and say hi. He'd like that. He's always down there.' She picked up a coffee pot and walked away.

I continued looking through the book as I ate. The football team had done well, the basketball team hadn't. The spring play was *West Side Story*. The make up on the kids was so bad, all of the actors looked like they were from *The Addams Family*. I flipped through the pages past the computer club, chess club, kitchen and janitorial staff. Ninth grade, tenth grade and then there it was: a face I didn't know, but a name I *did* know, and a memory as large as my life: Pauline Ostrova.

'Jesus Christ! Donna? Could you come here a minute?' My voice must have been way too loud because both she and the moving men looked at me with wide eyes.

'Yeah?'

I pointed to a picture. 'Do you know her? Pauline Ostrova?'

'Yes. I mean I know her, but she's not like a *friend* or anything. Why?'

'What's she like?' For a moment I didn't realize I was holding my breath in anticipation.

'Sort of weird. Smart. Into computers and stuff. She's a brain. Why, you know her family? You know *about* them?'

'Uh huh. I know a lot about them.'

She leaned in closer, as if about to tell me a secret. 'You know about the other Pauline? Her aunt? What happened to her?'

'Donna, I found the body.'

I left the diner feeling so good that I could have rhumbaed around the parking lot. In the car I turned the radio on full blast and sang along to the Hollies' song 'Bus Stop'.

I *had* it. I finally had it again and the fact was so glorious and exciting that I felt bulletproof. I HAD IT! It was almost nine at night when I picked up the car phone and started dialing the office number of Aurelio Parma, editorial gargoyle, afrit and human Ebola virus to tell him HA! I have the idea for an incredible new book! Plus everything is already *there*: no need to create a thing. The phone rang in his office until, through the rocket's red glare of my enthusiasm, I realized he had gone home hours before. But I had to talk to someone about this. I got out my address book and found Patricia Chase's home number. In all the years we had worked together, I had never once called Patricia at home. Now I knew I'd have an embolism if I didn't.

I waited while her phone rang. Across the street was a gas station that had once sold Flying A, then Gulf, Sunoco, then Citgo. Now it was Exxon and looked very Hi-Tech modern, although there was no garage where cars could be repaired. Just the gas pumps and one of those tiny markets that cater to people's addictions – cigarettes, lottery tickets, junk food and *The National Inquirer*.

In its earlier incarnation, the station had been where we always rode our bikes after school to the bright red Coke machine in front. Drinks cost a dime and that vaguely green glass bottle would come banging down from inside, ice cold and curving perfectly into your hand. We'd stand with our bikes balanced between our legs, drinking in long bottle-emptying glugs. In between, we'd watch cars pull in and out for gasoline or to be repaired. We'd name the makes if they made the grade. 'Fuckin' 4-4-2.' 'Nice 'Vette.' 'That Z-28'd kick *your* ass!' Eavesdropping on the mechanics' conversations as they worked in the garage had taught us the importance of these great machines, as well as all the dirty words a nine-year-old needed to know. At home, the pictures on our walls were of Shelby Mustangs or Cobras, a Chevrolet 327 engine, a tucked and rolled custom leather interior, the drag racers Don Prudhomme or 'Swamp Rat' Don Garlits.

'Hello?'

'Patricia, it's Sam Bayer.'

'Sam! Is Aurelio holding you prisoner?'

'Better, Patricia, much better! Listen to this—'

I told her the idea for the book. When I was finished, there was a long silence which could have meant anything coming from the formidable Chase. She has a strong, impressive voice but when she did speak, it was the softest and most tentative I had ever heard it. 'You never told me about that, Sam.'

'It happened a long time ago.'

'It doesn't matter. It's a hell of an experience!'

'It is, but what do you think of my idea? Do you like it?'

'I love it and so will Aurelio.'

'But it doesn't necessarily mean I'll *find* anything, Patricia. I'm just going to look.'

'I think it could be that big book we were talking about today, Sam. The gods must be happy with you to offer this idea seven hours after we talked. Where are you, by the way?'

'In Crane's View! I just had a California burger at Scrappy's Diner and am going down to the river now to see what I can remember.'

'I think it's going to be great, Sam. I'm very excited.'

'You never say that!'

'You never wrote anything like this.'

I was about to answer when I saw something that knocked me back into my past with the force of a punch.

While we spoke I had watched the comings and goings at the gas station. My window was down so I heard the constant mutter of traffic and street noise outside. Nothing special, until someone nearby started speaking in a deep, dead monotone that part of my brain recognized instantly. It was repeating word for word a Honda Accord commercial I had seen on television so many times that, against my will, I'd memorized the words to it, like a terrible pop song that will not leave your head. I recognized the slogans a moment before recognizing the voice. That voice doing exactly the same thing it had always done when I was a kid – perfectly repeating the words to television commercials. Thirty years ago it had been ads for Cocoa Marsh and Newport cigarettes, Tide detergent and Rambler cars. Today it was a Honda but that made no difference: it was a Crane's View ghost alive in my ear. Shocked, I slowly turned to look for the face.

There he was, still walking in those big galumphing steps, arms swinging too high up from his side, his feet encased in shoes that looked as big as the boxes they'd come in.

'Holy shit, it's Club Soda Johnny!'

'What did you say?'

'I'll call you tomorrow, Patricia. I gotta go. My past just walked by, doing a Honda ad.' I put the phone down and jumped out of the car. Johnny was walking towards the school and as always, moving so fast that I had to jog to catch up.

He was forty pounds heavier and had lost most of his hair. The rest was a crew cut which made his face look even larger and squarer.

'Johnny! Hey Johnny!'

He stopped and turned around. When he saw me he only stared.

'Do you remember me? Sam Bayer? I used to live here a long time ago?'

'No.'

'I didn't think so. How are you, Johnny?'

'Okay.'

'Whatcha been doing?'

'Not much.'

Johnny Petangles lived with his mother and grandmother on Olive Street down by the railroad station. He was slow in the head, as they used to say, and worked odd jobs around town. What he really liked to do was watch television. Although I don't think he was an idiot savant, he had one great talent: he could repeat verbatim every television commercial he had ever seen. 'And away goes trouble down the drain; Roto Rooter!', 'Take Sominex tonight and sleep . . .', 'Puff Puff Cocoa Puffs.' Club Soda Johnny's gospel came straight from the blue tube and slow as he was, he still knew every chapter and verse. Sometimes we'd be sitting around, bored stiff. Along came Johnny on one of his never ending marches through town. 'Hey Johnny, do the Clark Bar ad. Do the Chunky. How does the Bufferin one go?' The ads didn't have to have music or jingles for him to get them right. Even doctors in white coats pointing to charts demonstrating the effectiveness of Bufferin aspirin or Preparation H hemorrhoid cream went right into Johnny's soft head and stayed forever. But because he was demented, the sentences, although perfect, came out flat and totally deflated, sounding like a computer voice. 'CHAR-LIE SAYS LOVE MY GOOD AND PLEN-TY!'

Being near him now was like bringing a bouquet of fresh flowers to my nose. The smell of nostalgia was overpowering.

He looked to the left and right. Then in an exaggerated gesture, pulled up his sleeve and looked at his wristwatch. I noticed the dial face was a picture of Arnold Schwarzenegger in *The Terminator*. 'I have to go now. I have to get home to watch television.'

I put out a hand and touched his arm. It was very warm. 'Johnny, do you remember Pauline Ostrova? Do you remember her name?'

He narrowed his eyes, touched his chin and looked at the sky. He began to hum. For a moment I wondered if he had forgotten my question.

'No.'

'Okay. Well, it was nice seeing you again, Johnny.'

'It was my great pleasure.' Surprisingly, he put out his

big hand and we shook. His face didn't change expression when he abruptly turned and strode off.

Watching him walk away, I remembered the *old* Club Soda Johnny, Frannie McCabe, Suzy Nichols, Barbara Thilly ... so many others. I remembered evenings in the town park, bored out of our skulls, happy to see crazy Johnny because he was a welcome five-minute diversion. We had so much time on our hands in those days. About all we had *was* time. Always waiting for something to happen without ever quite knowing what. Something about to happen, someone about to come and save our day, week ... from just *being*.

Johnny stopped, spun around and looked at me impassively. 'Pauline is dead. You're joking around with me. She was killed a long time ago.'

'That's right, Johnny. A hell of a long time.'

I drove past Sacred Heart Church, Stumpel Ford, Power's Stationery Store. It's interesting how some shops, no matter how many times they change owners, always stay the same. Most locations go from pizzeria to boutique to whatever every few years. The stationery store in Crane's View had a new owner but was still the place to buy a newspaper, rubber bands, candy. As a kid, my first allowance had been twenty-five cents. Enough to buy a Payday candy bar and a *Sugar and Spike* comic book there. I'd walk out not knowing what to do first – open the comic or the Payday. Usually I'd do both at once – read, eat, cross the street without looking and not realize until I got home that I'd finished everything.

At the traffic light in the center of town Main Street forked. If you went straight, you took Broadway uphill towards the nicer sections. If you veered right, Main Street continued through the heart of beautiful downtown Crane's View, all six minutes of it. When I brought Michelle on our pilgrimage to my roots, she'd said, 'But what did you do for fun here? There's nothing.'

Which was almost true. A pretty town an hour up the Hudson River from Manhattan, Crane's View had a Waspy name but was populated by mostly lower middle-class Irish and Italian families. People there needed only a good hardware store, market, clothes store that sold chinos, Maidenform brassieres, house dresses, Converse sneakers. The most expensive thing on the menu at the best restaurant in town was 'Surf and Turf'. There was a decent library but few used it. The Embassy movie theater too, but you went there to make out with a girl because it was dark and usually empty as a tomb. The bars were named Shamrock and Gino's. Michelle was right – it was a town where people worked hard during the day then went home at night, drank beer, and watched the game on TV.

A few residents didn't fit the description. They were mostly white collars who worked in Manhattan and commuted so they could own a decent house, a yard and some green around them. One rarely seen couple who lived way up on Pilot Hill drove a Rolls-Royce, but they had no kids and whenever we encountered them they were like aliens from another planet.

At the other end of town was Beacon Hill, the only apartment complex. For some unknown reason, a good number of Jewish families lived there. I remember in sixth grade going to Karen Enoch's apartment when I was deeply in love with her. The first menorah I had ever seen was on their dining room table. I told Mrs Enoch it was a beautiful candelabra that reminded me of the one Liberace had on his piano in his TV show. Later that day she tried to explain Chanukah to me, but all I understood was it was Christmas times twelve.

I grew up in a small American town in the 1950s. Part of the reason why I didn't have much to say about my childhood was simply because nothing much happened. No one grew their hair long, the only thing you protested was having pot roast again, drugs were only a whispered rumor, and any guy who behaved any differently from the norm was a fag. We played a lot of sports whether we were good or not. Most of my friends were named Joe, Anthony, John. Most of the girls we sweated and dreamed about were generally the kind who peaked physically at seventeen but then quickly started looking like their mothers once they got married far too early.

Driving through the center of town, I passed the police station and was tempted to go in and ask for Frannie McCabe, but that could wait. If things went the way I hoped, I'd be back soon and spending a great deal of time in Crane's View.

At the end of the small commercial district, Main Street curves steeply down and ends at the railroad station and river. As I took my foot off the gas and let the car roll down the hill, I remembered the many times I'd walked to the station from our house. All dressed up and full of expectation for a day in New York, I'd saved my allowance for weeks and had an agenda worked out to the minute. I'd be going to the Automobile Show at the Colosseum or a wrestling match at Madison Square Garden, sometimes to the Broadway Sports Palace to spend all my money on the arcade games. Lunch would be a hot dog and Coconut Champagne, or a stringy two dollar steak at Tad's Steaks. New York wasn't frightening then. A twelve-year-old wiseguy could walk around Times Square alone and the worst that would happen was a panhandler would come up and ask for a dime. I was never afraid to be there and thought of the city as a kind of flashy friend with a toothpick in its mouth.

I drove over the bridge that crossed the railroad tracks and took a sharp right towards the station. Some enterprising soul had built an expensive-looking steakhouse at the river's edge. I felt a spurt of dismay to think life had gone on here without me all these years. Who did they think they were, changing the landscape that had once been mine? Part of you thinks you own the terrain of your memories; a law should keep things looking just the way they were.

I parked the car in front of the station and got out. A moment later, the express train from Chicago blew down the track towards the city. As it passed in a violent *whomp* of air and a thousand metal clicks, the world inside its cars was once again all romance and possibilities. The train we took from Crane's View to New York was always a local. It stopped twelve times in its easygoing ramble before pulling into Grand Central Station. Commuters took our train, old ladies going to the matinee of *Hello Dolly*, thirteen-year-olds in pants that were too short, purple V-neck sweaters and wearing enough Brylcreem in their hair to give the family car a lube job.

Sighing, I looked towards the water and saw a young couple playing frisbee while a dog chased back and forth between them. It was having the time of its life. Every few throws they would let him catch one. He'd run around in a crazy triumphant dance before they wrestled it back and sent it flying again. It's interesting how many times in life you'll have a deeply sad moment only to be reminded an instant later that things are okay. I watched the couple. They sent out such strong waves of happiness that I felt them where I stood. The girl whirled around in a circle and threw the frisbee as hard as she could. It came right at me and dropped a few feet away. I started towards it but the dog rushed over and I stopped. So did he. He stood inches away from the bright red disk, but looked up at me as if I was in charge.

'Go get it. It's okay.'

He tilted his head in that classic 'Huh?' look dogs have that make me laugh every time. 'It's okay. Get it.'

He snatched it from the ground and tore off. I started toward the water.

'Excuse me? Could you tell me what time it is?'

I don't know how long I had been standing there, looking at the river and remembering. It seemed the night was ripe for reveries. Whatever, I came out of the trance and looked first at the girl, then my watch. 'It's a quarter past nine.'

'Are you all right?' She had a sweet face, all concern.

I looked at her and tried to smile. I didn't know what to say.

'Did I ever tell you about the time I found the girl's body?'

The person I loved most looked at me and smiled the smile I would remember on my deathbed. Her long brown hair fell in a perfect part over her shoulders and her thin nightgown had little birds on it.

She shook her head. 'That's one of the things I like about spending the night with you. In the morning you always tell me a story I never heard before.'

She was sixteen years old going on thirty. I reached across the table and caressed her cheek. She took my hand and kissed it.

'It never ceases to amaze me you're my daughter.'

Cassandra Bayer frowned. 'Why? What do you mean?'

'I mean exactly that. How did your mother and I manage to hatch such a good kid? Your mom's lived a life that would make a nun blush. I've got more neuroses than Woody Allen. Yet here *you* are – solid, smart, funny ... How'd it happen?'

'Maybe my genes skipped a generation.' She picked up the bottle of spooky black nail polish and went back to work on her thumb.

'Can I paint my nails black after you?'

She rolled her eyes and groaned. 'So what about this body you found?

I got up and poured myself some more coffee. Without

looking, she extended her cup to me. I filled it and looked at the top of her head. 'I have a good idea: Why don't you shave your head and have "Dad" tattooed there? That would go with the nails and then I'd really know you loved me.'

'I know a girl who got a tattoo down below.'

'*What*? What'd she put there?'

'A lightning bolt.'

I looked out the window, trying to absorb that one. 'Cass, sometimes you tell me things that make me feel a hundred years old. I mean, I'm pretty hip for a guy my age, you've said so yourself. But if I went to bed with a woman and saw she had a tattoo there, I'd call the police.'

'I don't think you'd want to go to bed with *this* girl, Dad. Her name is Spoon and the only thing she eats is lamb. It's some kind of new religion, like the Malda Vale.'

'What do Spoon's parents say about that?'

She finished her thumb and screwed the cap back on the bottle. Her gestures were all so delicate and precise. 'Are you going to tell me about the dead body or not?'

'Okay. When I was fifteen, a bunch of us went down to the river to swim.'

'You *swam* in the Hudson River? Dad, that place is *glowing* with pollution!'

'Yeah well, I'd rather swim in a dirty river than tattoo my genitals! Anyway, it wasn't so bad back then; just a little smelly. But we didn't really go to swim. All the cool girls went there in their bikinis. Someone would have gotten beer, everybody'd be smoking Marlboros, there'd be a portable radio ... W.A.B.C. with Cousin Brucie. It was nice. I always think of it as the day of "A Hard Day's Night". I'll tell you why in a minute. Joe O'Brien and I were the first there.'

'Joe O'Brien – your best friend who you once knocked out in a fight?'

'That's the guy. Politics were rough back then. It was

that kind of town. Everybody was tough or pretending to be. You could be best friends but if the guy crossed you, BAM! you'd be in a fight in a minute.'

Cass shook her head. 'Nice place to grow up.'

'It *was* a nice place to grow up. It was innocent. We believed in loyalty, most of the girls were virgins. The music we listened to was about going steady and not eating someone's cancer. We could come and go as we pleased without worrying about being murdered in a drive-by. Girls weren't raped and no one carried a gun. Well, *almost* no one.'

'I bet Frannie McCabe did. Is this a Frannie story?'

'No, and he never forgave us for it. Frannie was the king of one-upmanship, but this turned out to be the biggest one-up in all our lives.

'Anyway, Joe O'Brien and I got there first. It was about ten o'clock in the morning. Hot day. Really a hot day. There was this spot by the water where we always went. A couple of hundred yards away from the train station. We laid out our towels and stripped down to our swimsuits.

'We were all revved up for the party to start. There was a new girl in town, Geraldine Fortuso, who had the greatest body we'd ever seen. She also had a mustache, but nobody's perfect. All the guys were vying for her and we knew she was coming. Joe and I stood at the edge of the water looking at the boats and talking about the divine Fortuso's figure.

'A speedboat went by and sent waves rolling into shore. I don't know who saw it first. It's funny because it's such an important detail, but I honestly don't remember. *Whoever* did, said "What the fuck's that?" The waves had made this big white, diaphanous thing out in the water about forty feet rise and fall like a gigantic jellyfish. Both of us stepped forward to get a better look but I went too far and slipped off the edge into the water.

34

'Joe said "You see that? Go out and see what it is. Maybe it's a parachute."'

Cass sat forward and said in the same doubting voice I had used that day 'Parachute?'

I shrugged. 'It looked like one. Either a little parachute or the biggest damned jellyfish you ever saw. You know how fearless kids are until they learn life has big jaws. Without a thought that it might be something bad or dangerous, I waded right out and then started swimming for whatever it was.'

'When did you see it was a body?'

'Not till I was only about five feet away. The water reflected the sunlight, and the color was a surprisingly light green so you couldn't make anything out till you were really close.

'She was floating on her stomach and wearing a man's shirt. It had been unbuttoned and that's why it looked so wide and filled out. I'm thinking back a long time now, but as I remember, first I realized it was a shirt, then that it was *on* something. That's what I thought – it was on some *thing* and not someone.

'I was calm, Cass. That's the amazing thing. If it happened today I'm sure I'd be a lot more scared or surprised. Maybe it's because when you're young, you still think things *should* happen to you. So since you're waiting for the adventures to begin, if you discover a dead body, it's just like a James Bond film. And that's only right because that's where you belong.'

'James Bond is dorky.'

'He wasn't then. He was the coolest dude on earth.

'So, now that I understand it's a shirt, and something's *inside* it, I let out a whoop that would have stopped a train. Joe started yelling from the shore but I barely heard him. I paddled over and just as I did, a big wave from a passing boat turned the body over. I saw her face. Even though she was just beneath the water, I saw every feature of her face

35

clearly. Her eyes were open but there was something white and cloudlike floating across her mouth.'

'God, Dad, weren't you scared at all?'

'No, that's the amazing thing. I was fascinated. Maybe it's just the different courage you have as a kid. I was only curious; I wanted to see everything. My parents thought I'd be traumatized by the experience, but it didn't touch me. It took a few seconds to sink in, and when it did, I called to Joe to get the police 'cause it was a *body*. He took off like a shot. I paddled around wondering what to do next. I kept looking at her and thinking "She's dead. That girl is dead." But what I most vividly remember is how close to the surface she was; like if she'd only lifted her head a few inches she could have breathed again and been okay. Strange, huh? You know what the reality is, but part of your brain is still thinking crazy things.

'I took hold of her arm; she was in rigor mortis by then and very stiff. I started in toward shore, pulling her next to me. It took a few minutes of awkward struggling but I finally got her in. I stepped on to the little shelf of beach and then was able to use two hands to pull her out of the water.

'As I said, she was wearing a man's shirt and only a pair of very brief bikini underpants. I shouldn't tell you this, but it was the first time I'd ever seen a woman like that. I could see everything. I couldn't believe it. The thing all us guys had been talking about and dreaming about for years was right there in front of me – an almost naked girl.'

Cass groaned. 'Dad, she was dead! You thought it was *sexy*?'

'I certainly did. She was beautiful and there wasn't much on her. I couldn't help staring.'

'That is gross. I can't believe it. You were staring at a dead body!'

'No! A fifteen-year-old boy with the hormones of a bull

moose was standing there and for the first time in his life he was seeing a woman. That's a big difference, Honey.'

She put her hands together as if about to pray. 'I am *so* glad I'm not a man! What happened next?'

'I reached down and wiped the film off her face with my hand. I guess it was mucus or something. Nothing else happened. I stood there and looked at her till Joe got back. The interesting thing was when he came, he wouldn't get near her. He stood up on the ledge and gaped but refused to come down.

'Nothing ever happened in Crane's View, so I'm sure the cops were thrilled to hear about a body. They were there in less than ten minutes. Captain Cristello and Pee Pee Bucci.'

'Pee Pee?'

'Peter. The cop we hated most. He'd graduated from high school a few years before. The one who always gave us the roughest time when we were caught doing things.'

'Were you really tough, Dad? I mean, all the stories you tell about when you were a kid make you sound like a real delinquent.'

'No, I faked it. I never fit in. I did bad things only because the guys I hung around with did them. I wanted them to like me but they knew I'd leave Crane's View as soon as I could. And I did. But when you're a kid, you go with the flow. That's part of the deal. You think the punks or the hippies were any different? It's just a different costume and haircut, but kids want to be accepted. They'll sell a lot of their soul for that. You're about the only one I've ever known who's stayed on her own path. I admire you for that.'

It was true. From the beginning, Cassandra had been strong-minded and genuinely independent. When her mother and I divorced, she handled it so well it disturbed me. Until now, boys had stayed away from her because she was mature and honest. Unfortunately she thought it was because she wasn't good-looking. She had a large, marvelous nose, her mother's cheekbones and slightly oriental eyes. She was tall, wore tortoise-shell glasses and generally hid the curves of a lovely body with no-nonsense work shirts and jeans.

I adored her and treasured the time we spent together. I had turned much of my life into a royal fuck up, but surprisingly I was, I think, a good father. We talked about everything and her candor educated me and made me very proud. One of the things I relished was what good friends we had become over the years, in spite of all the fallout that comes with a broken marriage.

'Okay, so Pee Pee and the Chief of Police came and you were there with the body.'

'Right. Joe's up on the bank, I'm down on the beach and here come the sirens. It was so typical. There were two police cars in town and both arrived with sirens screaming. Couldn't they have just taken one—'

'Dad, the story?'

'The cops arrived and took over. Cristello ordered me away from the body. A minute ago she was mine but now she was public property. Pee Pee made me climb up the bank and give him a statement, which I thought that was the coolest thing: I was actually giving *my statement* to the cops! It was just like on *Dragnet* or *Naked City*, my favorite television shows. I could see Pee Pee was jealous. He kept asking me ridiculous questions like, "What do you mean, you saw a shirt in the water?" and "What were you doing by the river anyway?"'

'What did he expect you to say? You were only a kid!'

'Exactly. That's why he was jealous. Cops in small towns wait all their lives to find a murder victim. Now two dopey kids had stumbled on one and all Pee Pee could do was take our statements. It was great. So we gave them while waiting for an ambulance to arrive from the town hospital.

Cristello got a bright yellow tarpaulin out of the back of the patrol car and covered her body. I remember that moment very well – it was as if I was saying goodbye to her. For all intents and purposes I was, because when the ambulance got there, the men took the body away quickly and I never saw it again.

'We had to go to the station house and give statements again. When we got into the police car, the radio was on and the disc jockey was saying "And now what you've all been waiting for: the new song by the Beatles – 'A Hard Day's Night'." It was the first time I ever heard it. Since then, whenever it comes on, I think of that day.'

'Did they find out who did it?'

'That's hard to say. Her boyfriend from college was convicted and sent away to jail but there were a lot of rumors afterwards. Plus we had our own ideas and you know how kids talk. The story that went out to the public was the night before, she had gone down to the river with the guy she was dating. He hit her on the head, panicked, and threw her body into the river. That's all.'

'Why didn't you try to find out? You were the ones who found her!' Cass sounded indignant we hadn't followed up on it.

'I know, and we did try, but no one tells kids anything. Especially not the cops. Not a word.'

'That's really strange. Who was she?'

'Pauline Ostrova.' I thought about the dead girl a moment, trying to frame what to say to describe her correctly. 'No matter how small a town is, you can usually find at least a couple of very good and very bad kids in it.'

Cass put up a hand to stop me. 'Wait! Let me guess – Pauline Ostrova was . . . very good. All A's, editor of the yearbook and dated the captain of the football team.'

'No. Much more interesting than that. I didn't know her well because she was a few years ahead of me in school.

She had already graduated by that time, but was still legendary because she was *both*. Completely wild, she had a reputation nine miles long. The word was she slept with whoever she liked, drank like an Irishman, and would do anything on a dare. But she was also brilliant and had a full scholarship to Swarthmore.'

'Swarthmore? Swarthmore's harder to get into than Harvard!'

'That's why she was amazing. God only knows what she would have become if she'd lived. There were so many contrasting Pauline stories floating around when I was in school, you never knew which to believe. She must have been remarkable.'

'But you didn't know her?'

'Not really. Sometimes I'd see her drive by in a car or walking down the street. But the stories made her so much larger than life that I could only stare at her a second before I had to look away. It was like looking at the sun; your eyes would burn out if you looked too long.'

'I can't believe you didn't find out how she died.'

I waited a dramatic moment and then said triumphantly: 'That, my pearl, is what I am about to do.'

She took a quick breath. 'What do you mean?'

I was going to play this one for all the effect I could, especially in front of my favorite audience. I walked over to a sideboard and took out the photograph from Pauline's senior class yearbook I'd borrowed from the high school library. I'd had it copied and then enlarged. I brought it to Cass and propped it in front of her. 'Pauline Ostrova.'

She took the 8"×10" and looked at it a long time before speaking. I watched her face to see if I could decipher what she was thinking. As usual, nothing showed because nothing would until she'd made up her mind. I knew my daughter well enough to know she didn't like any kibitzing until she was good and ready to pass judgement. 'Tall or short?'

'Kind of tall, as I remember.'

'Where'd you get the picture?'

'It's her senior year portrait. Out of an old yearbook.'

She shook her head. 'Her face is so small. And the teeth are so tiny and perfect. I could imagine her being the class brain from this picture, but not the other. Not if this was the only picture I ever saw of her. Do you have others?'

'Not yet, but I'm working on it.'

Cass looked at the picture again. 'She looks too sweet to be dead.'

That evening I brought her to the railroad station. While we were waiting for her train to arrive, she told me a story that stuck in my mind like a piece of chewing gum on the bottom of my shoe.

One of her friends' mother was an airline stewardess. She was taking a shuttle bus from London out to the airport when they hit a bad traffic jam. Apparently the woman is very good-looking. During the ride, she and this handsome well-dressed guy across the aisle were making heavy eye contact. But the whole time he was also talking nonstop on a pocket telephone and from what she overheard, he was in the middle of pulling off a big deal. She was already late and the bus wasn't moving. Her flight took off soon and finally it was clear she wasn't going to make it on time. Desperate, she went to the sexy guy and asked if she could borrow his phone to call her airline and tell them about the delay. The guy sputtered a minute and then said very sheepishly he'd like to help her, but the phone was a fake.

After putting Cass on the train back to Manhattan, I sat in the car and looked at my hands on the steering wheel. Mr Telephone gave me the creeps because his story sounded too much like mine. I had been walking around pretending to be a successful bigshot too, when in fact I was a stuck buckaroo with a mediocre novel sitting on my desk, staring at me like a gargoyle every time I entered the room. What if I was finished as a writer? There were too many stories about novelists who simply dried up one day and never found another drop inside. The idea of writing Pauline's story excited me, but what if that came out flat and lifeless too? I'd have no excuses then.

My still fingers began drumming and jumping around on the steering wheel. What if? What if? I didn't need any more doubts in my life, but sitting there alone on a pretty Sunday evening in summer with nothing to do, the 'What ifs?' poured out of my brain like a swarm of killer bees.

There was a large billboard on a wall advertising a new kind of yogurt. It pictured a beautiful female hand holding a silvery spoon with a blop of violet yummy on the tip. The tag line read 'Heaven is only a spoonful away.' Looking at it, I suddenly remembered Spoon, Cassandra's girlfriend who'd had her vagina tattooed. One tattoo led to another and reaching into my back pocket for my wallet, I took out the bunch of calling cards I kept in it. Shuffling through them, I found Veronica Lake's with the picture of the tattooed Russian criminal. I looked at it a few seconds, considered what other prospects I had for the night ahead, and picked up the telephone.

It rang four times before her machine clicked in. Answering machine messages tell a lot about people. Cassandra's mother said only 'You know the drill' and then came the beep. The most humorless man I know has the most embarrassingly unfunny attempt at being funny on his tape. My credo is if it ain't there, don't try to record it. Veronica's voice came on, crisp and friendly. 'Hi. This is 308–2338. Leave a message and I'll call you as soon as I can.' I felt a small tug of disappointment that she wasn't there, but thought it best to say something so she would know I'd been thinking of her.

'Ms Lake, this is Samuel Bayer—' Before I could say more, the phone clicked and her voice came on.

'Hello, Mr Bayer.'

'Are you hiding behind your answering machine?'

She chuckled. 'Yes. I like answering machines. They're like a bouncer at the front door: they only let in people you want to talk to.'

'I never thought of it that way. Listen, I'm sure you're in the middle of ten things right now—'

'I'm not doing a thing. Did you have something in mind?'

'Actually yes. I was wondering if you'd like to have a drink?' The words were out before I really knew what I wanted to say.

'I would love to! Are you nearby?'

'No. I'm at a train station in Connecticut. But I could be there in a couple of hours.'

'Wow! You'd drive all that way to have a drink with me?'

'It's a nice night. It's a nice drive.'

'Wow! *Belle parole pascon i gatti.*' Whatever language she was speaking, her accent was perfect and she slipped into it without a blip.

'What's that?'

'Beautiful words don't feed the cats. Actions speak louder than words. I love it when someone is straight and direct. It saves so much time. Where should we meet and when, Mr Bayer?'

Hawthorne's is the nicest bar in Manhattan. The drinks are big, the clientele quiet and discreet, and the surroundings comfortably worn in. By the time I arrived it was almost nine. I'd driven straight to the city from the train station so I was still wearing my Sunday at home clothes. That was all right for Hawthorne's and for Veronica too. I saw her when I walked in the door and felt a second's worth of eerie because she was wearing almost exactly the same outfit I had on – a white button down shirt, khakis and sneakers. Only *her* shoes were industrial strength, high top basketball jobs with enough Home Boy decoration on them to rate her a free pass to a Crips meeting. She looked delicious – that big blond ice sculpture of hair, long neck, and erotic rise beneath her shirt to make you wonder what it looked like underneath . . .

On seeing me, she clapped her hands in front of her face like a child. 'We're twins!'

'I was just thinking that. Who's your tailor?'

She patted the seat next to her for me to sit down. 'How was the drive in?'

'Clean and fast. Sometimes it's bad on Sunday night, but I guess everyone decided to stay in the country another day. What are you having?'

'Iced tea.'

'You don't drink?'

'I do, but not tonight. I needed a clear head if I was going to meet you.'

'Why?'

'Because you're my hero. I don't want to chance saying something dumb and scare you away.'

'You're the dream date, Veronica. Before I sit down, you say I'm your hero. I don't even have to tell my stories to try and impress you.'

'No, but I would love to hear your stories, Mr Bayer.'

'Sam.'

'Do you know how often I've dreamt of hearing you say that? Dreamt of sitting with you in a place like this, just the two of us, and hearing you say "You can call me Sam?"'

'Are you always so, um, honest?'

'Lying is too much trouble. You have to make sure to taste each word before letting it off your tongue. I hate that. It's hard enough making people understand without lying.'

The waiter brought my drink. Sipping it, I tried to get a better read on Veronica while we both thought of the next thing to say.

She looked younger than I remembered; more voluptuous and desirable. I had a bad habit of getting involved with skinny, neurasthenic women. They were often good lovers which got me hooked in the beginning, but their early sass in bed later turned into ugly static electricity that made me feel like a lightning rod in an electrical storm. Of course some of the trouble in the relationships was my fault due to my own defective wiring and various deadly sins. I was an optimist who loved women, two things that never failed to get me into trouble. Even now, five minutes after greeting Veronica Lake and having begun the mating dance, my spirit was already racing down the runway towards take off. Already thinking 'I wonder when I can ask her to Connecticut?' I wanted to know what her back looked like, what other authors she read, how her breath smelled. I enjoyed her honesty, the direct eye contact, the way she threw her hands around like a Greek when she spoke. I liked her before I knew her, but that was par for my course.

'What are you working on now? Can I ask that question, or is it too personal?' Her voice had some doubt in it, a little unsureness.

'No, not at all. I was writing a novel, but something happened recently that got me going on another project. I'm very excited about it.'

'Can you say what it's about? By the way, are you a Pisces?'

I stopped, cleared my throat. I don't like astrology. Don't like people asking my sign. Too often when you tell them, they nod sagely as if your birthdate explains why everything about you is so fucked up. It didn't surprise me Veronica guessed correctly.

'Yes. How did you know?'

'You're a fish. I can smell it.' She smiled and left it at that.

'What do you mean? I smell like a fish?'

'No, *you* smell like good cologne. Probably . . . Hermès? Hermès or Romeo Gigli. You smell great. I don't mean that.'

I signaled to the waiter. 'Time for another drink.'

She leaned forward and took firm hold of my elbow. 'Listen, I'm just a fan. I'm nobody. The last thing in the world I want to do is offend you. Your face says I've pissed you off. Please know I didn't mean to. Should I leave? Shit. I'm so sorry.'

She slid back. I touched her hand. 'Veronica, I just drove two hours to New York. Four minutes into our conversation you say I'm a fish and now you're *leaving*? I think we should run our tape back and start again. What do you think?'

'I think I'm scared to open my mouth now.'

'Don't be; I like your honesty. You asked what I was working on. Let's start there.' I sat back. She stared at me and didn't move.

'When I was fifteen, I found the body of a girl who had been murdered.'

Telling the whole story took only a few minutes. When I was finished, she sat silently looking at the table. Only after a good long pause did she raise her eyes. Her expression said she had figured something out. 'Pauline Ostrova was your dead mermaid. The end of childhood. All those impossible combinations we can only know and accept when we're young. Woman and fish. Young and dead. Sex and murder . . .'

'Oxymoron.'

She nodded slowly. 'Precisely. Childhood's all opposites. You're either too hot or too cold. It's hate or love, nothing else, and it shifts back and forth in a second. What *you* had in that fifteen-year-old minute, was all of 'em together in one. Right then in your life, a dead girl *was* sexy. Of course you wanted to stare at her underpants. That makes sense to me.'

'You mean I wasn't a burgeoning fifteen-year-old necrophiliac?'

'Sam, at fifteen everything made me think about sex. You have a wonderful mouth, you know. I think I will have a drink.'

She had vodka with ice. Her large hand with its salmon colored fingernails wrapped around that glass of clear liquid was so alluring that I sighed. When my eyes rose to her face, she was looking at me. Her smile said she knew exactly what I was thinking.

She stirred the drink and took a small sip. 'I heard an interesting story today. A friend of mine owns a restaurant on Sixty-Eighth street. A few months ago, a man came in and ordered filet mignon. My friend prides himself on buying the absolute best and freshest meat every day. So the customer had the filet and when he was done, said it was the best steak he'd ever eaten. The place is expensive, but every day for the next week he comes in and orders filet. Big tipper, completely satisfied, always full of compliments.

'One day my friend didn't get to the market, or something went wrong. Whatever, they didn't buy fresh meat. It was like from yesterday, but still good, you know? The customer comes in for his filet. When it's served, instead of taking a bite, he immediately bends over and sniffs it. Then he cuts a tiny piece, tastes it, and puts down his silver. "This meat isn't fresh." Calls for the bill and walks out. They never see him again. What I can't understand is why they didn't just tell him the steak isn't fresh today – have something else.'

'Come on, Veronica, you don't lie at *all*?'

She emptied her drink. '"It's easy to believe in yourself

when you're lying, because you're talking about someone else." You wrote that. I have it stuck above my desk.'

I put up both hands in surrender. 'But writers are notorious liars.'

'Could I ask you not to lie to me? I promise I can take a punch. You don't have to impress me because I already am. I like what you look like, and I swear to God it doesn't matter to me if you were on the varsity basketball team or know Bill Clinton.'

'What if I told you I was married three times and all my ex-wives think I'm a dog?'

'I knew about the wives because I read all the articles I could find about you. I don't care because they're them and I'm different. Give me a chance and I'll show you.'

'Boy, you really take it to the hoop, don't you?'

'The first day we met, at your book signing? I was dying to talk to you. But when we did, I chickened out. I wanted to tell you . . . No, I can't do it even now. I'm afraid.'

'What about the truth you were talking about?'

She took a deep breath, held it, let it out in a hard rush. 'Okay. I guess there's no difference between chickening out and lying. I want to go out with you, I want to *be* with you.'

'No boyfriend?'

'No boyfriend. No AIDS. I'm not a feminist and I'm not promiscuous, but sitting here with you this close, I just want to kiss your mouth for a long time.'

She sang in her sleep. It was only one of a number of unanticipated discoveries I made that eventful night. We went back to her apartment, but everything happened so fast after we got there that I forgot to look around the place to see how she lived.

We walked in the door, she kicked it shut with her foot – BOOM! – and took me straight into the bedroom. No matter how experienced you are, no matter how cool or worldly you think you are, nothing prepares you for a woman who leads you into the bedroom two seconds after you've entered her apartment on the first date. I felt twelve again and as innocent as a member of the Mickey Mouse Club.

She took off her clothes while staring at me the whole time. Shoes first in the most impossibly erotic way I had ever seen. Then her white shirt fell open more and more as she undid the buttons until there were none left. She hitched her shoulders and it fell off. No bra. Breasts worth fighting a war for.

A thick silver belt buckle which she unhitched with a couple of quick movements of her hand – right, left, open. The khakis were open just as quickly and then that sound any man will remember when he's old and horizontal and gasping for his last breath – the hiss of a zipper going down. Black panties. Off.

'Come here.'

I'd been sitting on the bed but stood quickly and went to her. She wouldn't let me touch her until she'd undressed me. 'Not yet. Enjoy no for a few minutes.'

Unlike her own strip, she undid the buttons on my shirt very slowly, stopping frequently to look at me and smile. I could smell her hair. It was some innocent child's shampoo. She had broad shoulders but her arms were thin and defined.

When my shirt was on the floor, she ran her fingertips across my chest, shoulders, down my arms and across my hands. She came in close and her hands went up my back. When I bent to kiss her, she shook her head and turned away, although her hands continued to move.

'Veronica?'

Her hands stopped and she pulled back.

'I don't have a condom.'

She bent down, reached into the pocket of her trousers and brought out a handful.

'How could you know?' I tried to sound lighthearted and skeptical in one.

'I didn't. I *hoped*.'

Although my novels *are* full of sleazy sex, I won't even attempt to describe what it was like to sleep with Veronica Lake. Translating sex into words is not meant to be. Sure, you can whip up all sorts of steam and whipped cream for dummies by verbally throwing body parts together, but it's so far from the real thing that it's like saying a picture postcard looks like the place itself.

Much of what she knew and did I had experienced before, but what thrilled me was her fluidity and ardor. Like being out on the floor with a superb dancer who knew every step, never wanted to sit down, and made you feel like you were Fred Astaire.

I don't know when we fell asleep but I awoke in the middle of the night with her hair across my throat and a quiet, sleepy voice somewhere nearby singing Billy Joel's 'Uptown Girl'. At first I thought we'd left the radio on, but then remembered there had been no radio on. Then through the cobwebs of sleep I thought it came from out on the street until I realized the voice was too close. I pushed her hair off my face and turned towards the woman I'd fallen asleep next to.

'Veronica?'

'"Uptown Girl—"'

'Veronica?'

'"You've been livin'—"'

'*Veronica?*'

Her head was turned away from me. It came slowly around. 'Hi' in that same sweet singing voice.

'You sing in your sleep!'

'I know.'

'You were singing "Uptown Girl"!'
'Press my nose and the song'll change. Kiss me?'

In the morning I woke before her and had a chance to look around her apartment. The things in it kept saying the word 'shipshape' to me. It was tidy but not obsessively clean. There were a few hairpins and women's things lying around the bathroom, some dirty cups in the kitchen sink. Despite that, there was an overall pleasing neatness and order to the place. There was a bedroom and a living room which doubled as her study. The nicest thing about the apartment was how sunny it was. Everything felt airy and open.

Writers are chronic snoops and these are some of the other things I noticed about my new lover's home. She read mostly novels, poetry, books on design and biographies of artists. The furniture was cozy rather than stylish. Her living room was full of exotic cut flowers in vases of wildly different colors and sizes.

Glancing at an unfinished letter left on her desk, I was struck by the handwriting. If I hadn't known it was hers, I would have thought a man had written it. Each letter was bold and perfectly vertical, extremely distinctive and elegant. Nearby was a fountain pen. Very large, it was a luminous blue with gold cap. I carefully picked it up.

'Isn't it a beauty?'

I turned as she touched my shoulder. Her hair was in a sexy sleep-frazzle around her head. Her hand was soft and warm. 'I love fountain pens.'

She leaned her chin on my shoulder. 'Are you looking around? That's what I do too after I've spent a night with someone. See them through where they live. What conclusion did you reach? Don't lie.'

I put the pen down and kissed her temple. 'Shipshape. Everything is right where it should be. You'd make a good sailor.'

'Fair enough. And what about my things? Do you get a read from them?'

'You like bundles of color, yet none of your flowers are alive. You're not into high maintenance. Biographies of maniac geniuses, but your apartment says you're orderly. Books on how things are designed. Let me guess – you're an Aquarius?'

'Nope. Virgo.'

I stiffened unintentionally. 'Veronica, one of my wives was a Virgo. You are *not* a Virgo. Virgos don't make love like you do. They make fists, freeze, and stare at the ceiling.'

She yawned and stretched languourously. When she was done, she brought her long arms down slowly around me. Her breath was stale and warm. I wanted to kiss her.

'I make love the way I am, not because I'm a Virgo. What else did the apartment tell you?'

'What are the stones?' In the upper corner of her desk was a small pile of uninteresting looking smooth stones piled in a large brass ashtray. She picked up a couple of them and rubbed them against her cheek. 'They're from Java. I'd always wanted to do a film on the Komodo dragon, so I got a small grant and went to Indonesia for a month.

'I was on a beach one day throwing stones into the water. I picked one up. *This* one, actually, and was about to throw it when suddenly a thought came to me. What if all the stones on all the beaches of the world were human souls?

'That's what happens to us after we die: our souls are turned into rock and thrown into one of the oceans. For thousands or millions of years, they're knocked around in the water until they're worn down and look like this. But the *real* purpose is to be worn away completely. Once that happens, the soul gets to go to heaven or Nirvana, nothingness, whatever.' She jiggled the stone in her hand. 'Or else the purpose is for the stone to get washed back up on to land after a thousand years in the water. Slowly slowly being pushed towards shore, up there where it's safe and calm and the sun beats down on it every day . . .

'It was one of those ideas which was so strange yet had enough *import* to it that it stopped me like a slap and made me wonder. So I picked up this handful and brought them home. My stone memento mori.'

The next time I went back to Crane's View, Cassandra came along. It was the week before school started and she was predictably cranky about having to go back to the grind for another year. When I suggested we spend a day in my home town she lightened up and agreed to go on the condition I didn't regale her with stories of my glorious good old days. I said that was no problem because I didn't have many back then. I was a good enough student, I had some unmemorable experiences, I watched too much television.

'Okay, Mr Happy Days, so what is your greatest memory of high school?'

'I guess finding Pauline Ostrova.'

'*Dad*, that's not a memory, it's a horror. I mean normal stuff. You know, like the prom or the homecoming game.'

'Being in love. Learning how to be in love. One day girls went from just being there to being the center of everything.'

'When did it happen with you?'

I lifted a hand off the steering wheel and turned it palm up. 'I don't remember. I just know I walked into school one day and everything was different. There were all these swirling skirts and bosoms and enticing smiles.'

She rolled down the window. The wind whipped her hair across her face. 'Sometimes when I'm really sad or depressed, I think *he's* out there somewhere and sooner or later we'll meet.

'Then I wonder what's he doing this minute? Does he

ever think the same thing? Does he ever wonder what I'm like or where I am? He's probably reading *Playboy* and dreaming of boobs.'

I thought about it a moment and had to agree. 'Boys do tend to do that. Judging from my own experience, he's either already somewhere in your life but hasn't materialized in your thoughts yet. Like people when they're beaming up in *Star Trek*. You know, when they're halfway there but still look like club soda bubbles? Or else he's in Mali or Breslau and you won't see him for a while. But you can be sure no matter where he is, he thinks about you, sweetheart.'

She shrugged. 'Speaking of such things, what's with your new girlfriend?'

'I don't know yet. She's still in a fuzzy pink frame for me.'

'What does that mean?' Cass put her bare feet up on the dashboard.

'It means she's still too much of a sweetie pie for me to have any perspective on the situation. Everything she does is adorable.'

'What's her name again, Greta Garbo?'

'Don't be a wiseguy; you know her name – Veronica Lake.'

'When do I get to meet her?'

'The next time I come into the city and can wrest you away from your mother. We're all going to have dinner together.'

We stopped for lunch at Scrappy's Diner and surprisingly, Donna the waitress remembered me from the last visit. She asked if I had gone to see her Uncle Frannie yet. I said today was the day. She looked at Cass curiously so I introduced them.

'Donna, this is my daughter Cassandra. Donna's uncle is Frannie McCabe.'

Cass whistled loudly, thoroughly impressed. 'Frannie

McCabe is my father's hero. Every bad guy in every book he ever wrote has some of Frannie in him.'

Donna giggled and asked if I would like her to call the station to see if he was in. I said sure. She went off and was back in five minutes. 'He remembered you! He says to come down.'

Half an hour later we walked through the door of the Crane's View police station. I found myself unconsciously shaking my head. 'The last time I was in here, a whole bunch of us were dragged in for fighting at a football game.'

A young policeman passed on his way out and gave Cass an appreciative look. The Dad in me clenched but I kept moving. Just inside the door a woman in uniform sat at a desk. I asked if we could speak to the Chief. After asking my name, she picked up a phone and called. A moment later the door behind her opened. A gaunt man in an expensive dark suit emerged wearing a smile I'd know a thousand years from now.

'Fuckin' A, it's Bayer aspirin! I just want to know one thing – you got cigarettes?'

'Frannie!'

We shook hands a long time while staring at each other, checking the wrinkles, the signs, the years across each other's faces.

'You aren't dressed too sharp for a famous author. That last book of yours – I laughed so loud at the end, I got a sore throat.'

'It was supposed to be sad!'

He took hold of my chin and squeezed it. 'Our bestseller. Sammy Bayer on the *New York Times* bestseller list. You can't imagine how happy I was when I saw your name there the first time.'

His hair was brushed back and gelled into place, *GQ* magazine style. His rep tie was elegant and understated; the shirt as smooth and white as fresh milk. He looked like either a successful stockbroker or a professional basketball coach. The same crazy energy I remembered so well glowed on him, but his face was extremely pale and there were deep blue circles under his eyes. It looked like he was recuperating from a serious illness.

'Who's this?'

'My daughter Cassandra.'

He put out a hand to shake, but Cass surprised both of us by stepping forward and embracing him. He looked at me over her shoulder and smiled. 'Hey, what's this?'

She took a step back. 'I know you already. I've been hearing stories about you since I was a baby.'

'Really?' He was embarrassed and very pleased. 'What'd your dad say about me?'

'I know about the Coke bottle bombs, the VFW Hall, Anthony Scaro's Chevelle—'

'Whoa! Come into my office before you get me arrested.'

The office was huge and bare of anything but a big scarred desk and two chairs facing it.

'It looks exactly the same as it did twenty years ago!'

Sitting on the other side of the desk, Frannie looked over his shoulder at the room. 'I took the Rembrandt down so you'd feel at home. How many times did they have us in here, Sam?'

'You more than me, Chief. They should have put up a memorial plaque for you in here.'

'I got tired of sitting on your side of the desk and havin' someone hit me on the head with the Yellow Pages. I thought I'd take over and get to do the hitting.'

My daughter the pacifist stiffened. 'Do you really do that? Hit people with telephone books?'

'Naah, Cassandra, the good old days are over. Now they make us use psychology. But now and then if they get fresh we sneak in and poke 'em with an electric cattle prod.'

As I so well remembered, his expression gave away

56

nothing. All innocent, calm, and empty, that perfected poker face had gotten him out of a lot of trouble twenty-five years before.

'Tell her you're joking, Frannie.'

'I'm joking, Cass. So, Mr Bayer, how come you've graced Crane's View with your presence after two decades?'

'Before we get into that, tell me how in God's name you ended up Chief of Police? I was sure you'd be—'

'In jail? Thank you. That's what everyone says. I didn't have a religious conversion, if that's what you're worried about. Better – I went to Vietnam. Things happened. Good guys died but I didn't. You remember Andy Eldritch? He was eating a can of Bumble Bee tunafish his Mom had sent and then suddenly he was dead two feet away from me. I'd just asked him if I could have a bite. Things like that. I got pissed off. Life couldn't be *that* worthless, you know? When I got out, I went to Macalester College in St Paul and got a B.S. Then, I don't know, I became a cop. It made sense.'

'Are you married?'

'*Was*, but no more. Now I'm single as a thumb.'

'Dad's been married three times.'

Frannie opened a desk drawer and took out a pack of Marlboros. 'No surprise. Your dad was always odder than a Brussels sprout. Guess he still is.'

'You can say that again. Now he's dating a woman named Veronica Lake.'

'Isn't she dead? Wow, *that's* original, Sam.'

'Fuck you, Frannie. Listen, remember Pauline Ostrova?'

'Sure, you pulled her out of the river. The day we all grew up.'

'You remember everything about that day?'

'Damn right I do! How many people get murdered in this burg?'

'How many *do*?'

'Two, as long as I've been on the force. That's seventeen

years. Both marital things. Very pathetic and uninteresting.'

'Who did it? Who killed Pauline?'

'Who do they *say* did it, or who did it?' He lit the cigarette and closed his lighter with a hard snap.

Cass and I looked at each other and waited for him to continue. He didn't.

Smiling, he wiggled his eyebrows. 'I should have been an actor. How's that for dramatic tension? I think they should cast Andy Garcia as me in the movie.

'The best part of being Chief of Police is I get to look in all the old files and see what really went on here when we were kids. There's still a file on you, Sam. Now that you're famous, you think I could get money telling the world you were a juvenile delinquent?'

'Frannie, what about Pauline?'

'The case was open and shut. She had a boyfriend from college named Edward Durant. They arrested him, he confessed, they cut a deal with the prosecutor and sent him up to Sing Sing for life. He's dead.'

Cass gasped.

Frannie ran a hand through his hair. 'This is ugly stuff, Cassandra. You sure you want to hear it?'

She licked her lips, nodded slowly, then quickly.

'As soon as he got up there, the bad boys started using him for a fu ... uh, love doll until he couldn't take it anymore and hanged himself in his cell.'

'Jesus! How old was he?'

'Twenty-one. Nice-looking boy. Dean's List at Swarthmore. But he didn't do it.'

'Who did?' I realized I was breathing too quickly.

'I've got my suspicions. You didn't know Pauline, did you? She was from another dimension. Why do you want to know about her now?'

'Because I want to write a book about what really happened to her.'

Frannie took a long drag on the cigarette and put his hand behind his head. 'Interesting idea.' He looked at the ceiling. 'Come on, I want to show you a couple of things.' He stood up and gestured for us to follow.

Out on the street he shot his cuffs and walked over to an unmarked Chevrolet. 'Hop in.'

Driving down the street in a police car with McCabe at the wheel made me laugh. 'Frannie, I wish there was some kind of magic available where I could go back and say to fifteen-year-old me "Do I have something to tell *you*."'

'He'd never believe you. Here, look at this shitty store. You buy a pair of shoes in there, you're barefoot in two months. Remember Al Salvato?'

'Green Light?'

'Right.' He looked in the rearview mirror at Cass. 'Al Salvato was a *svacim* we grew up with. Whenever someone said something he agreed with, he'd say "Green light." He thought it was cute.'

'But Frannie didn't. He punched him in the nose for it.'

'That's right. Salvato owns three stores here now. This is one of them. He brought cheap shoes, a sex store and bad Greek food to town. Ran for mayor last year and lost, thank God.'

Chief McCabe's tour of Crane's View went up and down and all around. He pointed out who owned what, who of our old friends still lived there, and gave a running, funny history of what had happened since I'd left. His information only furthered what I already assumed: new money had moved up from Manhattan, thus terminally yuppifying much of the old homestead. There was a café now that served cappuccino and croissants, an Audi dealer, a vegetarian restaurant. What was left existed in a time warp that made the rest of the village look like it hadn't changed a bit. Witness Scrappy's Diner.

Cass asked more questions than I did. From them, I was

touched to hear she remembered many of the stories I had told her over the years. She and Frannie chatted away as he drove us around. After a while I tuned them out.

We drove up Baldwin Street and took a right on Broadway. I smiled, knowing where we were going. He stopped the car in front of a well-kept red and white house with a wraparound porch. Large chestnut trees flanked it on both sides. It was in much better condition than when I had last seen it.

'You know this house, Cassandra?'

'No.' She was leaning forward, her elbows resting on the seat between Frannie and me.

'This is where your Dad lived.'

'Really? He never showed it to me. Can we go look?'

We got out and stood on the sidewalk in front. 'How come I've never been here before, Dad?'

I was about to answer when Frannie climbed up on the porch and went to the front door. 'You want to look inside?' He held up a bunch of keys and jigged them to show he could get in.

'You have a key?'

'To my own house? Sure!' Without waiting for our reactions, he opened the door and walked in. I caught up as he was walking into the living room. I wanted to ask a dozen questions, but also wanted simply to stand there and remember.

'You *live* here? You bought my house?'

'Yeah! I've had it seven years.'

'What'd you pay for it?'

He looked to see if Cass was near. 'None of your fuckin' business. Bought it when I was married. My wife was an executive producer at NBC so we had a lot of money then. When we split up, she gave me the house.'

'Congratulations! Every time *I* got divorced, I had to check to see if I still had all my body parts after the settlement. Can we look around?'

'Sure. You want something to drink? Cassandra, you want anything?'

'Could I have a beer?'

'Sam?'

'Nothing. I'm in too much shock. Frannie McCabe owns my house. You bought it from, who, the Van Gelders?'

'Their son. They moved to Florida and gave it to him.' He started for the kitchen. 'You wanna look around, go ahead. Go upstairs if you want.'

'Dad?' Cass look at me expectantly.

'Go ahead. I'm going to sit here a little while.'

Frannie was back in a few minutes with a can of beer in one hand, a glass of milk in the other.

'Milk? *You*?'

'Good stuff. Now what's with the Pauline thing? How come you want to write about her?'

'Because it's too interesting to pass up. I've been thinking about it a while now. Why don't you think her boyfriend did it? You've got to tell me everything because I don't know a thing.'

He sat down across from me and cradled his glass in both hands. 'I'll show you the files. She and this Edward Durant went out the night it happened. He'd come down for the weekend to be with her. His story is, they went to the river to drink and make out. What he remembered was they drank too much and got into a bad fight. Really bad. They were hitting each other. Then they stopped and drank some more.'

'Why were they fighting?'

'Because she wanted to break up. Said she didn't respect him and wanted out. The last thing he remembered was her getting out of the car and him following. She went over to the water and he was right behind her. She said get away. He hit her. Slapped her across the face. She fell down and started screaming. Said all kinds of nasty things and kinda went nuts. Way over the top, even for crazy

Pauline. That spooked him, so he went back to the car, hoping she'd cool off. While he was waiting, he kept drinking till he passed out.

'When he came to, it was an hour later. Eleven thirty, because he looked at his watch. She wasn't back. He got out again and looked all around, but she was gone. He thought she'd walked home. He was so angry at what had happened that he just drove right back to his house in Bedford.'

'But you said he confessed when they caught him.'

'He confessed to being there alone with her, to fighting, to hitting her, to passing out. They had a lot of proof from his past that whenever he drank he got violent. They put two and two together. And that, my friend, is usually enough to convince a jury.'

'But why would he admit to all that if he *did* kill her? That they fought and he hit her? It makes no sense. He never actually admitted to killing her?'

'No.'

'And you don't think he did it?'

'Nope.' He finished the glass of milk in one slug.

'Who did?'

'We're talking off the record here?'

I held up both hands. 'I'm not taking notes and I ain't wired.'

'Take it easy, Sam. What do you think this is, *NYPD Blue*? Do you remember David Cadmus?'

Cass came back into the room. Frannie stood up and handed her the beer. 'Sure you remember him. Little guy? Hung around with Terry Walker and John Lesher?'

I thought about it until a picture from our high school yearbook came to mind: Three boys standing stiffly around a 16mm movie projector, all wearing formal white shirts buttoned to the top and thick black Clark Kent eyeglasses. 'The worms! Of course I remember.'

Frannie sat down on the couch next to Cass. 'Back when we were in school, any guy who carried around a slide rule, was good in math or science, and didn't take baths was a thumbs down kinda guy. We called them worms.'

Cass rolled her eyes. 'Worms? God, you guys were so mean.'

'And proud of it! But Cassandra, you kids got your own terms for them now. How about geeks? Nerds? Call 'em what you like, for us they were worms.

'But I found out something I bet you didn't know, Sam; David Cadmus's father was Gordon Cadmus. *The* Gordon Cadmus.'

'The *gangster*?'

'That's right, bud. Crane's View's very own Mafia man. We just didn't know it then. We thought he was a business guy. He owned some companies in the city. We wouldn't have teased his kid so much if we'd known who his dad was.'

Cass looked at me, then at Frannie. 'Who was Gordon Cadmus?'

'Eleven years ago in a New York restaurant three men were having dinner: Gordon Cadmus, Jerry Kargl and George Weiser. Two men in raincoats walked into the restaurant and shot all three. Nobody in the place remembered what the shooters looked like of course, only that they were both wearing raincoats. See no evil, hear no evil. Story has it that after they finished shooting, one of the guys walked over to Cadmus's body and stuck a chocolate eclair in his eye. Then they walked out and that was that. You had something like it in one of your books, right, Sam?'

'*The Tattooed City*. That's how the damned story ends! My God, if I'd known one of the real victims was Cadmus's father ... But what did he have to do with Pauline's death?'

'*Pauline* knew who he was back then. She had been seeing him on and off for two years.'

'Frannie, she was nineteen years old when she died!'

He shrugged. 'Some kids start young. Especially ones like Pauline.'

The room was silent a while. Frannie tipped his empty glass up to get the last drops. To my surprise, Cass was first to speak.

'Dad, remember the girl I told you about, Spoon? The one with the tattoo? She sounds like Pauline in a lot of ways. Her motto is "do it now because you might not get a chance later."'

Frannie laughed strangely. 'Exactly! When you start looking into Pauline's life, you'll see she was either fearless or totally nuts. I've never been able to figure out which.'

I looked around the room where I'd spent so much time as a kid. In that corner we'd always put the Christmas tree. Over there our dog Jack used to stand on his hind legs and look out the window. Frannie had been here too. Sitting uncomfortably on the edge of a chair, utterly ill at ease talking to my parents while waiting for me to come downstairs so we could go out and make trouble.

'This is serious business, Frannie. Why haven't you done something about it? Talked to people?'

'I've talked to a lot of people. I'll tell you about it some time.'

'Now you're suddenly getting mysterious on me? Where's David Cadmus now? Do you know?'

'Hollywood. Runs an independent film company. They put out that big hit recently, *The Blind Clown*?'

'Sounds like your worm turned, huh?'

Frannie pointed a finger at Cass. 'Touché.'

'Why would Gordon Cadmus kill Pauline if she was his mistress?'

'Because Edward Durant's father was a federal attorney

investigating racketeering. Guess whose case he was assigned three weeks before Pauline died?'

Unfortunately I had to go out on a book tour to promote the paperback edition of *The Magician's Breakfast*, so I wasn't able to return to Crane's View for a while. Before leaving, I arranged to rent a room in Frannie's house so I could set up an office and not worry about bringing things back and forth from Connecticut on the many trips I knew I would be making to my old hometown. Frannie said I didn't have to pay rent so long as I dedicated the book to him. I didn't know if he was serious but I'd promised the next one to Cass.

From the way he lived, it seemed my old pal could use all the money he could find. His house was beautifully furnished. I knew enough about furniture from my second wife to recognize some of the pieces he owned were very expensive. He also drove an Infiniti and had a closet full of clothes that reminded me of the Great Gatsby's shirt collection. When I asked how he afforded these things, he laughed and said he'd once been married to a rich woman. I didn't know how far that explanation would fly but it wasn't my place to probe. Despite the fact he was Chief of Police and had apparently turned his life around since I'd known him, I had a lingering suspicion somewhere behind Mr Solid Citizen, old rogue McCabe was up to some kind of mischief that allowed him to live way beyond his means.

Book tours can be irritating and exhausting. Too many cities in too few days, 'interviews' with people who haven't read the book but need you to fill up a few desultory minutes on their TV or radio shows, meals alone in dreary restaurants ... When I'd first done them, I thought tours romantic, exciting; now they were only part of the job. Worse, I found I lived in a kind of empty-headed limbo for

65

days after they were finished. This time I resented the fact I couldn't get to work on Pauline's book until this was out of the way.

Trying to find some way to cheer up the inevitable, I hit on the idea of asking Veronica to come along. I was hesitant at first because two weeks on the road with anyone could end in disaster. But by the time I did ask, we had been having such a nice time together that I was willing to try. So was she and the way she accepted the invitation gave me hope. Her face lit up, but she said, 'What a nice idea. Are you sure we won't drive each other crazy?'

'No, I'm not sure.'

'Me neither, but I'd like to try.'

Because of earlier commitments, she couldn't go to Boston or Washington, but would catch up in Chicago and we'd go west together.

The trip began dreadfully. In Boston, the tail end of a hurricane was visiting the city. As a result, about twenty sodden people showed up at the bookstore for my signing.

When I got back to the hotel, there was a message for me to call a Rocky Zaroka who said he was a friend of Veronica's. She'd called him to say I was in town and suggested we get together. I couldn't imagine anyone wanting to come out in that weather, but Mr Zaroka sounded happy to hear from me and we made a date for a drink in the hotel bar.

Half an hour later, one of the handsomest men I've ever seen stood next to me and smiled. 'Mr Bayer? Rocky Zaroka.'

'How'd you know me?'

'I was at your reading. The wet guy in the back row?'

'You went out in this weather?'

'Veronica said she'd kill me if I didn't. And when Veronica says go, you go.'

He was engaging, smart, and told great stories. He'd been places in the world I'd never even heard of and had once had drinks with Gorbachev. I listened and listened to him and finally couldn't stand it anymore.

'How do you know Veronica? Were you two together?'

His smile faded. He moved his head slowly from side to side. 'I *wish*! I fell in love with her on sight when we met years ago and have pursued her ever since. It's become a joke between us now. Whenever we meet, the first thing I do is propose. She always says no, and then we talk about other things.'

'*I'd* marry you.'

He laughed and slapped a hand on the bar. 'Thank you, Sam. Tell that to your friend! Veronica knows exactly what she wants but unfortunately I'm not it. Once I proposed to her in a hot air balloon over Saratoga Springs. She was teaching a semester course in documentary filmmaking at Skidmore.'

'Where did you meet?'

'In Burkino Faso.'

I stared uncomprehendingly.

He smiled. 'That's in Central Africa. She was working on a goat breeding project for the government.

'There's a restaurant called Mama Marie's in Ouagadougou. That's the capital. They make great fou fou. The first time I ever saw Veronica, she was sitting in there reading one of your books. I remember that specifically because it was a vision: this *magnificent* woman sitting alone in that funny place, reading a book in English and looking totally content. I went over to her and lied that I had read it.'

'What'd she do?'

'Looked at me real cool a minute and then said "What does Milena Cappetta do?" She gave me a *quiz* about your book! Which I failed!'

The next morning while the weather continued to eat Bean Town, I dutifully showed up on time for an interview with an 'alternative' newspaper. The woman asking the questions arrived half an hour late and immediately started launching verbal Scud missiles at any person who'd ever been on a bestseller list. In ten minutes things between us went from polite to open warfare. When she smugly asked if I ever read 'serious' writers, I suggested she should stop reading George Bataille a while and go get laid instead. Then I got up and left.

Because of the weather, the plane to Washington was delayed two hours so I sat in airport hell wondering once again why there is nothing to do in airports. Why hasn't some enterprising genius yet realized all us bored ticket holders would adore, flock to, pay hard cash for ... any diversions that lasted longer than a cruise through the magazine racks or dull necktie store?

In contrast to Boston, Washington was going through an ugly heat wave that melted your brain into mozzarella. Who wants to leave the great god air conditioning to go listen to some thriller writer read from a book they've already read?

When it was over, I ate sushi across the street from my hotel and stared at a couple nearby. Watching them was like seeing a terrific film in a foreign language with subtitles: no matter how much you enjoy it, you know it would be even better if you understood what was really being said. Looking at the passion and electricity between them, I knew I wasn't in love with Veronica yet, but it was a real possibility. I loved seeing her, and hearing Zaroka's stories made her even more intriguing and elusive. Goat breeding in Burkino Faso? Why hadn't she ever mentioned that?

She seemed full of the kind of engaging contradictions I like in a woman: tough in her profession but vulnerable and affectionate with me, strong-minded and intelligent but also curious about the workings of the world and thus open to suggestion. One of the best things about our relationship was how well we communicated, including long conversations in bed after sex – that dangerous, sometimes magical time when people tend to tell the truth more than usual.

In Chicago, she was waiting for me in the hotel room. Sitting on the edge of the bed with the TV remote control in her hand, she was wearing a bright white T-shirt, black skirt, white socks and black Doc Martens tie-up shoes. Her hair was back in a ponytail and the whole package made her look eighteen years old.

When she started to stand up I walked to the bed and put a hand on her shoulder. She turned off the television and smiled at me.

'I hope you don't mind me sneaking into your room, Mr Bayer. I'm your biggest fan. Will you sign my heart?'

I moved my hand to her cheek. 'It's nice to touch your face again. I'm glad you're here.'

Her eyes were all eagerness. 'Are you really? You weren't worried or anything?'

'I'm worried and everything, but I'm still glad you're here. How come you never told me you were in Africa?'

From Chicago we went to Denver, then Portland, Seattle, San Francisco, Los Angeles and finished in San Diego. One radiant morning in Seattle while walking by the water, I told Veronica all I knew about Pauline Ostrova and the book I wanted to write. I told her about Frannie McCabe and growing up in Crane's View, what came after, and then about some of the people who had mattered along the way.

We were sitting at a Starbuck's coffee shop when I finished. The air outside was cool and crisp, full of delicious smells that kept changing with the breeze – wood smoke, ground coffee, the sea. Veronica wore a pair of large black wire-rimmed sunglasses that made her look alluring and powerful. Her face was so changeable. One moment she was Lolita, the next, the president of some multinational conglomerate.

'Thank you.'

'For what? You look famous in those sunglasses. Aren't you Veronica Lake?'

'I mean it, Sam. Thank you for telling me your story. It's a dangerous thing to do. Telling someone leaves you open and vulnerable. I think I've done it a total of three times in my life.'

'Think you'll ever tell me your story?'

She slipped off the glasses and put them on the table. Tears glistened in her eyes. 'I don't know yet. Whoever says I love you first, loses. That line has always frightened me. You already know I love you. If I tell you my whole story too and then things go wrong between us, I won't have much left.'

'You sound like a member of one of those tribes that believe if someone photographs them, they lose their souls.'

She put the heels of her hands to her eyes and rubbed them back and forth. 'Your story *is* your soul. The longer you're with someone, the more you trust them, the more you're willing to tell. I believe when you find your real partner, you tell them everything until there's nothing left. Then you start from the beginning again, only this time it's their story as well as yours.'

'No separation of church and state? You even have to use the same toothbrush?'

Her voice was low but very firm when she spoke: 'You buy two blue toothbrushes exactly the same and keep them in a glass so you never know which is which. Yours is mine and mine's yours.'

'Those are pretty tight quarters, Veronica.'

The offices of Black Suit Pictures were in a modern high rise a few streets back from the ocean in Santa Monica. You parked below the building and rode up in an elevator to an altitude you did not want to visit in that forever shaky part of the world. Two nights before in San Francisco, a small earthquake had jolted us very much awake minutes after we got into bed. Sex that night was more 'please hold me' than anything else. We laughed about it, but that didn't stop either of us from sitting up very straight any time we felt the slightest anything the rest of the time we were in California.

A beautiful receptionist was facing the elevator so that the moment the door slid open, you were blasted with one of those million white teeth smiles that are supposed to make you feel welcome and comfortable.

'Can I help you?'

'I have an appointment with David Cadmus. My name is Samuel Bayer.'

'Would you have a seat while I call?'

I sat on a slinky leather couch and looked around. Nothing new. The place looked like every other film producer's office I'd seen: tony furniture, the requisite posters of the films the company had made. I recognized the titles of some. Two had been genuine hits.

I almost laughed when David Cadmus entered the reception room because he looked exactly as he had twenty-five years before. Same spiky porcupine haircut, square eyeglasses, white dress shirt buttoned to the top. Yet his 'look' was today's ultimate cool, as opposed to ultimate asshole when we were young. Black chinos, dress shoes . . . I'm sure the labels on his clothes were Prada or Comme des Garçons rather than Dickies, but the look was the same.

I stood up. He kept his hands in his pockets. We stared at each other. Out of the corner of my eye, I noticed the receptionist watching us. We hadn't even said hello but were already in a High Noon standoff.

'He didn't do it.'

Without thinking, I cocked my head quizzically to one side. 'Excuse me?'

'My father. He didn't kill Pauline Ostrova.'

According to his son, by the time Gordon Cadmus fell in love with Pauline he had forgotten how to laugh. Certainly there's a lot less to laugh at as we grow older, but that's beside the point. Here was an immensely powerful man who controlled half the crime in Westchester County. People did what he said without thinking. He had private bank accounts in countries whose names you couldn't even pronounce. He had what he wanted, he'd achieved his dream. But he was a morose sourpuss, convinced years before someone actually shot him that one day he would be murdered.

So shocking to the Cadmus family was the sound of the old man's laugh – a surprisingly deep and delighted Har de Har Har – that both son and mother froze when they heard it. In their separate bedrooms on that Saturday afternoon, the boy had been reading *Famous Monsters of Film Land* magazine, the mother one of Jack Paar's autobiographies. Within seconds, both appeared at their doorways wearing similarly worried expressions.

'Did you hear that?'

'Yes! You think something's wrong?'

'Dad never laughs.'

'Maybe we should go see.'

At the top of the long staircase, they bent down to see Gordon Cadmus at the front door, talking to a girl.

It was Pauline Ostrova who, among other things, wrote for our high school newspaper. Someone had told her there were rumors Gordon Cadmus was involved with 'the mob'. Being insanely self-confident, she decided to do an in-depth interview with our local gangster. She put on her nicest dress, combed her hair, and rang his bell.

When he answered the door (a thing he rarely did), a

nice-looking girl stood there, looking as if she might be selling magazine subscriptions or tickets to a church raffle. She said, 'Mr Cadmus, my name is Pauline Ostrova. I write for the Crane's View High School newspaper. It's well known you're associated with organized crime and I'd like to interview you.'

That's when he laughed and invited her in.

Almost three decades later, his son said, 'You've got to understand most people couldn't even *look* at my father without breaking into a sweat.'

'Aw, come on, David. We were nosey kids. We knew what everybody did in Crane's View. How come we never knew about your father? How come we didn't know he was in the Mafia?'

David smirked. 'Because on paper he *wasn't*. He was in waste removal and olive oil importing. He had a construction company.' He could have filled a wheelbarrow with all the cynicism in his voice.

'All synonyms for the Mafia, right?'

He smiled and nodded.

'So how *did* a high school girl find out who he was?'

'Because at the time, the high school girl's lover was the Chief of Police.'

'*Cristello*? Pauline was Cristello's lover too? Who was this girl, Mata Hari?'

Policeman Cristello told his lover about Mobster Cadmus and she went right out and became his lover too. Simple as that, or according to the mobster's son it was.

Cadmus fell for her. Why? Because she made him laugh. Years later, he told David the whole story. The two men had grown very close over the years and one Christmas the old man asked his son what he wanted for a present. David said the truth. He wanted to know about his father's life because he knew absolutely nothing and it mattered very much to him. In one astounding night, Gordon Cadmus told his son everything.

I didn't probe, but *did* ask how he felt after he'd heard his father's story. 'I never loved him more.'

As I was leaving, I asked David how he knew I was going to ask about his father's connection to Pauline. His answer shocked me.

'Because your pal McCabe called and said so. He's been taunting me for years about it but has never been able to find even the smallest shred of proof that Dad killed her. Because there isn't any. My father loved Pauline. He was crushed by her death.'

'Wait a minute! Your father could have found out who killed her. He must have known people who could have found out.'

'Dad believed the boyfriend did it. Edward Durant.'

It made real sense. Durant killed her and went to jail. When he got there, Cadmus arranged to send in the clowns who used Edward as a sex toy until his brains were scrambled eggs and he saw no way out but a permanent necktie. What a neat and evil way to get your revenge.

It sounded plausible, but what had seemed so simple a few days before had suddenly become a surreal three-ring circus of motives, love and revenge.

David walked me out of the building into a scorching California afternoon. We talked by my car a few minutes. I noticed the heat didn't seem to bother him. No sticking shirt, no squinting against the sun.

'This is a long way from Crane's View, New York. Have you been back there recently?'

He shook his head. 'I remember you and Frannie McCabe walking down the halls of the school. I never knew if I envied or hated all of you in that gang. No, I haven't been back, but McCabe keeps calling me. He's a strange motherfucker. I'd be flattered by his attention if I didn't know it was my father he still wants to get.'

We were staying at the Peninsula Hotel but when I got back to the room, Veronica wasn't there. That was okay because we had been as inseparable as Siamese twins throughout the trip. It was good having time alone to think through my meeting with Cadmus and make notes.

I write all my books by hand. There is something ceremonious and correct about putting things down a letter at a time, your hand doing that slow work instead of fingers tap-dancing across a keyboard. For me, something is lost in all that speed. On the computer screen, the work looks finished even when you know it isn't.

From my briefcase, I took out a beautiful leather notebook Cass had given me for my last birthday. Then the forty-year-old mustard-colored Parker 51 Custom fountain pen that was the only one I ever used for this purpose. I am superstitious about everything and over the years the pen had become a fundamental element of whatever mysterious chemistry was involved in writing a book. I filled it with ink and opened the notebook to the first page.

In that graceful anonymous room with the air conditioning purring around me, I began the story of Pauline Ostrova's death – with my dog Jack the Wonder Boy.

He looked at you seriously and appeared to listen to what you said. He was smart and generally reasonable, but there were certain things he insisted on and refused to stop doing even if you went after him with a broom or an angry hand. Bones could only be eaten on a rug, he had to sleep on the corner of my bed, any food left too close to the edge of a table was his if he could somehow get to it.

Every morning of his life he stood by the front door at a reasonable hour, waiting to be let out. We all knew to check the hall as we walked to breakfast to see if he was waiting by the door. In all of his fifteen years, I don't think his neck ever knew the feel of a collar or the tug from a leash. Jack took care of himself, thank you, and didn't need to be led by any human. None of us ever followed him on his rounds, but he was a dog of such fixed routines and dimensions that I'm sure he walked the same route, lifted his leg on the same trees, sniffed the same places thousands of times.

I began the book with our front door opening and Jack stepping out into a new day in Crane's View. My words took him out to the street and then on his morning jaunt.

I wrote for an hour, then got up and walking restlessly around the room, flicked the television on, channel surfed, turned it off. Looking out the window, I remembered the book signing at Book Soup at seven and wondered if Veronica would be back in time. I sat down again and went back to work.

Jack trotted through town. Stores were beginning to open. A few cars were parked in the Grand Union lot on Ashford Avenue. Three teenagers stood in front of the firehouse smoking cigarettes and watching cars go by. Victor Bucci. Alan Tarricone. Bobby LaSpina. According to McCabe, LaSpina died in Vietnam, Tarricone ended up running his father's gas station, Bucci left town and no one heard from him again.

Why did Frannie keep calling David over the years? Even if his father *was* guilty of Pauline's murder, what could David do about it, especially now that the old man was dead? And what else was McCabe up to? What other inexplicables did he have up his sleeve?

Pauline Ostrova hit our dog Jack in front of Martina Darnell's house. At the time, I had a crush on Martina but she wasn't interested in me. The only time we ever spoke for more than ten seconds was when she described hearing the screech of tires in front of her house, the thud, Jack howling.

That morning, I was the only one home when Pauline knocked at our door.

'Hi there.'

I was so involved in writing that Veronica's voice gave me a jolt. I turned around. Her face was a foot from mine. 'Hey you.'

'I didn't hear you come in.'

'I see that! You're writing away like a little engine. Whacha doin'?' She had a couple of bags in her hand which she tossed on to the bed. A piece of anthracite blue lingerie slid provocatively out of one. Pushing her hair up with one hand, she fanned her face with the other. 'Can you tell me what you've been writing?'

'After I talked to David Cadmus, I started writing notes and think I might even have begun the book.'

'Really!' Her eyes widened and she clasped her hands to her chest. 'That's wonderful, Sam! Can I give you a hug?'

'I'd love one.'

The moment we were in each other's arms, the phone rang. We kept hugging, but the insistent ringing made it feel like someone was in the room, waiting. I broke off and answered. A very deep woman's voice asked for Veronica. Taking the receiver, she looked at me like she couldn't imagine who it might be.

'Hello? Oh hi, Zane. What?' She paused to listen, then both her voice and face went from blank to fierce in a split second. 'So *what* if I'm here! Am I required to check in with you every time I come to LA?' Listening, she started tapping her foot and shaking her head. 'Zane ... Za ... You don't need me anymore. What? It's a big town. I doubt we'll bump into each other. No, I'm not going to Mantilini's. What? Because we *shouldn't* see each other!' She raged on like that a few more minutes and then making an exasperated face, hung up. 'That was Zane. We used to go out. She wanted to meet.' She frowned.

I pointed to the phone. 'You hung right up on her.'

'Life's too short.' She took a deep breath and looked hard at me. 'Does it upset you that I was with a woman?'

'Makes you more intriguing. That and raising goats.'

The book signing went well. Afterwards we had dinner at the restaurant next to the store. Both of us were in good moods and we gabbed away throughout the meal. It was the kind of conversation only new lovers can have – a combination of discovery, recognition and sexiness that comes as a result of knowing one facet of a person extremely well and almost nothing about the others.

I said something about how magically our relationship had evolved and I wished I knew how that magic worked so I could spread it over other parts of my life. She stood up and said, 'The only ones who want to know how a magician does his tricks are children and fools. I'll be right back.'

Although to the eye there is nothing immediately wrong, there are wrong faces. All the features are in the correct places and the nose has only two holes, but something is *off* and without being able to say exactly what, you know it. The restaurant made a wonderful *crème brûlée*. I liked it so much that I had my eyes closed in ecstasy over a mouthful of it when I heard that deep voice again.

'You're Samuel Bayer, aren't you?'

I didn't know whether to open my eyes or swallow first, so I did both. Every feature on her face was sharp as a Cubist painting – nose, cheekbones, chin. Her eyes were as black as her hair, which was short and very à la mode. She was good-looking in a combative, don't-fuck-with-me way and had a long thin body that matched. She would have been a good villainess in a James Bond film, dressed in patent leather, knowing every lethal karate move in the book.

'Yes I am. Do I know you?'

'My name is Zane. I was the one who called Veronica before. The one she hung up on. I've been waiting to talk to you, but it has to be fast, before she comes back.'

'How did you know she was in Los Angeles? How did you know where we were?'

'She had lunch today with a mutual friend. They told

me.' She kept glancing toward the bathroom. Tough as she looked, she was clearly apprehensive. Was it a crazy face? Mean? Maybe it wasn't her face that was so disturbing: maybe it was the incredibly negative, mad mouse running in a wheel energy she shot out in all directions. 'Ask Veronica about Gold. Ask her what happened with her and Donald Gold.'

'The actor?'

'That's the guy.' Once again she looked towards the bathroom, saw something, and without another word walked quickly out of the restaurant. I watched her go. Outside, she paused on the street, looked at me, mouthed 'Donald Gold' and took off.

Veronica returned a moment later and said coolly, 'Was that Zane?'

'Yeah. Strange woman.' I hesitated, then said, 'She told me to ask you about Donald Gold.'

'Good old Zane. Still Miss Terminal Toxic Nastiness. Did she think that would ruin things between us? Before I met her, I lived out here with Donald. We were bad for each other. We fed on each other's weaknesses. He threw me out and was right to do it.'

'That's all?'

'I was lost then, Sam. Maybe a little more than is safe. I was living a life which if you read about in a book, you'd say "How could she let that happen?" But here I am now and you seem to like that me, right?'

Taking her hand, I kissed it and intoned pompously: '*Omne vivum ex ovo.*'

'What's that?'

'The only Latin I remember from school. Everything alive has come from the egg.'

I don't remember what television shows we watched as kids on Saturday mornings, but all of them were sacred.

Television itself was sacred then. That big square altar in the middle of the living room that held you captive any time it was on.

I was watching TV that Saturday. My parents and sister were off shopping. I was sitting on the living room floor eating a donut when the doorbell rang. White powdered sugar was all over my fingers and mouth. The only thing I did to prepare myself for whoever was out there was rub an arm across my mouth, then my hands over my filthy jeans. Unhappily I went to the door.

When I opened it and saw Pauline Ostrova was facing me, looking gorgeous and scared, I was speechless. Of course I knew who she was. I was in lowly junior high while she lived in the upper echelons of high school, which would have given her god-like status even if her unprecedented reputation hadn't preceded her.

When she saw me she smiled a little. I almost peed my pants. 'Hey, I know you! You're Sam, right? Listen, I ran over your dog.'

'That's okay,' I said cheerfully. I loved Jack the Wonder Boy but so what compared to Pauline Ostrova knowing my name.

'He's all right, I guess. I took him to the vet. The one on Tollington Park, Dr Hughes?'

'We use Dr Bolton.'

'Yeah well, I thought he was going to die, so I took him to the vet closest.'

'Okay. You want to come in?' I had no idea what I was doing. She'd run over our dog. Shouldn't I be frantic? What would I do if she came in? Just the idea of Pauline Ostrova breathing the same air made my heart race around my chest.

I was twelve, so she must have been sixteen then. At school even I knew she was all things to all men – adult, whore, scholar, artist ... A few years later they would have called her liberated, but in those black and white Dark Ages before Betty Friedan and feminism, Pauline was only one word – weird. Everyone knew she slept around. That would have been acceptable if it had only been that. Then we would have had a category for her, ugly and simple as it was. But she made everything complicated by also being so smart and independent.

Waiting for her to say something else, I suddenly remembered the donuts I had been eating. Frantically, I rubbed my mouth in case any crumbs were still there.

'Don't you want to know more about your dog?'

'I guess.' I leaned against the door, then stood up straight, then tried leaning again. In her awesome presence there was no comfortable position on earth.

'He ran out in the street and I hit him and broke one of his rear legs. Actually, it was kind of cool because the vet let me stay and watch him put the leg in a splint.'

She was talking to *me*. I was only a little tool in seventh grade who watched her float by every day with upperclassmen, all of them carrying reputations nine miles long behind them like bridal trains. Yet for the moment, this high honor roll/slut goddess who knew my name was saying words meant only for my ears. The fact she was doing it as a way of apologizing for running over our dog was irrelevant.

'Listen, Sam, I really have to go to the bathroom. Could I use yours?'

Bathroom! Not only was she admitting she peed like the rest of us mortals, she wanted to use *ours*! Pauline Ostrova's bare ass on our toilet seat!

'Sure. I'll show you.' I started down the hall and heard her footsteps behind me. The nicest bathroom in the house belonged to my parents. It was big and light and had thick powder blue shag rug on the floor – very fashionable back then. But it was upstairs and I didn't think it appropriate to take her up there, no matter how much I longed to show off the blue carpeting. So I went towards the smaller one just off the kitchen.

Naturally when she was inside with the door shut, I wanted to glue my ear to it so as to hear every sound she made. But I was equally afraid she'd know and come bursting out of there like a Nike missile, intent on catching me listen to her tinkle. I went into the living room and quickly scarfed down the donut I had been eating before she arrived.

She didn't come out. The toilet didn't flush. Nothing happened. She just . . . *stayed* in there. For a while I thought maybe she was only taking her time, but that time grew too long and I began to grow apprehensive. Had she had a heart attack and died? Was she having trouble going? Was she snooping in our medicine cabinet?

I grew so nervous that I ate another donut without thinking. I wanted to ask if she was okay, but what if that question angered her? What if she had taken sick and for some reason couldn't speak? I pictured her grabbing at her throat, her face cyanic. With a last gasp, she'd reach weakly for the toilet flush so when they found her, at least she wouldn't be embarrassed by what she'd done before dying.

When I could no longer stand it, I purposely walked to the corner of the kitchen farthest from the toilet and shouted, 'Pauline? Are you okay?'

Her answer was immediate. 'Yeah. I'm reading one of your magazines in here.'

When she re-emerged, we drove across town to the veterinarian to get the dog and then she took us home. I wanted the whole world to see me in Pauline Ostrova's car and misinterpret why I was there. Unfortunately, the only person I recognized on the streets was Club Soda Johnny Petangles, the human commercial.

As I climbed out of her red Corvair with the dog fussing in my arms, she said, 'I took that magazine out of your toilet 'cause I want to finish the article. I'll give it back to you in school.'

'That's okay. What's the article?'

'It's in *Time*. About Enrico Fermi?'

'Oh yeah, I read that one.'

Enrico who?

I was delighted because something of ours would stay with her and there'd be reason for further contact with her.

Sadly, despite a desultory 'Hi' from her now and then in the halls at school, I never spoke with Pauline again.

That night the telephone in our room rang while Veronica was taking a bath. It was David Cadmus. 'You didn't tell me you know Rocky Zaroka.'

'I *don't*. I've met him. Once.' I looked at the closed bathroom door.

'Well, he knows you. I talked to him this afternoon and he said you and I should talk some more. I'll be in New York at the end of the month. I'll call when I get in and we can meet if you want.'

'Is there more you have to say, David?'

'Maybe. Let me think about it.'

After hanging up, I knocked on the bathroom door and walked in. Veronica was lying in the giant tub, water up to her chin. Her face and slicked-back platinum hair shone from the moisture.

'David Cadmus just called and said he knows Zaroka. Said Rocky called him this afternoon and suggested we talk some more.'

She splashed water on to her face. 'Rocky's a powerful guy. He doesn't have money, but has open access to other people's and they trust him with it. I know he's done some work financing films.'

'Did you tell him to call Cadmus?'

Looking at me, she crossed her eyes and stuck her tongue out the side of her mouth. It was amusing seeing a beautiful woman looking so silly but right then I wanted an answer to my question.

'Veronica? *Did* you?'

She waited a moment, then nodded. 'Now you're wearing your winter face. Are you angry? I want to help, Sam. I want you to give what you want.'

When the book tour was over, I returned to Crane's View. Working in the old guest room of my childhood home, I continued writing the first pages of the book. That was the easy part – just letting memories roll in and carry me along, like waves on their way to shore. There was no way I could tell this story objectively, so I decided to tip my hand early and begin it with my personal involvement.

I spent two days at Frannie's writing and talking to people who had been around at the time of the murder. Pauline's father was dead, but her mother and sister still lived in town. I decided not to talk with them for a while because I wanted an overview of things before going to the heart of their matter.

Frannie had kept a good file of the records of both the murder investigation and subsequent trial of Edward Durant, but I held off reading those too. I pictured my investigation as a kind of circular labyrinth. Entering somewhere on the outer edge, I would inevitably make many wrong turns but hopefully close in on the center eventually.

That meant first finding out who were the peripheral people in her life and seeing them. A couple of teachers were still at the school who had taught her. Two old lizards who had long overstayed their welcome in academia. Wizened and cranky, they were not the most reliable sources in the world. Yet because they spend so much time with kids for a specific, concentrated block of their young lives, teachers experience them in a singular way no others do.

Her French teacher remembered her because good as she

was at the mechanics of the language, Pauline could never say the words so they sounded like anything French. 'Bonjour' became 'Bone Jew' on her tongue and hard as she tried, it always stayed right there. He remembered her ramrod posture and love for the poetry of Jacques Prévert. What I got from him was a picture of every teacher's favorite student – eager, inquisitive, occasionally remarkable.

The same wasn't true with her English teacher, Mr Tresvant. I had had him too while in school. He was one of those sanctimonious sour balls who made us read dinosaurs like Hope Muntz's *The Golden Warrior*, and then had the audacity to call them literature. He appeared to be wearing the same brown tie and dead corduroy suit he had three decades before. What was uncanny and perversely wonderful was that on entering his room again after all those years, I felt my asshole tighten with the same fear I had felt back when his grades meant life or death.

The first thing he said to me was 'So, Bayer, you're a bestseller now, eh?'

I wanted to say 'That's right, you old stump. No thanks to you and Hope Muntz!' But I gave an 'Aw shucks' shrug instead and tried to look modest.

I asked if he remembered Pauline Ostrova. To my surprise, he silently pointed to a picture on the wall. I continued looking at him, waiting to hear if he was going to say anything about it. When he didn't (Tresvant was famous for his menacing, pregnant pauses), I got up and went over. It was a fine drawing of Shakespeare's Globe Theater. Whoever had done it had spent a long time because every possible detail was there.

'Did Pauline draw this?'

'No, of course not. That was, that *is*, the English award, Mr Bayer. Obviously you've forgotten the goings on here. Every year I give away a copy of that drawing to the best

English student in my classes. Pauline Ostrova should have won it because more often than not, she was an excellent student. But you know something? She turned out to be too excellent for her own good. She was a cheat.'

I reacted as if he had said something obscene about one of my best friends, which was ridiculous because she was dead almost thirty years and I *hadn't* know her. Finally I managed to weakly repeat 'She was a *cheat*?'

'A very adept one. And not always. She read everything. Wayne Booth, Norman O. Brown, Leavis ... Send her to the library and she took everything she could lay her hands on. But once too often what she read appeared in what she wrote, whole cloth, and she was dangerously *stingy* about giving credit where it was due.'

'That's hard to believe!'

He smiled but it was an ugly thing, glowing with scorn and superiority. 'Did you love her too, Bayer? Much more than the cheating, that was her sin. She made it easy to love her, but she never loved back.'

'Did *you* love her, Mr Tresvant?'

'The only thing that went through my mind when I heard she was dead, was a mild "Oh." So I would guess not. Anyway, the less old men remember about love, the better.'

Skin cuts the easiest. Even the thinnest paper resists – a moment's 'no' before the knife slices through its surface. But a knife into skin is like a finger into water. I was slicing open a package of legal pads when the knife slipped and slid through the top of my thumb. Blood shot out and splattered across the yellow paper.

It was ten at night. Frannie was downstairs eating Mongolian barbecue take-out and watching a Jean Claude Van Damme video he had rented earlier. I wrapped my thumb in toilet paper and called down, asking if he had medicine and bandages. When I explained what had happened, he raced up the stairs with a gigantic orange first aid kit. He looked at my finger and dressed it like a pro. When I asked where he learned to do that, he said he'd been a medic in Vietnam. Surprised he had spent his time as a soldier bandaging and not flame-throwing people, I accused him of not telling me much about himself. He laughed and said I should ask any questions I wanted.

'How come you keep calling David Cadmus?'

'Because the fucker's father killed Pauline Ostrova.'

'The fucker's father is *dead*, Frannie.'

'But the crime isn't. Turn your hand over so I can get the other side.'

'I don't understand what that means.'

'It means I want someone besides Durant to admit killing Pauline.'

'Why? Why's it so important?'

He held my wrapped hand in both of his while he spoke. I tried to pull it away after what he said next, but he wouldn't let go.

'What do you believe in, Sam?'

'What do you mean?'

'Exactly that. What in your life do you believe in? Where do you worship? Who would you give a kidney to? What would you go to the wall for?'

'A lot of things. Should I list them?' My voice went way up on the last word.

'Yes! Tell me five things you believe in. And no bullshit. Don't be cute, don't be clever. Say five things right out of your heart, and don't think about it.'

Offended, that's when I tried to pull away. He held tight, which made me even more uneasy. 'All right. I believe in my daughter. I believe in my work, when it's going well. I believe in . . . I don't know, Frannie, I'd have to think about it some more.'

'Wouldn't do any good. Listening to you talk, all that cynicism leads you to one big fucking wall of nothing. You know the saying "The fox knows many things, but the hedgehog knows one big thing"? The difference between you and me is I have at least one big thing that matters and gives me direction. I'm sure Edward Durant didn't kill Pauline. One day I'm going to prove who did.

'Even with all your success, you've got a fox's eyes, Sam – nervous and edgy, they don't stay on any one thing too long.

'I think you're back here because you're trying to get away from your life. Trying to return to some old part that's dead but safe. But maybe there'll be something in it to save you. That's really what attracts you, because where you are now is some Sunday in the middle of your life and the rest of your week looks pretty grim.'

He let go of my hand and left the room. I heard him go down the stairs and then the sound of the television again. What was most interesting was the calmness of my heart. Normally bells and alarms would have been going off in there. I have a quick temper and an even quicker emergency defense system that throws up the walls in my soul whenever it is attacked. This time, however, my insides were as calm as the truth because that's exactly what he had spoken and I knew it.

We didn't see each other again that night. Around two in the morning after rolling over and over the phrase 'one big thing', I gave up hope of sleeping. I went downstairs to do whatever I could find to do in someone else's house after I'd just had my skin peeled off.

In the kitchen, the McCabe cupboards were an explosion of circus-colored junk food boxes and a vast array of bottled hot sauces. The fridge had a hodgepodge of nasty-looking survivors from various take-out joints. When it came to food, Frannie called himself a 'gourmutt' and seemed pleased about it.

There was nothing else to do but turn on the Van Damme video and spend time with the Muscles from Brussels. I went to the machine to put in the video. Lying on top of it was a porno film titled *Dry Hard*. It starred Mona Loudly and from her picture on the box, Mona looked like better company for the midnight hour than Jean-Claude, so I put it in, figuratively speaking. A little porno now and then is good for the soul, and mine could have used a spicy diversion.

Before the film started, the company advertised some of its 'COME – ING ATTRACTIONS!' A few minutes of sleaze to rev up our appetites for another trip to the dark corner of the video store. I laughed at the clip of the first one, settling into the mood.

Then the second preview came on, *Swallow the Leader*. Veronica Lake opened a door to a hunky-looking repairman. *My* Veronica Lake. One and a half minutes of my lover doing guess what with a Jeff Stryker lookalike.

I bet *you've* never had that experience: the woman who is charmingly modest about undressing, always closes the door when she goes to the toilet, and likes to wear simple white nightgowns or men's pajamas to bed is suddenly in front of you on a television screen, doing things only prisoners and misogynists dream of women doing.

My Veronica Lake.

What is the decorum for asking your lover why they didn't tell you they acted in porno movies? Where is Miss Manners when we really need her?

The next morning I called a friend who is a movie buff and also happens to be plugged into every Internet station in the galaxy. I asked him to find out how many movies 'Marzi Pan' had made. Two. *Swallow the Leader* and *The Joy Fuck Club*.

While I was sitting in a semi-coma, trying to think of what to do next, Veronica called. I tried to be normal but my voice must have sounded like it was coming from the other end of the Alaskan pipeline. She picked up on it immediately.

'What's the matter?'

'I found out about "Marzi Pan", Veronica.'

Whatever I was expecting, what she said next wasn't it.

'Oops, the jig is up.' Her voice was light, giggly.

'What do you mean, "The jig is up"? For Christ's sake, Veronica, why didn't you tell me?'

'Because it's stupid. And it doesn't mean anything, Sam. Do you hear me? It doesn't *mean* anything! I did something idiotic and then it was gone. It was a bird that flew out the window a long time ago. Oh Jesus, I was afraid you would react like this.

'What do you want me to say, Sam, I'm sorry? Sorry for being a person I no longer am? Sorry you had to find out before you cared or knew enough about me to understand? Which sorry do you want?'

'I'm spinning, Veronica. I feel like I'm inside a clothes dryer.'

Her voice became petulant. 'Do you want to hear about it now? The whole story? That's what Zane meant in LA when she told you to ask me about Donald Gold. It was his fault, but I went along because I wanted him to love me. I would have done anything and that's what he wanted. He even thought up that name for me.

'But it's *over*, Sam. That was years ago. Aren't you ashamed of anything in your past? Something you can't change now, so you just have to be sorry and move on? What am I saying? I'm not even ashamed anymore. It's old history.

'I'm proud of myself now, my friend. Proud of who I am and what I've done. Proud that you want...' Her voice faltered for the first time and she took a quick breath. '...that you want to be with me.' She had begun to cry. Her voice was breaking up. She tried to say something else but stopped.

Shit that I am, I could think of nothing to comfort or

console her. Instead, I whispered I would call her back and
hung up.

The cemetery in Crane's View is wedged between the
Lutheran church and the town park. It's nondenomina-
tional and some of the gravestones date back to the 1700s.
Ironically, both Gordon Cadmus and Pauline are buried
there, not far from each other. It's a small place where you
can have a good look around in less than an hour. When I
was a kid we'd go there at night to mess around, sneaking
up on each other or making noises that were supposed to
be scary but fooled no one.

I got out of my car and climbed over the low stone wall
that enclosed the grounds. It was a beautiful morning,
warm and still, the air full of birdsong and the smell of
flowers.

I found Pauline's grave first. The stone was a small black
rectangle, engraved only with her name and dates. The
plot was well tended: clearly someone spent time there
bringing fresh flowers, weeding, keeping a candle burning
inside a small protected lamp. I stood above it, thinking
not very original thoughts – what a tragedy, what would
she be doing now if she had lived, who killed her. I
remembered the time I saw her at school bent over a
drinking fountain. She was wearing a white blouse and
long red skirt. Her hair was in a ponytail which she held
to one side while she drank. Passing by, I purposely veered
so as to pass within inches of her. For one instant I was the
closest person in the world to Pauline Ostrova. Her hair
was shiny, her fingers so thin and long on the silver knob.

Kneeling down, I ran my hand across the lettering on
her gravestone and said, 'Remember me?' I stood up
slowly.

I started away, thinking to look for Gordon Cadmus
next. A car slowed and stopped out on the street. Thinking
it might be Frannie, I turned and saw it was only a brown

UPS van making a delivery. Then because of my position, I saw the back of Pauline's gravestone for the first time. Written on it in thick white letters was 'Hi Sam!'

After Pauline's death, a number of strange occurrences took place in Crane's View. Some of them we were aware of, others Frannie told me about years later.

The day after we found her body, someone went around town writing 'Hi Pauline!' in large white letters on walls, the hoods of cars, sidewalks, you name it. We saw it on the side of the Catholic church, the huge glass window at the Chevrolet showroom, on the cashier's booth at the movie theater. Our gang was used to rowdy acts, but this was sick. Never for a moment did we think any of us could have done it. Gregory Niles, the class brain, said it was 'pure Dada'. We didn't like the sound of that, whatever Dada was, and threatened to kill *him* if he didn't shut up. Pauline's death was bad enough. Murder doesn't belong in a small town and we were dazed by what had happened. But someone, someone we probably knew, thought it was *funny*. Writing a greeting to a murdered girl was funny. For the first time since returning to my hometown I felt real foreboding.

When I got back to Connecticut, my darling child was sitting in the backyard, feeding popcorn to Louie, my unpleasant dog. Of course when he saw me he growled, but he always did that. I could feed him steak, pet him with a fur glove, or take him for hour-long walks. No matter, he still growled. Cass thought he blamed me for the breakup of my last marriage. So I tried to tell him Irene didn't like him either but to no avail. We put up with each other because I fed him, while he was at least some kind of company when my empty house got too large. Other than that, we gave each other a wide berth.

Cass had been babysitting him while I was in Crane's View. Normally, she lived with her mother in Manhattan during the week and came up to my house on the weekends.

I sat down next to them. 'Hi, Sweet Potato.'

'Hi Dad.'

'Hi Lou.' He didn't even deign to look at me.

She turned to me and smiled. 'How was your trip?'

'Okay.'

'How's Greta Garbo?'

'Okay.'

The three of us sat there like Easter Island heads, staring into the off. Louie saw something in the corner of the yard and skulked off in that direction.

'How come when I was a kid we used to have great dogs, but when I grew up I chose him? The only male on earth with permanent PMS.'

'Gee Dad, you're in a good mood. Want to have a catch?'

'I would love to.' I got up and went into the house for the baseball gloves and ball. They were on a table in the hall next to the mail. I looked it over and saw an express letter from Veronica. I appreciated the fact she hadn't called, but wasn't in the mood to listen to her right then, so I put it down and went back outside.

As a youngster, Cass was the best Little League baseball player around. She threw like a pro and could hit the ball into next week. Things changed as she grew older, but she was still the best person on earth to play catch with. For her birthday a few years before I had bought her an expensive baseball glove. Opening the package, she took the mitt out and buried her face in it. Then she rubbed it up and down her cheek and said in an ecstatic voice, 'It smells like the gods!'

We tossed the ball back and forth, the first throws slow lobs to warm up our arms. That sound, that immortal American sound of a hard white ball slapping into the pocket of a leather glove: father and kid together. After a few minutes, I nodded at her and she began throwing much harder. I loved it. The knots in my head from the last few days began to undo themselves. This girl could throw both a curve and a knuckleball, two things I had never been able to do in my life. Sometimes I could catch them, sometimes they were so tricky and well thrown that I was completely baffled and they sailed by, back to the fence. I was in the midst of retrieving one of those when Cass broke her news.

'Dad, I've met someone.'

About to throw the ball, I dropped my arm instead. A smile grew on my face. 'Yeah? And?'

She wouldn't look at me, but she grew a smile too. 'And, I don't know. I like him.'

'What's his name?'

'Ivan. Ivan Chemetov. His family's Russian. But he was born here.'

This was dangerous ground. I knew anything I said now would determine how open she would be with me about what was really going on. Forget it. 'Have you slept together yet?'

Eyes widening, she giggled. 'Dad! How could you ask that? Yes we have.'

'Were you careful?'

She nodded.

'Is he a good guy?'

She opened her mouth to speak, stopped, closed her eyes and said, 'I hope so.'

'Then mazeltov. I'll kill him the minute I see him, but if you like him, I'll wipe my tears and shake the man's hand.' I flipped her the ball. She caught it with the most subtle little twist of her hand. My beautiful girl. 'Does he play ball?'

'You can ask. He's coming over in half an hour.'

We continued our catch until Ivan the Terrible rang the bell. The dog moped towards the door to see if anyone was bringing him food. Cass sprinted, while Dad held the

baseball a little too tightly and tried not to scowl. I had
been dreading this moment for years. Like the character in
the Borges story who tries to imagine all the different ways
he can die, I had created a hundred different scenarios of
what it would be like to meet the fiend who deflowered
Cassandra Bayer. Shake his hand? Spit on it, more likely.
Perverse as it sounds, even when she was a little pixie I
had thought about the day when . . . and now here it was.

Ivan. Ivan the Terrible. Ivan Denisovich. Ivan Bloom-
berg, one of the biggest assholes I knew. What was his last
name, Chemetov? Cassandra Chemetov? Say *that* one fast
three times.

'Dad, this is Ivan.'

Half a head shorter than Cassandra, he had the kind of
chiseled Slavic features and brushed back long hair (short
on the sides) you often see in fascist art of the twenties and
thirties. A handsome boy, but hard enough looking to open
a can of peas with his stare. Add to this the fact he was
wearing a T-shirt that covered arms roughly the size of
Popeye's and Bluto's combined.

'Mr Bayer, it's a pleasure.' His shake was surprisingly
gentle and long. 'I've read all your books and would love
to talk with you about them.'

I asked the pitty-pat questions fathers are supposed to
ask on first meeting the suitor – What do you do? Freshman
at Wesleyan University, wanted to major in Economics.
Where did you two meet? In New York at a Massive Attack
concert. Not knowing whether that was a rock or a military
group, I wasn't about to ask. We chatted and I half listened
to his answers. What really caught my attention was the
look on Cass's face. The way she gazed at Ivan resembled
the expression of a saint having a religious ecstasy on one
of those camp Italian postcards. No sexy 'I wanna eat you'
or 'Ain't he sweet' look. Hers was 100 proof adoration.
Coming from my notably cool and rational daughter, it
said everything.

The phone rang. I walked over to the porch to pick it up. 'Hello?'

'It's Frannie. You were at the cemetery today, right?'

'Yes.'

'So you saw what they wrote on Pauline's stone? Why didn't you call me?'

The kids were watching. I turned and walked a few steps away. 'To tell you the truth, Fran, I thought *you* might have done it. To get me stimulated or something.'

'Stimulate yourself, Sam! I'm not interested in desecrating gravestones to get you off your ass. Whoever did it's going to have me breathing in *their* face, believe me. Mrs Ostrova's a nice old woman and this upset her. She was the one who discovered it. I guess she was up there right after you. Jesus, who the fuck would write "Hi" on a gravestone?'

'Hi *Sam*. They were saying hello to me, Frannie. That's what I don't like.'

'Yeah, whatever. Listen, next time anything like this happens again, you call. Okay? You want my help on this, you help me back. Otherwise, I'm going to kick your ass like I used to. Got me?'

'Gotcha, Chief.'

'And one other thing: Hi Sam!' He sniggered and hung up.

I took the lovebirds out to dinner. After forcing myself to stop thinking about his fingertips on her skin, I realized Ivan was an outstanding young man and could easily understand her infatuation. He was intense and enthusiastic in equal measure. He spoke respectfully to Cassandra and gave her his complete attention whenever she spoke. More importantly, he seemed genuinely interested in what she had to say. He was also one of those fortunate people curious about all sorts of things at the same time. Economics was no more important than the last novel he had read. He had been a state champion wrestler in high school.

Granted, he exuded a faint aura of arrogance. But I would have been arrogant too if I'd been as sharp and engaged as him.

At the end of the meal, Ivan said he'd heard about my new project and had brought along something he hoped would interest me. Reaching into his knapsack, he pulled out an inch-thick wad of papers that looked like an unbound movie script.

Since hearing the story from Cass, he had been doing some research for me. Another Internet cadet, he had driven his Porsche brain all over the information super-highway, picking up a variety of available data that he thought might be helpful. Thumbing quickly through the pages, I saw documents from the county District Attorney's office, articles from regional newspapers about the murder, an old piece in *Esquire* magazine by Mark Jacobson I'd already read about the death of Gordon Cadmus . . . It was a treasure trove.

'Wow, this is terrific stuff! Thank you very much, Ivan.'

'I would really like to help out in any way I could. I love doing research.'

'I may take you up on that. Let's see what's needed and then we can talk some more about it.'

When we got back home, they went out again. I stood at the window watching them leave. The silence in that room was very loud. I was happy for Cass, but knew tonight marked in some profound way the beginning of the end of our relationship as it had been for so many years. She had a lover now, someone who wanted to hold her and hear her secrets. Letting go of the curtain, I sadly wondered if she had played catch with him yet.

Feeling a wave of middle age break over me, I shook myself like a wet dog and decided to do some reading – Veronica's letter, Ivan's information.

The dog was planted in my favorite chair, sound asleep

and making unattractive wet sounds. More than once he had snapped at me when I tried to rouse him from said chair. I wasn't about to go through that again. I sat on the couch and pulled some reading glasses out of my pocket.

I heard a noise upstairs. There had been a series of break-ins around the neighborhood. That made any sound ten times more suspect when you were alone in the house. I stood up slowly and walked on tiptoe to the staircase. I listened for more, but nothing came. There was a hammer on a side table and I picked it up. For a while I had considered buying a gun for the house, but that only made you part of the problem. The hammer would have to do.

At the top of the stairs I saw a light on in my bedroom. I hadn't turned it on. Stupidly, I strode over and kicked the door open. Veronica was sitting in the rocking chair by the window. Heart racing, anger and relief chased each other around in my stomach. 'What are you doing here? How did you get in?'

'I know how to open doors.'

'You know how to open doors. That's great! Welcome to my house, Veronica. Why didn't you just call and say you were coming?'

'Because I was afraid you'd tell me not to. You didn't answer my letter.'

'I just got it!' I went to the bed and sat down. There was this hammer in my hand. I looked at it and dropped it on the floor.

'I was frightened, Sam. I thought you'd never want to talk to me again. I was going crazy.' Her voice cracked on the last word. When she spoke again, it was too loud and agitated. 'But it's *my* life! Not yours or anyone else's! Why am I apologizing for what I've done? Don't you think I feel bad anyway? Don't you think I look back and say "How could you have done that? What got into me?"'

I turned and looked at her. 'Did *you* write on that gravestone?'

She stared at me, shook her head. 'What are you talking about? What gravestone?'

'Forget it. Never mind.' But the problem was I didn't know if she was telling the truth. She'd already lied to me, acted in porno films, broken into my house ... What else was Veronica Lake capable of doing?

As if reading my mind, she said, 'You don't trust me at all anymore, do you?'

'You're not who I thought you were.'

'Who *is*, Sam? Who is?'

The next morning Veronica and Cassandra met. It went very badly. Veronica and I had slept, fully clothed, on my bed. In the middle of the night I woke up and saw her ten inches away, staring at me. I got up and went into the guest room.

Cass was in the kitchen eating breakfast when I got downstairs. I told her Veronica was there and she raised an eyebrow.

'I didn't know she was coming.'

'Neither did I. We'll talk about it later.'

Veronica appeared a few minutes later looking like hell. I introduced them. Cass tried hard to be friendly and warm but Veronica was withdrawn. She wouldn't eat anything and answered Cass's questions with short, curt sentences that were just short of rude. It was one of the most uncomfortable meals I had sat through in a long time. By the end of it we were all silent and the only sound in the whole house was the clink of cups and silverware. Luckily Ivan came by and left with Cass to happier lands. When they were gone, I suggested we take the dog for a walk.

'You want me to go, don't you?'

'If I wanted you to leave, Veronica, I'd—'

'No you wouldn't, Sam. You're too polite.' She gave a derisive snort. 'But you know, when you start being polite with a lover things are getting bad.'

I threw up my hands and left the room for my coat.

It was overcast and chilly outside. Veronica wore a light shirt. I offered her a jacket but she wouldn't take it. Crossing her arms tightly over her chest, she walked with her head down.

'Did you read the letter I sent? There was nothing in there except a poem, or part of one, by Neruda. Can I say it to you?

"'And our problems will crumble apart, the soul
Blow through like a wind, and here where we live
Will all be clean again, with fresh bread on the table.
For the dark-faced earth does not want suffering;
It wants freshness-fire-water-bread, for everyone:
Nothing should separate people
But the sun or the night, the moon or the branches."'

We walked on silently. A car passed and honked its horn. I jerked at the sound and looked up quickly. It was a neighbor, giving a big wave. I waved back.

'Do they like you around here, Sam? Do you have a lot of friends?' She licked her lips. There were tears running down either side of her face.

'No. Just people to wave to. You know me – I'm not very social.'

'But I'm your friend. I'd do anything for you!'

She said it with such anger that my own reared and shot right back. 'That's the trouble, Veronica. You were friends with Donald Gold and look at what that led to.'

She gasped and put a hand to her cheek. 'You son of a bitch!' She ran down the street before I could say anything else. Stopping once, she turned and looked at me, stumbled once turning back around, then started running again.

Later, when I went to my bedroom to take a nap, I found a small package on the table next to my bed. Inside was a small box filled with cotton. Lying on it was a glass tube with a dead insect inside. It looked like a tiny army helmet covering a bunch of legs. A white piece of paper was stuck on the side of the bottle. It said only. 'Hemispherota. Look it up.'

'He don't look dead to *me*. But maybe that's 'cause we're in LA; out here they tan a body before showing it.'

'Frannie, shut up. The guy's *dead*.'

'Good riddance – he and his dad are playing ping pong together in Hell.'

We moved past the open coffin of David Cadmus and sat down on folding chairs nearby. There were only two other people in the room – a smoky-looking brunette and a guy whose beeper kept going off. Welcome to LA.

A day before, McCabe called to tell me David Cadmus had been murdered in a drive-by shooting. 'Boy, that completes the Cadmus circle, huh? Like father, like son.'

He said he had friends with the Los Angeles police who would fix it so we could have a look around Cadmus's house before anything was removed. We were on a plane six hours later.

What was strange was the last time I had seen Cadmus, he had been white as a sheet. In death, he had the deep tan of a beach volleyball player.

Los Angeles is a town where you take your chances, but other than my editor Aurelio Parma having been held up at gunpoint at the convention of American Booksellers Association, I'd never known anyone there directly touched by crime.

After a minute or two of silence, Frannie leaned over and said, 'Let's get out of here. I don't have that many respects to pay to the Cadmus family.'

Outside he pulled a pair of snappy-looking sunglasses out of a pocket and slid them on.

'Nice glasses.'

'Armani. What else? You want something, you get the best.'

'Then how come you rented a Neon, Giorgio?'

He kissed the air between us and walked over to the beige rental car that looked like a large lump of bread dough. 'Hey, this car's okay, Sam. It gets about a thousand miles to the gallon and that's what matters out here.'

Inside it was like a microwave oven. Thank God the seats were made of cloth or else our asses would have melted on to them like grilled cheese sandwiches. Frannie turned on the air conditioning but that only made it hotter.

We drove out of the funeral home parking lot on to Pico Boulevard. 'Cadmus's house is not far from here. About ten minutes. There's a fabulous place for ribs on the way – you ever been to Chickalicious? They also make these hot wings . . . ummm, wait'll you taste them!'

'Don't you think we'd better go to his house and look around before we eat a ten ton meal?'

'Fuck no! Crime makes me hungry.'

Pico Boulevard was still showing the haunting effects of the last LA riot. The farther away we got from Beverly Hills, the more burnt-out shells of buildings we saw. It reminded me of the after-effects of a tornado – why had the funnel touched down here and destroyed one place, while the building next door was business as usual? I said that as we passed what was once an Indian food store.

Frannie ran his hand through his hair. 'Riots are always a good excuse for kicking your neighbor's ass. The guys who owned that place probably overcharged their customers for years. When the riots came – payback!'

The stores along the road were a weird and entertaining combination of Jewish this, Black that, and a bunch of other nationalities thrown into the mix. Roscoe's Chicken and Waffles restaurant was next door to a Swedish bakery. An Ethiopian record store boomed reggae music while a family of Orthodox Jews waited on the sidewalk in front for the bus.

'How do you know this area?'

'I had a girlfriend who lived around here. Lucy. Lucy Atherton. Big beautiful thing; head like a lion. Lied more to me than any other woman I've ever known. The things I found out about her after it was over . . .'

'What were you doing in California?'

'I told you, my wife was a TV producer. I used to come out here all the time.'

'To see Lucy?'

'Sometimes. Here's the restaurant and hey, look! That's where we want anyway – Hi Point Street. Sounds like a 1950s pen. Let's eat.'

We pulled into one of those omnipresent pocket shopping plazas you see all over California. A video rental store, fish and chips restaurant, hairdresser, and gourmutt McCabe's choice for the day – Chickalicious. He parked in front so we had a good view into the place. 'Frannie, everyone in there is wearing a Malcolm X T-shirt and hates us.'

He waved it off and got out of the car. 'They may hate you, but I'm a Brother. Watch.' He walked to the door and threw it open. His brothers didn't seem thrilled to see him. In fact, first they gaped at him like he was nuts, then the real hard looks started. I followed as slowly as I could, ready to make a Road Runner U-turn in a micro-second. Then from behind the thick glass windows a big black man came out, looking the meanest of all.

'Frannie McCabe! Ronald, get your ass out here and see Frannie McCabe!' Built like a Rottweiler, the owner was wearing a Chickalicious T-shirt and an emerald-green baseball cap, the name of the restaurant spelled out on it in fake diamonds. He and Frannie embraced. When another guy in a full apron appeared from the back, McCabe hugged him too. The customers looked at each other and slowly settled back into their chairs and rib dinners. I could feel relief leaving my pores like steam.

'Where the hell you been, Frannie? Lucy comes by here all the time. I was afraid to ask her what happened to you.'

'She wouldn't care. Albert, this is my friend Sam Bayer. He's a famous writer.'

'Nice to meet you. You here for lunch? Sit down. What do you want to eat?'

I wanted to see the menu, but Frannie rattled off a stream of things he'd obviously memorized. Albert was smiling after the fourth item.

'You gonna eat all that, or you just want to remember what it looks like?'

After taking the order, Albert sat down with us. He and Frannie talked for a while, and then he turned to me. 'This guy saved my life once. Did he tell you 'bout that?'

I looked at Frannie. 'No.'

'Well, he did and that's all that's important.'

McCabe said nothing more about it. A medic in Vietnam, a lifesaver, but from my childhood memories of him, ferocious as a badger when he didn't like someone. I honestly didn't know how to feel about my old friend and it was getting more confusing as time went on.

The food came and was sensational. We went through it as if our tapes were on fast-forward. Dessert was 'Sock It to Me' cake, but I was already down for the count. Frannie wasn't and ate two pieces.

As we were leaving, Albert gave each of us a green and diamonds cap like his own. Frannie wore it the whole time we were in Los Angeles.

Hi Point Street was directly across from the restaurant. It was a black middle-class neighborhood where people showed their pride by keeping their houses and lawns in perfect condition. The front yards were mostly small while above them loomed huge palm trees. Expensive cars were parked in many of the short driveways next to the houses.

104

The Cadmus place was near the corner where Hi Point and Pickford streets intersected. The largest house on the street, it was a 1920s Spanish-style beauty with a front porch flanked by two palms. A metallic blue Toyota Corolla was parked in the driveway. Frannie stopped to look at it. 'That's funny. All these other showboat cars on the street, but the big movie producer owns a Toyota.'

'*Owned*.'

'Yeah, right, past tense. Interesting that a white guy with some money would choose to live in an all-black neighborhood.'

'I'd live here too if I could have this house. What a great place.'

We walked up the path to the front door. Frannie went first and rang the bell. When no one answered, he took a key out of his pocket and opened the door.

Off the entrance hall was a large, nicely furnished living room with two Mission-style chairs, a black leather couch and festively colored rug. Windows on three sides filled the room with dappled light. A large fireplace was against one wall. On the shelf above it were several knickknacks. I walked over to look at them. There was a polished wooden ball perched on a metal stand, a primitively carved dark wooden pig, and a photograph of David Cadmus and his father.

'Look at this.'

Frannie picked up the picture and grunted. 'The family that lies together, dies together. Come on, let's look around.'

Bedrooms flanked either side of the hallway. One was quite dark although painted a bright salmon color. Inside was a desk with lots of scattered papers, a computer and printer on it. Frannie said he'd check them out and told me to go to the next one.

Whatever money Cadmus had, he certainly hadn't invested it in goodies for his home. His bedroom was a bed and a night table. On the table was a cheap portable telephone and a gay porno magazine. I picked up the mag, took a look at one page and closed it.

The bedroom opened on to a wooden deck overlooking a small well-trimmed backyard. Two black director's chairs and a table were out there. I sat down in one of them. A few minutes later McCabe walked out of the house wearing a gray wool baseball cap with the word 'Filson' in a corner.

'Cool hat, huh? I love Filson stuff. You think Dave'd mind if I took it?'

'Don't do that, Frannie. For God's sake!'

'Why not? Your friend won't be wearing it anymore. You see his reading material in there? Deep in the Heart of Tex's Ass, huh? I didn't know he was gay. There's enough costumes in his closet to outfit the Village People. You find anything?'

'No, but I didn't look very hard. I feel weird doing it. Like I'm grave robbing.'

'Not me. It's all possibilities, man. I'm going to look around some more.' He walked back into the house.

I sat and watched airplanes take off from LAX a few miles away. The day was dying and the sky was turning that strange LA copper color. I could hear the constant whoosh of cars on the freeway a few miles away. Next door someone began playing the organ and they were very good. The smell of barbecued beef was in the air, along with that of flowers and gasoline. I thought of Cadmus sitting out here alone or with a lover at night, content that the day was over. A few nights ago he got into his car to drive to the market for some milk or Ben and Jerry's ice cream and ended up with a hole in his chest for no reason at all.

'You fucking dilettante!' Chief McCabe was glaring at me from the doorway. 'You write those novels full of crime and murders and clever whodunits. But when you're down here at mud level with a real murder, you don't want to get involved. Fuck you, Sam! Get back in here and help me look around this dead man's house. Idiot!'

The truth didn't set me free but did send me back into the house. We spent a good hour going through each of the rooms top to bottom, opening drawers, snooping in closets . . .

The papers on his desk were all work related. Frannie sat at the computer and expertly brought up as many files as possible. Some were protected but he figured out many of the passwords. There was not much left in Cadmus's life in that house we didn't know, or have at our disposal, by the time we were finished.

'He hung out at a bar in West Hollywood called the Emerald City, wrote love letters to a guy named Craig, most of his money was with Fidelity investments. I can't find anything interesting about him.'

'What did you expect?'

'I was *hoping* for something that might link him to his Daddy. You know, secret funds or something. Something nice and ugly. I'm going to check out his buddy Craig but I'm sure nothing's there. Our big movie producer's as dull as a basset hound.'

'I think you're out of luck, Fran. Just like he was out of luck to be where he was the other night. But it sure is ironic, isn't it? How often do both a father and son get shot to death?'

We had one last look and then went to the door. Frannie turned and looked around. 'It's a lovely house, though, you know? Simple, good taste. I don't know. Let's go.'

He opened the door and gestured for me to go first. I took a couple of steps on to the front porch and kicked something. It skittered away across the red stone tiles, hit a large planter and bouncing off, skidded back almost to where it had been. It was a videotape. Stuck to it was a bright green Post-it note. Across it was written in thick black letters 'Hi Sam!'

I reached down slowly and picked it up. Frannie snatched it away. 'Motherfucker!' Without another word, he went back into the house. I followed, not knowing what to think.

He walked into the living room, turned on the television and video machine. Slotting the tape, he jabbed 'Play' and crossing his arms, stood back to watch. I stayed in the doorway, not sure I wanted to be too near what we were about to see. I was right.

The tape started with the usual fuzz and jittery black/white lines. What came next took no more than two minutes. Whoever shot the film was sitting in a parked car, aiming the camera out the window. Across the street is a Von's supermarket. It's night and the large parking lot is brightly lit. Cars pull in and out, people come and go from the store. One of those people is David Cadmus. He's carrying a brown bag full of groceries. The camera follows him out of the parking lot. He crosses the street.

The picture blacks out, then comes on again a moment later. The car is now parked on a dark street. Walking down the sidewalk towards the camera is David Cadmus, still carrying his groceries. He gets closer. He's wearing a Walkman and is smiling. It is unbearable to watch.

When he is parallel to the car, the window on the passenger's side slides down. Whoever is filming must have said something to Cadmus because he stops and comes over, still smiling. A gun comes up and shoots him two times point blank in the throat and chest just as he is bending down to answer his killer's question.

The movie ends.

PART TWO

'How many people know you're writing this book?'

The stewardess bent towards us with a tray of drinks. Without taking his eyes from my face, McCabe told her in a growl to buzz off. Looking absolutely astonished, she buzzed off in a hurry.

'How many? Quite a few now. My agent, editor, some people in Crane's View. I don't know.'

We were sitting in the rear section of the plane. The air around us was stale and stinky. Since he couldn't smoke, Frannie had been fiddling in his seat since we got on. 'That doesn't make this any easier. If it was just a few ... It doesn't matter. Whoever killed Cadmus knew about your book. That's why they wrote on the grave and put that Post-it note on the tape. They want us to know they know what you're doing.'

'Obviously.'

He shook his head. 'Nothing's obvious, Sam. Everything that used to be obvious about this case isn't anymore. I was flat wrong for years. I can't tell you how that makes me feel. Whoever killed Pauline also killed the Cadmuses and God knows who else.'

'Do you really believe that? I thought Gordon Cadmus was a mob hit.'

'It once looked that way, but not anymore. I feel like Alice in fucking Wonderland. What is the motive? Okay, Gordon Cadmus and Pauline were lovers, that fits, but

111

why thirty years later does Mystery Man kill the son for no reason at all?'

'Maybe there was no reason.'

'Or else David knew something.'

'But why would they *film* it, Frannie? What was the point of that? And then give me the film?'

He stared straight ahead and was silent so long that I finally poked him on the shoulder. 'Huh?'

'Because you found Pauline's body. I hate to say it, but they may be thinking about doing you next. But I don't think so. Way down deep I gotta feeling they said Hi Sam because you're famous and writing about it. A book could make *them* famous. You've read about serial killers. They all got big egos. Think of this for a moment – what if you wrote your book about the death of Pauline Ostrova and came to the conclusion either Cadmus or Edward Durant killed her? Whoever really did it's left with nothing but a perfect crime. They got away with it. Nobody will ever know the truth. Maybe that's not what this killer wants anymore. Maybe after all these years, a little ego bird is flying around inside his goddamned murderous head singing "Me Me Me" and the song is driving him nuts.

'Remember Henry Lucas in Texas? The guy said he had killed over five hundred people, which would have made him the biggest serial killer since Dracula. But he was lying. Can you imagine lying about *that*? You know why it's dangerous for famous people to go to jail? Because some loser in the can thinks if I kill them, then I get to be famous too. And since I ain't never going to be famous for anything else, why not? That's why that fuckhead murdered Jeffrey Dahmer. And you know how worried they were about Mike Tyson getting hit when he was in? Some people get famous writing books. Those who aren't so creative get famous killing people.'

'Then why was this killer silent so long?'

'Maybe they were content with what they did, but *aren't*

anymore. For thirty years, no big best-selling author was interested in writing this story. Now you are and he knows it. I think you're safe so long as you're working on it. They want the book finished so long as it tells the real story. They want credit.'

'But then they're cutting their own throat!'

'Maybe not. They've been damned clever so far. You know about female spiders? They can store sperm up to eighteen months, and they have this nice little tendency to eat the male after he's done his duty. What we have here just might be similar – someone's stored this up for thirty years, but now wants to make some babies with it.'

As if David Cadmus's killer and my problems with Veronica weren't enough, I had to give a speech. Months before, students at Rutgers University had organized an arts festival and invited me to speak on the future of the popular novel. I agreed to go because I didn't have anything else to do and the kids sounded so enthusiastic.

After returning from California, I glanced at my calendar and realized with horror the thing was two days away. I whipped up some drivel in an afternoon, asked my neighbor to watch the dog, and drove south to New Jersey, cursing all the way down the turnpikes.

They put me up in a nice hotel and had me scheduled to do so many things I didn't have time to think about my problems. There were interviews, book signings, a visit to an advanced creative writing class. Fine.

The night of my speech, I was sitting in the hotel room watching television. Suddenly I had such a panic attack that I ran out of the room, went downstairs and bought a pack of cigarettes to get me through the rest of the evening.

The problem was they had put me in a no smoking room at the hotel and that was the only place I wanted to smoke. America has been so cowed by health Nazis in recent years that lighting up, I felt as guilty as a fifteen-year-old. The guilt got so bad that I went to the window and tried to open it, thinking I'd stick my head out and blow my poisonous Winston into the already ruined Jersey air. Unfortunately, the hotel was ultra-modern and the room had all-but-sealed windows. The management thought it best to control your environment, whether you liked it or not. But I wanted real air. I managed to wrestle the window open enough inches to get my head and my hand out. Feeling quite accomplished, I smoked the cigarette down to the butt and flicked it, sparks flying, towards the parking lot. I slid my hand back into the room but not my head. It, *I*, was stuck. Tonight's feature speaker, full of wisdom and insight into the plight of the contemporary novel, was stuck halfway out a window on the fifth floor of the Raritan Towers Hotel.

In my terror, I kept thinking about all those people downstairs waiting. People who had come to listen and consider. If they only knew where the featured mouth for the evening was. Then I thought about someone coming up to get me and seeing me half-guillotined in that window . . .

The trapped rat inside took over and I battled until I was able to make it budge an extra few inches. When all of me was back in the room, I looked in a mirror and saw an angry red line down the side of my neck, the window's souvenir. Rubbing it hard, I tried to get some blood flowing there again, but then someone was knocking at the door and it was time to go.

The lecture hall was full – there must have been three hundred people there. Totally flustered by my war with the window and now all these attentive faces, I raced through the speech. There was a question and answer session afterwards which I handled a little better. When it was over, what seemed like half the audience came up to get their books autographed. I left my notes on the podium and stood at the front of the stage signing. It took about an hour.

When I was done, I went back to the podium to pick up the papers. Another green Post-it note was stuck on top of them.

'Hi Sam! What happened to your neck?'

The package arrived almost simultaneously with Ivan's next 'report'. It was a small orange envelope addressed to me in Veronica's memorable handwriting. Inside was Stephen Mitchell's translation of *The Book of Job*. Nothing else.

It was the first time I had heard from her in days and I didn't know what to think. Life had been quiet since my return from Rutgers. I spent most of the time working on Pauline's book. Frannie and I spoke on the phone almost every day, but he hadn't been able to turn up anything of importance. The only fingerprints on the videotape were his and mine. The same with the Post-it notes. Because there were so few written words on them, done in block letters, no graphologist could do an analysis. His friends with the Los Angeles police had canvassed Cadmus's neighborhood, but no one had seen a person on the front porch the day we were there.

When I told him about what had happened after my speech, all he could say over and over was 'asshole!' Home seemed the best place to be. Other than a couple of visits from Cassandra and Ivan, I saw no one. Aurelio called once to ask how the book was going. The only thing I could think to say was 'It's movin' along.' I wasn't about to tell that loudmouth what had been happening. If McCabe was right, I was relatively safe so long as I continued writing. I assumed Mr Post-it was aware of what I was doing. But did he peek in the window to keep tabs on me? Sneak into the house when I was out and read what I had written?

I read Veronica's book in one afternoon and was awed by the beauty of the language, Job's brilliance at verbalizing his fears and anger in front of the Almighty. But why had she sent it to me? What was she trying to say? Besides loving the story, I couldn't help thinking she was using it as some kind of Trojan Horse to sneak up on me. I wasn't wrong. A few days after it arrived, I received a postcard from her. Written on it was a quote from the text which I remembered immediately.

> Remember: you formed me from clay . . .
> Yet this you hid in your heart,
> this I know was your purpose:
> to watch me, and if I ever sinned
> to punish me for the rest of my days.
> You lash me if I am guilty,
> shame me if I am not.
> You set me free, then trap me,
> like a cat toying with a mouse.
>
> Why did you let me be born?

P.S. don't forget the hemispherota.

Did she see herself as Job? And me as *God*? I couldn't even coax my dog off a chair! The thought made me pick up the phone. She wasn't home. I left a message, saying please call because we have to talk. Nothing. I waited two days and called again. Instead of her voice, she sent another card with another quote:

> Is it right for you to be vicious,
> to spoil what your own hands made?
> Are your eyes mere eyes of flesh?
> Is your vision no keener than a man's
> Is your mind like a human mind?

For you keep pursuing a sin,
trying to dig up a crime,
though you *know* that I am innocent
and cannot escape your grasp.

Job or no Job, we had to talk. I left another message on her machine, saying I'd be at Hawthorne's bar in the city at a certain time and would she please meet me.

All other things aside, I missed her. She had more secrets than the Turkish ambassador, and what little I knew now of her past gave me the willies. Still, I missed her. I sincerely hoped by talking we could find both common ground and reason to connect again.

The day I was to go into the city, Cass and Ivan showed up, both of them looking serious. When I asked what was up, Cass made a sign to Ivan. He handed her some papers and walked back outside.

'Dad, don't get mad, but I asked Ivan to do this.' She held out the papers to me.

'What's this?'

'Have a look and then you can ask anything you want. If you want.'

Veronica's name was at the top of the papers. Ignoring Cass, I read quickly. I had been chewing gum but my mouth stopped halfway down the first page.

'Cassandra, why did you do this? Where did Ivan get it?'

She cringed, but her voice was defiant. 'It's my fault, Dad. I asked him to find out whatever he could. Ivan's a good hacker – he can get into a lot of places.'

'You're not answering my question – Why did you *do* it, Cass? It's none of your business.'

'I don't care about her, Dad. I care about *you*. I've never, ever messed in your life. But . . .' Tears came to her eyes. Her face softened and for a moment she looked seven years old. 'I don't like her, Dad. The minute I met her, I thought something was really wrong. Something was really off. You know me. I like most people. I don't care what they do. I don't care what they are. But I just *really* didn't like her, so I—'

'So you did this? You have no right! What if I didn't like Ivan and did this to *him* after the first time we met? Would you have been angry? Would you have thought I was out of line? It's meddling in someone else's life. If you don't like her, fine, we could have talked about it. But this is absolutely wrong.'

I walked past her and out to the car. I opened the door and got in. Before starting it, I looked back at the house. She was standing in the doorway, hands pushed tightly against her sides. I could tell by her expression she was crying. She looked so alone and helpless, but she had gone way over the line this time. Way over. But what her boyfriend had discovered made me feel even more uneasy about my appointment with Veronica.

It is common practice for authors to create characters and then fall in love with them. It makes sense, though, because we live so intimately and so long together that it's difficult to keep them at arm's length. Part of the joy of being a writer is creating people and situations we long for but know will probably never happen to us.

When we were on the book tour, Veronica asked which characters were my favorites and why. Georgia Brandt. Only dear Georgia. I fell in love with her about five pages into her existence and it got worse as time went on. I created her when I was still young enough to have the hope someone like her existed in the world and one day we would meet.

What is important to know now is what she looked like. Tall and thin, she had very short black hair that she washed every morning in the sink and then never thought about again. Her skin was preternaturally white, eyes large and green. People mistook her for Irish. Her mouth was long and thin, set in a kind of perpetually bemused smile. If she had used makeup she would have been stunning. But her skin was allergic to it (an important part of the story) and that didn't bother her a bit.

When I walked into Hawthorne's that day, Georgia Brandt was sitting at the bar. I thought I'd died and gone to literature. I honestly thought Mother of God, there she is, she really *does* exist. Even wearing one of the same outfits I'd described in the story: a dark blue sleeveless linen dress and white tennis sneakers. What's more, on the table in front of her was the book Georgia was always carrying around: *Russian Verbs of Motion for Intermediate Students*. A black-haired wonder in a linen dress, reading that nutty book – how could a man *not* love her?

But what do you do when someone you have created on paper is sitting ten feet away? You swallow the toaster that is suddenly in your throat, go over and say 'I think I know you.'

Veronica/Georgia patted the seat next to her. 'Is that so? Why don't you sit down?'

'Is this your new Fall look?'

'Veronica couldn't come, so she sent me instead. I'm her union negotiator.'

'This is beyond strange.' I asked the bartender for whiskey.

She turned in her seat so she faced me square on. 'Not at all. You're having a drink with your favorite woman. You said so yourself. Tell *her* what's bothering you. She loves you too, so you can say anything.'

'Good. All right. Okay, I've been going out with someone for the last few months. Until recently it's been great. I thought I was beginning to know her, but now I've discovered things about her that make me really uneasy. I don't know what to think anymore. Veronica, were you really in the Malda Vale?'

She nodded casually. 'For two years. How did you know?'

'My daughter. She looked you up on the Internet. You have your own Web page.'

She sighed, then gave a very slow shrug. 'A lot of good it's done me. I *knew* she didn't like me. It's my fault. I was so upset that day. That's why she wanted to know more. It's sweet, Sam. She was worried for you.' She smiled and sighed.

'There, see! That's what I'm talking about: suddenly I've discover this great woman was a lesbian, acted in porno films, and was in the Malda Vale, the most famous suicidal religious cult of our age!'

Her voice was calm and reasonable. 'But is she good to you? Have you been happy together? What else matters?'

'Come on, it's not that simple. You were in the *Malda Vale*! That group was up there with the Branch Davidians and Jim Jones! Add in all of those other things ... What kind of person does these things?'

'If you ask me? An interesting one.' She reached up and pulled off the black wig. Her blonde hair was tightly pinned to her head and it was a while before she had it undone. 'What kind of person? After Donald threw me out, I was suicidal. That's when I met Zane and we were together. But I wasn't *with* Zane – I just needed to be around someone. She was there, turned out to be a terrible person and life got even worse. That's when I met some people from the Malda Vale. The truth of the matter is, they saved me. I'll always be grateful to them for that. I was in the group for two years. That's why I made the film about them afterwards – I wanted people to see they weren't *all* just a bunch of crazies. I left when things became frightening and dangerous. None of them tried to stop me. They wished me well. That's the whole story.

'I need to believe in things, Sam. Whether it's a person or a group, that's the way I function. I never dreamed you and I would get this close. I hoped you might be nice and

120

let me make a film about you, but then all this happened. It's unbelievable and I'm devoted to you. But I'm not promiscuous about that devotion. You're the first person I've slept with in three years.'

'Three years?'

'Uh huh.'

'Why did you dress up like Georgia?'

'Because besides your daughter, she's your number one. I know a lot of artists. The greatest loves of *all* their lives are their creations. Unfortunately, most of us don't have that kind of talent, so we have to make do with falling in love with real people.

'Did you look up the hemispherota?'

'No.'

'Well, then I'll tell you about it. It's a little beetle that looks like something out of a cartoon. But what's most interesting is it has sixty *thousand* bristles under its shell which, when attacked, it uses to glue itself into place and makes it impossible to turn over. That's its defense system. It just hunkers down and holds its ground.' She seemed satisfied with that.

'But why did you give one to me?'

'Because that's what you need to do. You need to stick with some things, Sam, especially when you're under attack. You just turn over; you give in too easily.

'I have what you want, but you just don't know it yet. No matter what I've done in the past, if you'd stay with me, you'd see I was right.'

'I should be like your beetle?'

'Yes. Don't let difficult things or other people's opinions or your first reaction to me turn you over. It's the worst thing you could do. Remember what McCabe said? That you need something to believe in? Well, right now you have only two – your daughter, Pauline's book and, if you let it happen, me. All three of them could save you.'

'Save me from what?'

'Yourself.'

At Veronica's place later while we were still thrashing things out, her phone rang. She ignored it and the answering machine came on. 'My name is Francis McCabe and I'm looking for Sam Bayer. He gave me this number. If you know where he is, please tell him to call me because it's urgent.'

I picked up the phone. 'Hi Frannie.'

'Bingo! I've been calling all over for you. Johnny Petangles' mother died and we had to go into his house to get her. Guess what I found there? Pauline's notebooks from school.'

Veronica asked if she could come with me and I was glad for the company. We got to Crane's View in an hour and drove straight to the police station. There was no time for the Bayer guided tour, but I pointed some things out along the way.

At the station there was only one cop on duty. With a tired waved he ushered us into Frannie's office. That big empty room was even gloomier at night with only two lights battling the shadows.

The Chief of Police was sitting with his feet up on his desk. Club Soda Johnny was facing him and the two of them were laughing. On the bare desk were two white notebooks with 'Swarthmore College' printed on the covers.

Frannie got up and straightened his tie as soon as he saw Veronica. After I introduced them, he went to get more chairs.

'Hi, Johnny.'

'Hello. I don't know you.'

'Well, I used to know you. This is my friend Veronica.'

'Hello, Veronica. You have hair like the woman in the Clairol ad.'

122

She smiled and moved to shake his hand. His first reaction was to pull back. Then like a frightened but interested animal, he slowly put his out and they shook.

She spoke to him in a gentle voice. 'Sam told me you know all the commercials.'

Frannie came back in with two chairs. 'Johnny's the king of commercials. That's what we were doing when you came in – he was doing the old "Call for Phillllip Mor-ris!" ad. So sit down, join the festivities.'

'My mother died. Frannie came to my house.'

We nodded and waited for him to go on. 'He was nice, but he went into my room and took my books. They're my books, Frannie. They're not yours.'

'Take it easy, big guy. I got a friend of mine to come over and talk to Johnny. He's a clinical psychologist over at the state hospital.' Frannie sat back in his chair, put his arms over his head and stretched. 'Tried every trick he knew, but Johnny isn't so good at remembering. Says Pauline gave him the books.'

'Pauline gave me the books and then she *died*.'

'Says he didn't kill her.'

'I never killed anybody. I saw a dead dog once but that's not a *person*.'

I gestured towards the door. Frannie got up and we left the room. Out in the hall I asked if he had found anything else at the Petangles house.

'Yeah, a lotta crucifixes and pictures of Dean Martin. Those houses down on Olive Street are like a fuckin' fifties time capsule, you go inside. It's strange he had the books, Sam, but I don't think he's involved. Maybe Pauline did give them to him for some cockeyed reason.'

'Where did you find them?'

'On a bookshelf in his room. He asked me to come in and look at it. Place was clean as a Marine barracks. Showed me all his comics and there they were, right up next to Little Lulu and Yosemite Sam.'

'Did you look at them yet?'

'There's nothing in them. Just scribbles and blah blah. I'll tell you one thing; it's an odd feeling seeing her handwriting all these years later. I'm going to copy them and give the originals back to her mother. I'll give you a set too. You haven't talked to her mom yet, have you?'

'No, but this will give me a good excuse.'

Back inside, Johnny was standing far across the room, glaring accusingly at Veronica. 'She's not nice! I don't like her.'

Frannie and I looked at her.

'He wanted to touch my hair. I said no.'

'That's not true! You liar! That's not true!'

I wondered if she *was* telling the truth. Despite the warm, close afternoon we'd spent together and everything we had talked about, I realized I still didn't trust her, hemispherota or not.

Jitka Ostrova's house was a shrine to her dead daughter. The walls were crammed with framed awards, pictures of the girl at all ages, high school and Swarthmore College pennants. Pauline's room, which we were shown almost immediately, was kept exactly as it had been thirty years before. Everything was dusted, all the figurines on the shelves arranged just so. On the wall above the bed was a giant, yellowing poster of Gertrude Stein looking like a fire hydrant in a wig.

No shoes tossed left and right, no underwear draped over a chair or flung haphazardly on to the bed. I knew how it should look because I lived with a teenage girl. Kids and Order rarely agree on anything. But no kid lived here, only ghosts and an old woman.

Outside that sad room, the rest of the Ostrova house was a cozy clutter. You liked being there, liked looking around and seeing this sweet woman's life in every nook and cranny. It was almost grandma's house from a fairy tale but that was impossible: two of the people she loved most who had lived here were dead. They left an emptiness that was palpable, despite all the *Gemütlichkeit*.

Mrs Ostrova was a gem. She was one of those people who came to the United States early in life but never really left Europe behind. She spoke with an accent, peppered her sentences with what I assumed were Czech words and phrases ('I took my five plums and left'), and rowed her little boat above a sea of bad fortune and pessimism a thousand feet deep. In everything she said, it was clear she loved her surviving daughter Magda, but adored the dead 'Pavlina'.

Magda was also there that day. She was a tough, attractive, tightly wound woman who looked to be in her early forties. She had the bad habit of watching you with the eyes of a museum guard who's convinced you're going to steal something. Very protective of her mother, she surprised me by speaking as reverently of Pauline as the old woman did. If there was any residual filial jealousy, I didn't see it.

When we handed over the notebooks, Jitka's face took on the expression of someone touching the Holy Grail. Until then very effervescent and chatty, she went silent for minutes while reverently turning the pages and sounding out some of the words her lost daughter had written so long ago.

When she was finished, she gave us a million-dollar smile and said, 'Pavlina. A new part of Pavlina is back in our house! Thank you, Frannie.'

She wasn't surprised when she heard where they'd been found. Johnny Petangles had told the truth: throughout her senior year in high school and whenever she came home from college, Pauline had tried to teach him how to read.

'Poor Johnny! He's so simple in the head but he tried so

125

hard for Pavlina. He loved her too. He don't take those lessons so he can learn to read – he wanted to sit next to her all those afternoons!'

Frannie said, 'Tell about *The Pirates of Penzance.*'

Jitka stuck out her tongue and gave him a raspberry. 'Yeah, that's the story you like just so you can laugh at me every time! Frannie, I wish you the black cheek!

'You see, that was *my* lesson from Pavlina. She was teaching everyone sometimes. You understand, my terrible English always embarrassed her. She'd put her hands over her ears like this and scream, "Ma, when are you gonna *learn*?" So she buys this nice record and makes me listen to it. This is *Pirates of Penzance* and after a while it is my lesson to try to sing along with it to make my English better. You know it?

'I am the very model of a modern major-general;
I've information vegetable, animal and mineral'

She sang so badly, so off-key and with pronunciations so horrendous that it could have made the whole of England shift on its axis. But she also looked so happy and proud remembering it that we all clapped. To my great surprise, Frannie picked it up where she stopped.

'I know the kings of England and I quote the fights historical.
From Marathon to Waterloo, in order categorical—'

'Impressive! Where'd you learn *that*?'

He pointed to Mrs Ostrova. 'Jitka gave me a copy for Christmas a few years ago. Now I'm a big Gilbert and Sullivan fan. You want to hear my favorite part?'

I was about to say no when he stood up and started singing again.

126

'When the enterprising burglar's not a burgling—
When the cutthroat isn't occupied in crime.
He loves to hear the little brook a gurgling
And listen to the merry village chime.
Ah, take one consideration with another
A policeman's lot is not a happy one.'

'Thanks, Fran.' I cut him off. *His* voice was good, but a little Savoy Opera goes a long way. A look of great affection crossed Magda's face when she watched him. Were they lovers? Who *did* my friend, this sexy divorced man, sleep with? He never talked about it.

There was so much I could have asked about Pauline, but I thought it better to simply let the two Ostrova women talk about her.

'I was her mother, but still I never really knew her, you know? This is something I still cannot get over. She came from right here in my stomach, but I did not know her because she changed and changed and changed and sometimes it was good and sometimes it was crazy. There was this old movie, *Man of a Thousand Faces*? This was Pavlina. A thousand faces. I don't know which girl she was when she died.'

An hour later, Magda said, 'My sister did her own thing and if you didn't like it, too bad. At the trial, it came out she had a lot of boyfriends. So? Big deal! A guy who has a lot of girls is a stud. A woman does the same thing and she's a slut. Know what I say to that? Bullshit! Pauline wasn't a slut – she was an individual and even I knew that when I was a kid. As a sister? She was okay, but mostly all I remember is her going in and out of our house in a hurry because she was always up to something, you know? Always had something going on.'

Jitka came into the room carrying a plate full of Czech pastries – *Buchty* and *Kolace*. 'Pavlina was a bird. That's what I say. She flew around and never landed anywhere too long. Then poof! Off she flies again.'

'Naah, Ma, you're wrong.' Magda picked up one of the sweets and took a bite. Powdered sugar dropped over her hand and fell like snow on to the floor. 'Bird are always jumping up and flying away 'cause they're scared of everything. Nothing scared Pauline. If she was curious, she'd charge it like a rhino. She wasn't any *bird*.'

They had given me permission to tape what they said. Not having to take notes enabled me to sit back and watch them interact. Sometimes they agreed, sometimes not. Once in a while they would compare notes about a shared Pauline experience. It gave me the feeling they had been going over these things for years. What *else* did they possess of the dead girl? What other things could they point to or remember and say *that's* who she was, that's what she did? Who else cared about their dead love? Worse, who else even remembered? I understood why they would cherish her notebooks.

I told them the story of the day Pauline ran over our dog and came to the house to report it. They were delighted and asked many questions.

'She never told me she hit a dog!' Jitka said crossly, as if preparing to have a word about it with her eldest daughter when she came in. 'When I was little girl in Bratislava, my mother got bottle of perfume for her birthday. She never wore it because she thought it is too nice to use. Typical mother, hah? But I would go into my parents' room all the time and smell it. If Mother caught me, ooh! She would get *so* angry, but she could not stop me from doing it; I *had* to breathe that smell at least twice a week. It said there so many exotic and wonderful things are in the world and one day *I* would go and know them. Adventure! Romance! Cary Grant! I didn't need to read Arabian Nights books – I just take the top out of her bottle and POP! – there was the *dzin* . . . the genie for me.

'But I grew up and married Milan and come to America. That was a little interesting, but my whole life wouldn't have filled up that bottle. I think, I really do think if Pavlina was alive, her life would have been everything I dreamed of when I smelled the perfume. She got into trouble and made me crazy, but she could have done anything.'

At that moment I happened to look at Veronica. She was leaning forward and had her hands clasped tightly. Perhaps I was just hypersensitive to her then, but I would have sworn from the look on her face that she was jealous of all this. She looked at me and then quickly away as if I had caught her when she didn't want to be seen.

'Who do you think killed her?' she asked in a calm voice that made the question a hundred times heavier.

Mother and daughter glanced at each other. Jitka nodded for Magda to speak.

'From everything we know? Gordon Cadmus. I mean, Frannie's been showing us all this stuff over the years, telling us things, and if I had to bet my life on it, I'd say it was him.

'It's getting cold in here! Hah, Ma? Isn't it cold in here?' Rubbing her shoulders, Magda stood up and left the room. No one said anything. Pauline's death was suddenly as fresh again as a just-dropped glass.

After asking if I could visit again, we thanked the Ostrovas and left. On the way to the car, Frannie's pocket phone rang. He was needed down at the police station. It was a five-minute walk from there so we said good-bye and he strode off.

Veronica was taking the train back to the city, but asked if I would show her Crane's View before she left. I'd done the tour first with Cass, then Frannie, and now Veronica. It had been different each time because it was always through another pair of eyes. Cass knew the town through my stories, Frannie because he had lived there his whole life, Veronica because of the death of Pauline. She made it plain she wasn't interested in Al Salvato's store or the spot where fifteen-year-old McCabe set a car on fire. She wanted to see Pauline's town.

We drove past the school, the pizza place, the movie theater. The tour ended down at the river/railroad station. I parked near the water and we walked to where I'd found the body. I described again what it had been like. We stood there silently looking around. The sun was going down and its gold set the water on fire. Her train was due to arrive in a few minutes. This companionable silence would have been a nice way to end the visit but then the big bats flew out of the Veronica cave.

The first one, a small and innocuous question, gave no hint of what was to come. 'Whatever happened to Edward Durant's father?'

'I'm interviewing him next week. He's retired. Lives across the river in Tappan. Sounded nice on the phone.'

To my great surprise, her voice came out a cold scold. 'Sam, you shouldn't have asked the Ostrovas who they thought killed Pauline. I was surprised at you.'

'*What*? You asked them.'

'Because I knew that you were about to. I could see it in your eyes. You're going to have to tell them about the videotape and the notes you've gotten. All of it's going to upset them. It's taken thirty years to get over her death and now you come in and exhume her. I think the less you upset them, the better. The less you tell them—'

'Don't *lecture* me, Veronica! I don't agree with you. When we find the real killer it'll give them some peace. The only way I can do that is to ask a lot of questions of everyone.'

'Do you think you can trust Frannie?' Her voice was innocuous enough, but the look on her face wasn't.

'Why shouldn't I?'

'I don't know. Just the way he is. He obviously has his

own agenda and maybe it's not the same as yours. Anyway, you don't need his help on this, Sam. *I* can do it with you. I'll do whatever you want. I'm great at interviewing and researching. That's my job! I make documentary films. Forget Frannie and that boy Ivan. I'll help you with everything. You can't imagine the connections I have!' She stepped in close. I could smell the hot tang of her breath. She put her cheek to mine and whispered, 'You don't need anyone but me. I'm your *harbor*.'

The tone of her voice and its absolute conviction made me shudder.

Thank God her train was due any moment. I reminded her of this and started towards the station. She took my arm. I didn't want her to touch me.

Pauline Ostrova and Edward Durant Junior were made for each other and never should have met. He was practical and thorough, she was not. The first time he ever insulted her, he said she was as complicated and bustling as a beehive. It became his nickname for her. She laughed in his face and said she'd rather be *that* than a pencil, like him, which served exactly one boring purpose and thus was constantly forgotten or lost.

Both kids were brilliant and moody. Durant had lived his life in the shadow of his important and powerful father. Pauline's dad was a mechanic.

That's how they met one afternoon when Edward's car wouldn't start. He had the hood up and was footzing around with the hoses and whatever else he could turn with his fingers. He knew nothing about car engines, but all men pop the hood and fiddle helplessly when their car doesn't start; it's in the genes.

Pauline had just finished a freshman philosophy class where once again college proved to be a disappointment. Her peers were mostly interested in doing things she considered old hat. Screwing and drinking, staying up all night, cramming for tests because of all the classes they'd missed screwing and drinking.

There were things Pauline needed to *know*, but no one was teaching them to her. Classes were hard, but not in a good way. She felt like a Strasbourg goose with a funnel jammed down her throat. Instead of food, Swarthmore force-fed her ontology and Ludwig Boltzmann, the Potsdam Treaty and other ho hum. Sure they filled her, but to what purpose?

She had argued with the philosophy instructor until both of them were ready to go for each other's throats. She argued with everyone in those days; it was getting bad. Her frustration was bubbling over.

A beige VW bug was parked in front of the building. Its back hood was up and a good-looking guy was looking at the exposed engine with suspicion and despair. Pauline stomped over, all fury and competence, and fixed it in fifteen minutes. Edward Durant invited her for lunch in an upscale restaurant that did not cater to students. They sat in a booth and talked a long time.

She didn't like him. He was too stiff, too straight, talked incessantly about his bigshot father, and wanted to be a *lawyer*, for God's sake!

Durant thought Pauline was dynamite.

Afterwards they went back to his room and had sex. He wrongly thought it was because he'd wowed her. She would have laughed if she knew. She only wanted to blow off steam and sex was always good for that.

In the following days he couldn't believe her indifference. She'd fixed his car. They'd spoken for hours. They went to bed! He'd told her great stories and made her laugh, but now she didn't seem to give a shit. She never returned his calls, ignored the love letter he spent one whole Saturday composing ... Nothing. What had gone wrong? He tracked her down after a class and asked the question point blank. She said, 'Nothing's wrong. You're nice.' And kept walking.

He wore her down. They didn't sleep together again for three months but that didn't matter. He loved the challenge and Pauline wasn't used to being wooed. She liked his eagerness and was flattered by his naive persistence.

She'd always been so quick to give herself to others. Since she was fifteen, sex was no big deal. She discovered the fastest way to know a man was through a few hours in bed with him. That way you saw his secret face and frequently he let his guard down.

After their one time in bed, Edward behaved like a perfect gentleman on a first date. He was happy to take walks with her, go to the movies, a meal. He proved to be much more interesting than she originally thought. He saw life and the world in ways she never considered before. He had never talked with a woman about these things. When he saw she was interested, he wanted to tell her everything. It unsettled him to know she had been around big time. She spoke of intercourse as if there were no mystery to it and only a little magic. He was dying to ask her a hundred questions about her many lovers, but never did. Partly because he knew she would answer every one without any hesitation.

Slowly college life improved for Pauline. Some of that was because of Edward's friendship and support. He knew the tide had turned the day she started calling him Eddie. The only person who ever called him that was his mother, and only when his father wasn't around.

The saddest thing about Durant was his fear of his father. But the truth was, Senior was so tuned to his own channel that Junior was rarely in his thoughts. The first time Pauline met the parents was on a weekend and the four of them went out to dinner. Despite his self-absorption, Mr Durant recognized this young woman's will was as strong as his own and he treated her coolly. Mrs Durant thought Pauline was sensational and because she loved her son much more than her husband, she encouraged the relationship. In the past, most of the girls Edward brought home were either awed or scared of him. This one stood her ground and was clearly his equal in the most important ways.

It would have broken Eddie's heart if he had known Pauline was sleeping with several other students. She never told him about it, but he heard rumors. It made him so upset that once he literally stuck his fingers in his ears and shouted, 'Shut up! Shut up!'

One night she was with one of these others. Just as they were about to get down to business, she sat up in bed. Looking around as if waking from a deep sleep, she said, 'No! I don't want to do this.' She got dressed again and ran across campus to Edward's dormitory where he was studying for a test. She called from a phone booth and begged him to come down. For one of the only times in his college career, Edward Durant flunked a test because he had better things to do with his evening. After that they were inseparable.

I patched all that together from interviews I did with Pauline's and Durant's college roommates. Both were now middle aged but remembered the smallest details and spoke of their dead friends as if the events of thirty years ago had happened yesterday. Pauline's roommate, Jenevora Dickson, cried through most of the interview. She had an important job at a major advertising agency and looked the part. Once she started talking about Pauline and Eddie, however, she came apart at the seams.

Durant's old roommate angrily paced the room the whole time we talked. 'Know what pisses me off most? This is off the record, okay? I still don't *know* if he killed her. Do you believe that? I lived with Edward for three years and was as close to him as a brother. But he might've done it. He really might've. He adored Pauline. Absolutely adored every part of her being, but it's possible he killed her.

'I saw him in jail, you know? Went up to goddamned Sing Sing and visited him. He looked like he'd shrunk two feet in that prison suit. No one was around and it was private in there, so I asked him. I said did you do it? All he could say was "I don't know. I swear to God I don't know." What's that supposed to mean? You killed her or you didn't. And I guarantee you – if he told anyone the truth, it would've been me. We were brothers.'

'What's his father like?'

'A bastard. A Paul Stuart suit with French cuffs. I once was in court against him. Remember Von Ribbentrop at the Nuremberg Trials? How arrogant he was right up to the last? That was Durant Senior. Everyone said he was broken by Edward's death, but he didn't look very broken to me.'

'Hi, Sam.'

'Hi, Veronica.' Although she was two hours and eighty miles away, I sat bolt upright in the chair and looked around the room as if she were on the phone and nearby at the same time.

'Hello, sweetheart. I'm sorry to disturb you, but I have incredible news. Did you know Pauline and Edward Durant were *married*?'

'Married? How do you know?'

She laughed like a child. 'I *told* you; I'm a great researcher! When I was looking at her notebooks I saw she'd written 'Forever Yours Motel, Vegas' with a big red question mark at the end. It was the only thing in there that made me curious. I played a hunch and contacted the town hall in Las Vegas. *Voilà!* There's a marriage license issued to them three months before she died.'

'Incredible! I don't know what it means, but it's gotta play into it somewhere.'

'I know! I'm wondering what if Gordon Cadmus had found out? If he was in love with her, or even just jealous, what would he do if he discovered she was married? Maybe he *did* kill her in a jealous rage.'

'Then why is someone sending *me* notes, and why did they shoot his son?'

'I don't know. But it adds a whole new twist, eh? You know what I was thinking? I could catch the five o'clock train up there and we could go out for a celebratory dinner. I don't have anything to do tomorrow and, well, it could be a nice night.'

My eyes narrowed. 'Do you mind if we do it another time, Veronica? To tell you the truth, I'm feeling kind of grumpy today.'

'I could make you feel better.'

'I don't think so.'

Her silence weighed a ton. One beat. Two. Then she started to whistle. I was so surprised that I didn't recognize the tune for several moments. The theme to Prokofiev's *Peter and the Wolf*. She just kept whistling.

'Veronica?'

Whistle.

'Veronica, I'm going to go now.'

'Okay. Bye.' And she was still whistling when I put the phone carefully down in its cradle.

Two things happened in quick succession that drove me even further away from Veronica.

I was at the supermarket doing my weekly shopping. Halfway down an aisle, I looked up and saw a staggeringly beautiful woman holding a package of chicken in one hand. It took some seconds to absorb her beauty. Only then did I realize she was talking *to* the package. I couldn't hear all that she was saying, but just enough to know she was completely mad. Both my heart and soul shivered, then froze.

One person rushed into my mind and took up all the space there. Veronica. Watching this beautiful lunatic talking to the chicken as if she were Hamlet and it was Yorick's skull, the only thing I could think of was my new lover. Particularly that whistling on the phone. Was she crazy too?

Then I discovered my favorite fountain pen was gone the day I was to interview Edward Durant Senior. I'm not a tidy person, but when it comes to my desk I'm fanatical. Both Cass and the cleaning woman knew never to even go near it. Everything had its place, especially that lucky pen. If something was missing, even dumb scotch tape, I'd get steamed and search until I found it. The loss of the pen was heart attack country. I scoured the house to no avail. I even looked in the dog's bed in the kitchen, so aggravated by then that I thought he might have taken it to spite me. I could just see him chewing it while smiling at the thought. But he didn't have it. I called Cass in the city but she knew nothing about it. When she suggested I ask Veronica, a stone door in my brain slammed shut with a tremendous bang. Veronica! She'd broken into the house once before. She knew how important the pen was to me . . .

'Yes, I have it.' No more than that. No explanation, apology, just yes. I hesitated to ask when she had taken it because I did not want to hear she had been in the house again without my knowing.

'I need it, Veronica. You know I need that pen.'

Most casually she said, 'Well, it's simple. I'll give it to you when we see each other.'

'Don't do this, Veronica! You're stepping over the line and it's wrong. This is a whole territory you don't belong in. Give it back to me. I need it for my work.'

'And what about *my* needs, Sam? What about the fact you've been avoiding me like I'm diseased! What's happening to us? What is going on in your head? Everything was fixed. We were going to work on your book together and—'

'No, *you* said that, Veronica, not me. I never collaborate. You're too close, do you understand? You're taking away all the air in the room. I can't breathe.'

'And what am I supposed to do, *Sam*, while you're in your room with the door shut and all that *air* around you?'

'I don't know. We have to talk about this another time. I must go now. Please send the pen back.'

'You make me feel like shit, Sam. I don't think I owe you any favors right this minute.' She hung up.

The pen arrived the next morning via express mail. It had been cut into two perfectly equal pieces.

Tappan was a pretty village with a cannon from some war plunked down in the middle of the town green like an old brown toad. Whoever came up with the idea of leaving large decaying weapons around as reminders of death and loss?

Driving beneath gigantic old trees that flanked the roads, I caught glimpses through them of the Hudson River below. Tappan's houses were a mixture of Colonial and modern. A great many were for sale. I wondered why. Following Durant's jovial directions, I found his house with no problem.

From all I had heard about the man, I expected his home to be a fifteen-room colossus with pillars and a lawn that stretched for acres. Instead it turned out to be a simple split-level fifties house with a driveway in front and a small but nicely kept yard. The man obviously liked to garden because there was a wide assortment of bright lush flowers all over. Two fat pugs lay in the middle of the driveway, their small pink tongues hanging out in the heat. I pulled up and got out. Both of them rose slowly and came over to have a look.

'Hey boys. Hot day, huh?' I bent down to pet them and they cuddled right up. The more I scratched their ears the more ecstatic their panting became. One fell over on his side and wiggled all his paws for me to scratch more. A screen door *heeched* open.

'Looks like they found a friend.' Edward Durant Senior did not look, as he had been described, like a tightass in a conservative suit and French cuffs. About five foot seven, he was thin and delicate. He had a large head and a closely trimmed white beard. He looked ill and carried himself carefully, as if certain of his parts were not working correctly.

His voice contradicted the rest. Deep and full, it had the pitch and timbre of a radio announcer or public speaker. It was easy to imagine that voice in a courtroom. Sexy. It was an extremely sexy voice and he used it well.

'I'm a great admirer of your work, Mr Bayer. A great admirer. In fact, if you don't mind, I would be very grateful if you would sign some of your books before you leave. '

When we went into his house it was like entering a small-town library. There were books everywhere and what was as interesting was the way they were cared for. It appeared every single one was covered with a transparent plastic jacket and they were all behind glass. The whole house was floor to ceiling bookshelves made out of some kind of rich dark wood I couldn't identify.

'It's a bit overwhelming, isn't it? A hobby that turned into an obsession. I was a sickly boy and books were my only way out of that bedroom for a couple of years. Best friends I ever had.

'Now, I have all of *your* books right over here—' He walked to a shelf and bending down, carefully opened the glass door. There they were, all my little chickens, standing together in perfect condition.

'I must admit I don't read a lot of fiction anymore. But yours has a wonderful snap to it.'

'That's very flattering. Thank you.' I looked around the room at his thousands of books. 'What *do* you usually read?'

'Biography.' He made a sweeping gesture with his arm, taking in the whole shebang. 'Since retiring, my time has been spent studying other people's lives and how they muddled through. It's a contemptible occupation.'

I was suprised both by the word and the mean way he said it. 'Why contemptible?'

'When you are my age, you feel you have the right to indulge in whatever appeals to you. I don't think it's wrong but it can be pathetic. Unfortunately, Mr Bayer, I am one of those pathetic fools who read about others' lives for solace because I made such a botch of my own. Although it's disgusting to take consolation in another's pain, it *is* reassuring to know the great stumbled as badly as we did. Would you like something to drink?'

What followed was one of the most engrossing afternoons I had spent in years. There are people who are as distinctive and delicious as a great meal. Edward Durant was one of them. He had led an incredible life but instead of showing it off as he had every right to do, he handed it over like a gift to be used whatever way you liked.

He was seventy-three and dying. Somewhere in the middle of the afternoon he mentioned that but only as a point of reference. It didn't seem important to him, certainly not in light of the other things he wanted to say. His wife and son were dead. He had failed both of them and that was his greatest sadness. Until their deaths, he had been a successful, confident man.

'Everything important is learned too late, Sam. The tragedy of being old is you can no longer apply what's taken you so long to learn. The thing scientists should work towards is a method that would allow us to skip to the end of our lives for a short while and then come back.

There is no *context* in the now, only greed and emotion. The language of my former heart does me no good now.'

He had gone to Swarthmore but dropped out to become a fighter pilot in Korea. At the end of the war he returned to college for his degree and ended up a Rhodes Scholar. He just missed being an alternate on the Olympic boxing team. One of the greatest moments of his life was sparring two rounds with the welterweight champion of the world, Benny 'Kid' Paret, in Stillman's Gym. 'How often are we allowed the privilege of having a master's full attention for six minutes? I argued cases in front of the Supreme Court, but it was nothing in comparison to seeing Paret's eyes size me up and then so perfectly kick my ass.'

It took some time for us to get around to his son, but as in everything else, he was painfully candid. 'I was a terrible father for all the reasons I mentioned. I was like a dishonest shoe salesman with Edward. You know, the kind who assures you the shoes you're trying on that are the wrong size will, by some miracle, fit beautifully as soon as you wear them around a while.

'My son was always a serious, steadfast boy who needed no encouragement to do what was right. I was egotistical enough to think he still needed both my discipline and guidance. Although it's not an excuse, you must remember this was in the fifties when all of us were so sure what we were doing was correct. Everything we needed to know was in books – Dr Spock, David Riesman, Margaret Mead. The only thing we had to do was connect the dots and we'd be home free.'

The doorbell rang. Durant was surprised. While he rose to answer it, I asked where the bathroom was. If it hadn't been rude, I would have stayed in there a long time. On the walls were framed letters from famous biographers – Boswell, Leon Edel, Henri Troyat. Intriguingly, the more recent ones were personal letters to Durant answering questions he'd apparently had about the biographers' subject matter. Richard Ellmann's letter about James Joyce's favorite music was alone worth the price of admission.

When I finally pulled myself away from the room, another surprise was waiting at the front door. Durant was standing there laughing with Carmen Pierce, the infamous defense attorney. She represented, among other flakes and dangerous beings, the Malda Vale religious sect. If only Veronica had been around they could have swapped stories and gossip about her old gang.

I was introduced to the flamboyant lawyer who seemed to be on television with one client or another every time I turned it on. We chatted a while. I told her a friend of mine had been a member of the sect before they went on their notorious last airplane ride to oblivion.

'I don't envy you, Mr Bayer.' She smiled.

'Really? Why's that?'

'Because the more I discover about the Malda Vale, the more dubious I am of its members, past and present.'

'But you're representing them!' I couldn't believe she was saying this out loud.

'No, I'm representing an *idea*. Religious persecution is not permitted in this country. What the government did to the Malda Vale is illegal. I don't have to like them to represent them. That's part of the fun of being a lawyer.

'Edward, I must go. Thank you so much for your help. Those articles were invaluable.'

She drove off in a ruby-red Jaguar while the two of us watched until her car was out of sight.

'Carmen is an exhilarating woman. I don't often agree with her methods, but her grasp of the law is phenomenal.'

'Are you helping her with something?'

He put his hand on my shoulder and steered me back into the house. 'No, not really. We've known each other for years. Now and again she calls up with a question and I do what I can. She lives just down the road in Nyack. Luckily when one retires, your profession becomes a hobby and with that sudden shift of perspective, it can become interesting again.'

'Your son wanted to be a lawyer.'

'Not really. My son wanted to please me, which I selfishly encouraged. Another of the great stupid mistakes of my life. He was a genuinely good poet, you know. Published two poems in *The Transatlantic Review* when he was twenty. An important magazine in its time! I'll find those poems and send them to you. They should be in your book. They'll show a side of him not many people knew about.'

'What did you think of Pauline?'

He looked at the floor and pursed his lips, then smiled. 'I've never admitted it to anyone, but she frightened me. She was one of the most erotic women I ever met. He called her "Beehive" and it was a perfect nickname. Always buzzing around, and you knew she could give you a hell of a sting! She made me admire my son more than ever. He had the courage to pursue and *win* this passionate woman. Never, even when I was young and full of myself, would I have had the guts to go after someone like her. And she loved him! It was so plain. They were mad for each other.'

'Did you know they were married?' I expected the question to stop or at least make him pause, but he only nodded.

'Yes, I knew. You really *have* done your homework.'

Edward Junior told his father about it the last time they ever saw each other. He must have been planning his suicide for some time because in their last conversation he said everything that was on his mind and in his heart. The single thing he did not talk about was how the other inmates were abusing him. He looked different than he had in the past – thinner and grayer, but the old man thought it was because the boy hadn't adjusted to the bleak life in prison.

'I had many friends in the penal system. They assured me they would arrange it so Edward would be protected. But a large prison is like a city. No one can be watched all the time. He was doing hard time. He was surrounded by bad men.'

'Do you think Gordon Cadmus ordered the abuse?'

'For years I did. I was convinced Cadmus was guilty of Pauline's death. I'm sure you know they were lovers. She was still sleeping with him when she began going out with Edward. For years I wanted a simple explanation and there was one: Pauline left Cadmus for my son. When I was assigned to investigate Cadmus, he killed her because he was afraid she knew something about his affairs. Or simply because he was jealous. He found the perfect time to kill her *and* frame an innocent man. Edward was sent to jail for the crime, suffered terrible abuse, and committed suicide.

'Cadmus, Cadmus, Cadmus. I was enraged when they shot him. Banal gangland killing, and you know what? He wasn't even the target. One of the other dinner guests was. I wanted him for *myself*. That's been proven. I wanted to take the law of the United States of America and shove it so far up his ass he would have had a second tongue. But then he was dead and there was nothing more I could do.'

'You don't think he killed Pauline?'

'No, Sam, not any more. For years I did, but not any more. Not since last week.' His voice was peaceful. Some part of his soul had come to the end of the line and was calm. A car drove by on the street outside. One of his dogs scratched at the screen door to be let in. Durant closed his eyes and didn't move. I got up and opened it. The pug waddled over to its master and tensing down a couple of times, finally jumped on to his lap.

'Who did kill her?'

'I don't know, but they've contacted me.' He gently

144

lifted the dog off his lap and put it next to him on the couch. It looked indignant but didn't move. Durant went to a desk in the corner of the room and picked up a manila envelope. He came back to the couch and handed it to me.

'As you can see by the postmark, it was sent from Crane's View. Whoever it is likes their irony. Open it. All of the answers are inside.'

It was nothing special – one of those brown manila envelopes you buy by the dozen at any stationery store. Durant's address was typed out in a nondescript font, no return address at the top left corner or on the back.

'I had a friend dust it for fingerprints but of course there were none. This person knows what he's doing.'

I put the envelope down and looked at him. 'From the look on your face I feel nervous opening it.'

'Better nervous than the way I felt when I took it out of the mailbox. I thought it was an advertisement so I opened it on the way back to the house. When I saw what was inside it felt like I had been punched in the heart. Go ahead, take a look.'

Inside were a typed note and four photocopies of original newspaper articles. The articles described separate murders spanning the last thirty-four years. The first was a teenage girl in Eureka, Missouri. The second Pauline Ostrova. The third a waitress in Big Sur, California, and the fourth David Cadmus. The words on the note were typed in the middle of the page: 'Hi Edward! I hear you're dying. Don't go before I tell you my stories. These are only some of them.'

'A serial murderer? That's what McCabe said in California!' I described the videotape of the Cadmus murder, the 'Hi Sam!' Post-it notes, other things, including the fact of the female spider preserving sperm inside her body for eighteen months. Durant listened without interrupting. While I spoke, he pulled the dog back on to his lap and scratched its head.

When I was finished, he reached into a pocket and took out a pack of Gauloises cigarettes and a battered Zippo lighter. The rich smells of summer in the room were quickly displaced by acrid cigarette smoke. He offered me one but I refused, remembering that smoking a Gauloise was like inhaling a volcano.

He looked at the cigarette and smiled. 'This is the only good thing about dying. I always loved smoking, but gave it up years ago with the provision that if I ever became very ill, I'd do it to my heart's content.

'I wouldn't have believed it was possible if there hadn't been one other thing in that envelope, Sam. *It* convinced me.' On the coffee table among the magazines, ashtray and many books was a small silver pocket knife. Durant pointed to it. I picked it up. Nothing special – a silver knife with two blades and no geegaws like a bottle opener or scissors. There was a long, deep scratch down the length of it. In the middle the name 'Sparky' was engraved.

'It belonged to my father. Sparky was his nickname. He gave it to me when I went to Korea. I gave it to Edward when he went away to college. It was a good luck charm for the Durant men. I wanted him to have it. Edward remembered using it the day of the murder to carve Pauline's and his initials into a tree. Whoever does that anymore? Then he explained its history and gave it to her.

'We talked about it when he was on trial. Despite all the terrible things happening, Edward became fixated on finding that knife. I looked everywhere and checked with the police, but it had disappeared. Killers often take souvenirs from the scene of their crimes. When I was practicing, we were often able to convict people on the basis of the mementos we found in their homes.

'It's quite remarkable. Practicing law all those years, I saw every kind of human aberration but never once, not *once* did I think Pauline's murder was only one of many. It never crossed my mind.'

All the crimes described in the articles were unsolved. Durant had used his considerable pull to find out as much as possible about each one. With the exception of David Cadmus, there were a great many similarities.

I asked the same question I'd asked Frannie. 'But why did they wait all this time? If they wanted to be known for these murders why didn't they advertise after they'd done them? The first girl was killed thirty-four years ago. Today she would be *fifty*!'

Durant chuckled and clicked his lighter open and closed a few times. 'You're asking a dying man that question, Sam. Believe me, your perspective changes when the Grim Reaper is on the horizon. Who knows why they're doing it? Maybe they're sick like me, or just *sick* and it's finally beginning to ooze out. Maybe they want to be on television like every other celebrity murderer these days.

'We . spend so much time looking for patterns and reasons, understandable motives and grudges, but it's fruitless. Some things just *are* and that irrationality terrifies us. We keep searching and saying "But there's got to be a reason!" Sorry, not always. Less and less frequently, if you look at the way the world is moving.

'Take your natural disasters. Whenever a tornado or hurricane strikes, some church is destroyed with a hundred good people inside. There's no explanation, so what do we do? Assess the damage and say a hundred million dollars. Count two hundred and nine dead. Hooray for numbers! Something we *can* understand. They may not explain, but they do create an ordering that we need to bear it.

'The contents of that envelope tells me that my son and daughter-in-law died because they had a fight one night and the wrong person was watching. Now they want us to know they were there.'

The next week felt like I was on one never-ending plane ride. I spent three days in Big Sur, California, flew down to

Los Angeles, then over to St Louis where I rented a car and drove to Eureka, Missouri.

Durant had loaded me down with information. When I told McCabe his story, Frannie was ecstatic and went to work finding out more. I spent most of the time in the air reading their combined research.

How many other people had this man killed? What had he been doing all the years in between? I kept picturing an old thin electrician in a nowhere town. Drinking at night in a dumpy bar and then going home in a beery haze to look at his souvenirs and clippings. I'd watched documentaries on television about mass murderers. They're often abused as children or the father abandons them when they're very young. Was this guy one of those? All of his victims had been hit on the head and then thrown into water where they drowned. No sexual abuse. Nothing of importance taken, other than a pocket knife here and who knows what else there. Did the killer keep these things in a box, a drawer, a special bag hidden in a closet? How did he know I was writing the book about Pauline?

That question was answered when I arrived in Los Angeles. In between sniffing around the death of David Cadmus, I stopped at Book Soup with an hour to kill. Browsing the magazine racks outside, I picked up a recent *People* magazine and riffled through it. I hadn't looked at one in a long time, basically because Cassandra's mother read it religiously. Every time I saw the magazine I was reminded of the pit viper who'd once been my wife.

'I saw an article about you in there a couple of weeks ago.'

I turned around and Ann English, the store's beautiful manager, was smiling at me. We kissed cheeks and I asked what she was talking about.

'You were in there, didn't you see?'

'This is news to me, Ann.'

'I saved the article and put it up on the wall in the office. Come in, I'll show you.'

We went into the store and climbed the staircase to the offices. Ann walked to a wall behind her desk and pointed. The date at the bottom of the page was two months past. In a section of the magazine I didn't recognize entitled 'What Are They Doing Now?' there it was – a large picture of me. I read that Sting was about to release a new album, producer Eric Pleskow was working on a film about Chernobyl, and bestselling novelist Samuel Bayer was writing a non-fiction account of the murder of a girl in his boyhood hometown Crane's View, New York.

I swore loudly and then asked if I could use the telephone. In a few seconds there was the hale and hearty voice of my editor, Aurelio Parma.

'Aurelio, you hamster dick, did you tell *People* about my new book?'

'How are you, Sam? Nice to hear your voice. It's been a long time, not that I mind your not returning my calls. Sure I told them. It's great publicity. Tell your fans what you're up to. Notice you were the only writer mentioned in the column?'

'I don't *want* to be mentioned! I didn't want anyone knowing about the book. You have no idea how you've complicated things.'

His voice jumped down the staircase to the cold and distant bottom. 'I have a job to do. Part of it is keeping you in the public eye. If you don't want to tell me how the work is going, that's your choice. But I have to sell it when you're finished. This is how it's done. Don't be naive.'

Three days later back home in Connecticut, I hunkered down and returned to work on the book. At first I thought it would be best to throw out everything I'd written so far and start again. This time tell the story of four murders and how they eventually connected.

I worked on that premise for a week but grew increasingly uncomfortable with the idea. It's easy to lose sight of what you want when you think you want everything. Discovering the very real possibility that Pauline might have been 'only' one of a series of victims threw me way off. Her killer was still alive, taunting Durant and me to come find him. Was his story the one that needed to be told instead? And what about the other victims? Were they to be only footnotes?

Veronica had said Pauline was my mermaid, a radiant mythical creature I had pulled from the water too late to be of any help. If I had loved her from afar back then, that affection only increased the more I learned about her now. Mermaid, Beehive, cheat, femme fatale, tutor to the retarded . . . In the end, I realized I wanted to tell her story and in the process try to do her justice. It would also be Edward Durant's story, but he was the moon to Pauline's earth; he may have affected her tides, but all of their light came from her.

I had a long talk over the phone with Durant senior about it.

'You're right, Sam. You either write about what you know, or what you *wish* you knew.'

I felt so good about this breakthrough that I called Cassandra to ask if she would like to go to a Yankees baseball game. Her mother answered the phone and filled my ear with her waxy woes. Out of nowhere, a memory of an event in our marriage came and I laughed out loud in the middle of her whine.

When Cass was a little girl, she had to do a report for school about Russia. Always the conscientious student, she came to us wanting to know if the citizens of Moscow were called Mosquitoes. The best part of the story was her mother looked at me for a few seconds and I *knew* she was wondering if it was true. Great beauty is like a fat person sitting down on a crowded bus. Everyone else has to shove uncomfortably aside to let this fatty in. Everyone else in this case meaning good sense, taste, intelligence ... I married a beauty and would be forever grateful to her for giving birth to our daughter. The rest was silence.

Cass was eventually able to wrestle the phone away and we made plans. We hadn't spoken much since I blew up at her for investigating Veronica. Our conversation began edgily, but when she heard about the Yankees game she dropped her defenses and we were back on keel. Before we hung up, she hesitantly asked if Ivan could come. I said sure. I would have preferred just the two of us, but there was a man in her life now and she wanted him around.

I took the train into the city and met them at the Grand Central Station information booth. When I walked up, they were having an animated conversation. Cass wore overalls and a Boston Red Sox baseball cap. Ivan had on a black T-shirt with the name 'The Evil Superstars' across it. On the back was the title of their album, *Satan Is in My Ass*. I realized they were speaking French. It was so impressive and flat-out cool that I couldn't resist putting my arms around both of them and moving us towards the subway.

The game was a pleasant bore and I spent much of the time watching the kids delight in each other. What is more exquisite than the first time you are in love? The first time you realize something this all-encompassing is possible and it's actually happening to *you*? The contrast between the kids was marvelous: where Cass was all liveliness, Ivan was grave and thoughtful. She was so different with him than with me. For years I had watched her tread the earth carefully, afraid of taking any wrong step or saying the wrong thing. How great to see her ignoring caution altogether now, exploding with happiness and all the things she had to say right this minute.

Naturally, with Pauline and Durant so much on my mind, I kept seeing parallels between the two young couples. Had they gone to baseball games together? Flirted the same way? Her hand on his arm six times in thirty seconds? His eyes gulping her down, his body tensing with joy every time she touched him?

During the seventh inning stretch I went to the bathroom and then to buy a beer. Standing in line at the counter, I was idly checking out a good-looking redhead nearby when I heard Ivan's voice.

'Mr Bayer?'

'Hey Ivan. Call me Sam. Wanna beer?'

'No thanks. I would like to talk to you for a minute. I didn't want Cassandra to hear. You know your friend Ms Lake?'

'Veronica?' Our eyes locked.

'Yes. She called me. I don't know how to say this, so maybe I should just say it. She told me to stop bothering you.'

The vendor handed me a beer but suddenly I wasn't thirsty anymore. 'Bothering me? How are you bothering me?'

'With your book. She said you didn't want me to help with the research. That's fine with me, don't get me wrong, I just thought it was kind of queer *she* was telling me and not you.'

'She had no right to say that, Ivan. I never said I didn't want your help.'

'She sounded adamant.'

'Well, so am I. I need your help. There are some things I would appreciate your checking for me. I can't believe Veronica called you.' We started back to our seats.

'She also said you didn't like my dating Cassandra.'

'Look, forget what she said. I think it's great you two are together. For whatever it's worth, you have my blessing. I like you and the way you treat Cass. I wouldn't just say that.'

He stopped and stuck out a hand. We shook.

*

The telephone rang at two o'clock in the morning. Late night calls mean only two things to me – disaster or wrong number. I hate both.

'Hello?'

'With whom am I speaking?'

Confused, I said my name.

'I hope I'm not disturbing you—' Veronica's voice was nervous and stilted.

I hung up.

Hearing her voice at that empty hour threw a pan of cold water on me. There was no way I'd get back to sleep for a long time. I would have roused the dog and invited him to go for a walk. But knowing my roommate, he would have ignored the invitation or farted – his one great talent. So it was just me in the dark with a lethal dose of adrenaline in my veins and too much Veronica Lake in my head. Switching on the light, I sat on the side of the bed.

The middle of the night has its own song and it's not one I like. In that deep silence, all your ghosts gather in a Greek chorus and each voice is brutally clear. Why haven't you? solos one. Why did you? People think you're a fool. You're getting old. You haven't done it. You never will.

Years ago I went to an analyst who told me not to worry, everything flows, nothing remains. If you don't like it today, tomorrow will be different. I laughed in his face and said wrong – everything *sticks*. Those big fat bugs of memory and loss stick to us, some dead, most still very much alive, buzzing and squirming.

The silence was growing louder. It was a nice night, so I decided to put on a robe and go sit in the backyard.

Why didn't it surprise me that Veronica was out there? Why did I do only a small double take, then walk over and lower myself tiredly into the lawn chair next to hers?

'Did you call from your pocket phone?'

'Yes. I've been sitting here a long time, trying to get up the courage to call.'

'What if I hadn't come out?'

'I would have stayed here a while and then gone away.'

'What do you *want* from me, Veronica?'

'The same thing Pauline wanted! I want to live ten lives at once. I've tried to do that, and I've tried to do it right, not hurt people, but—' And then she wept. It went on and on. She cried until she was gasping for breath, like a child when they know it's no use crying anymore because nothing will change.

I was thunderstruck. Why hadn't I realized it before? Veronica *was* Pauline! A grown up, electrifying, confused woman with so much to offer but who kept putting it in the wrong places. How often had I *yearned* to know what Pauline Ostrova would have been like if she'd lived. Here she was a foot away, crying herself inside out.

I went over and kneeling down in front of her, put my head on her knee. She put a hand on the back of my head and we stayed that way some time.

'I'm cold. I'm going into the house. Would you like to come?'

She looked at me with hope. I hesitated before smiling and nodded as if to say, yes, that's what I mean.

We stood up together. I started for the house but she stopped me. 'I have something for you. It was going to be a surprise, but . . .' She reached into her pocket and took out a piece of paper. 'This is the phone number of a man named Bradley Erskine. He's one of the men who shot Gordon Cadmus.'

'How did you find him?'

'I did my homework and called in a lot of favors. He said he would talk to you, but he'll arrange it. Just call that number.'

'I don't know what to say. Thank you.'

She waited for me to move. I took her hand and we went back into the house.

Although she had always been a great lover, sex with

Veronica that night went way beyond everything else I had experienced with her. Some of it was due to desperation on both our parts, some of it relief that we were back to a place where the human equation worked without words, motives, thought. We went at it a long time and when we were done, minutes passed before I stopped feeling my heart pounding throughout my body. Veronica was lying next to me, her arm extended over my chest, the tips of her fingers just touching my ear. Neither of us had spoken for a long time and I was beginning to doze when she asked, 'Have you ever seen a ghost?'

I rolled my head to look at her. She was already looking at me, her white hair plastered across her face and the dark blue sheets.

'A ghost? No. Have you?'

She rolled her head up and stared at the ceiling. 'Yes, twice. Once in Nepal, in a town called Salyan up by the Tibetan border. But the second time was much more important.

'A couple of years ago I was walking down Twenty-Ninth Street one night. I'd been to a lousy party and had left early. I just wanted to go home and be by myself. Nothing was wrong in my life then, but nothing was great either.' She turned to me to be sure I understood. 'I'd gone thinking maybe I'll meet some interesting new people, but there was no one and I wasn't in the mood to talk blah blah for hours. Better to go home and watch TV.

'So I was walking down Twenty-Ninth Street for no reason other than I was twenty-nine too at the time. It was cold that night and I was all bundled up. You know how when you're out in the cold like that, when you look in people's apartments from the street, they always look more cozy and warm than they probably are? Only because you're out in the cold and at least it's warm in there.

'But then I passed this one place and stopped. I could only see the living room but I took one look and was absolutely frozen in place. Because *everything* in that room was exactly what I would have bought and exactly in the same place where I would have put it if I lived there. It was one of the strangest experiences I've ever had. In the whole city of New York that night I had found *my* room, Sam. Everything in it was, or *should* have been, mine. The Paul Strand photograph on the wall, the *bunraku* puppet hanging from the ceiling, the oat-colored couch. I can't tell you – everything was as I had dreamed of it for years when I would have enough money to pick and choose and select the place I wanted to live in for the rest of my life. But suddenly it was right there in front of me down to the last detail. Everything. Even the color of the telephone and the mauve tulips in the yellow vase.

'Naturally I was mesmerized and stared until my nose started to run from the cold. At the other end of the room was a door and suddenly it opened.'

'And it was you?'

'I don't know. I didn't *want* to know. I just turned around and ran.'

'Did you ever go back?'

'Nope.'

We lay there silently until she said quickly, 'The hair made me run. I saw the door swing open and before I could get out of there, I saw hair. There was a lot of it and it *was* the same color as mine.'

I called the telephone number Veronica had given me, half-expecting it to be a phony. The recorded voice said to leave a message. I did and two days later a woman called back. There was a phone booth on the corner of Fifty-Eighth Street and Lexington Avenue in the city. I was to be there at five o'clock the next day. Don't bring anyone, don't carry anything, just be there.

When I arrived, someone was in the booth using the

phone. I tried to bribe them out but they told me to fuck off. At 5:07 they hung up and left wearing a spiteful smile. I waited another half hour but nothing happened. I called the Erskine number again and left a message, saying I was at the booth and would wait another half hour. Nothing.

Another week passed while I fumed and tried to work on the book. I didn't tell anyone about Bradley Erskine because I was afraid McCabe or Durant might do something that would ruin it.

The woman called back and said I was to be at the booth again the next day, same time. When I got there it was empty and the phone was ringing. I snatched it up. The woman said only, 'Subway station, Seventy-Second Street and Central Park West in half an hour.'

Once there, I didn't know if I should wait outside or go in. I went in, paid my fare and sat down on a bench. Several trains came and went. I was looking the other way when he sat down next to me.

'Ask away.'

He was in his fifties. Short cropped black hair, a face that could only be described as soft and pleasant. There was a slight sheen to it, as if he was sweating or had just applied cream.

I didn't know whether to shake his hand but since he didn't offer, I didn't try. But I couldn't resist *looking* at his hands. He was the first murderer I'd ever met and I wanted to remember as much as I could. Fat hands. Pudgy fat hands.

'Mr Erskine?'

'Mr Bayer?' He smiled and raised his eyebrows expectantly.

'My friend told me you know something about the death of Gordon Cadmus.'

'I do. I had a ringside seat. Do you mind?' He reached over and tore open my shirt. I was shocked and didn't move. He pulled so hard two buttons flew off and rolled down the platform. His face was impassive. Leaning over, he looked down the open shirt.

'Gotta be careful. Don't want you wired or anything. So, okay, Gordon Cadmus. Whaddya want to know?'

'You were involved?'

'Yep. I was the second coat from the left.' He laughed so hard tears filled his eyes. Then he repeated the line as if it were too good to lose. When he was done, he sighed. 'You're not even gonna ask why I'm talkin' to you?'

'Well yes.'

'Because I need the money. Don't we all? Your girlfriend paid me half up front and the other half after we talk.'

'She gave you money?'

'Hell yes! Twenty-five hundred now, twenty-five hundred after.'

'Jesus! Five thousand dollars?'

'You didn't know? Nice girlfriend you got. So yeah, I was there.'

'Who ordered it?'

He looked at the ceiling. The thunder of an approaching train got louder. 'The name wouldn't ring a bell.'

'Say it anyway.'

'Herman Ranftl. But the rumor was the order came from the mysterious East, you know what I mean? Ranftl just set it up for some warlord or general in Burma. Cadmus and those other guys were messing around with smack importers. I guess they stuck their hands too far into the cookie jar. Fortune cookies!' He laughed again, delighted with his own wit.

'What happened to the other man you did it with?'

'He got colon cancer. Nice way to go, huh? First they give you a bag for your shit, then you're in a bag and all you *are* is shit.

'You know your girlfriend? How she find me? I mean,

it's not easy, you know? She just waltzed in and said hey, can we talk? Very gutsy. I like that in a woman.'

Cass had given me Ivan's number weeks before. I called and asked how good a hacker he was. He said the best. I asked him to find out whatever he could about Herman Ranftl and Bradley Erskine. I gave him all the details I had but insisted he not tell Cass anything. Good man that he was, he didn't ask any questions other than what was relevant to his search.

I went back to Crane's View to talk with Mrs Ostrova again and read some pertinent police transcripts at the station. I called Frannie to say I was coming. He wasn't in when I arrived, but left a note on the front door telling me to keep dinner free: he had a video of the new Wallace and Gromit film (an addiction we shared) and it was time to eat some steaks together.

The phone in the car rang as I was driving down Main Street. It was Edward Durant. He was entering the hospital for a few days and wanted me to have his telephone number there just in case. He asked if there were any new developments. Instead of answering, I asked if he'd ever heard of a man named Herman Ranftl.

'Sure I knew Herman. He was a big *macher* for years. Used to go to Giants games with Albert Anastasia. Ranftl ordered the deaths of Gordon Cadmus and the other two. He died in his sleep a few years ago in Palm Springs. A happy old man.'

'What about Bradley Erskine?'

'Erskine? But Sam, I *told* all this to your friend when she came to visit. She took copious notes. I assumed she gave them to you. No? What a charming woman. And certainly a fan of yours!'

'*Veronica* came to your house? *You* told her about Ranftl and Erskine? When was this?'

'A week ago. More. Maybe ten days.'

Sirens were wailing somewhere nearby but I barely noticed them after what Durant said. I wished him well in the hospital and got off the phone as fast as I could.

For a time I forgot where I was going. Why hadn't Veronica told me she'd spoken with Durant? Why had she lied about finding Erskine through her own research when she must have known he'd tell me? The only reason I could think of was so she could find out everything possible about the men and then hand it to me as a gift.

I came out of my fog when an ambulance swerved around my car and roared on to the end of the block. Two police cars were stopped precariously in the middle of the street, doors still open. Crime scene in Crane's View! Had someone snitched a magazine from the stationery store? A jaywalker caught red-handed crossing against the light?

As the ambulance pulled to a stop, I slowed and saw McCabe's silver Infiniti. It had gone up over the curb and was now blocking the sidewalk. What was going on?

I parked as close as I could to the scene. A crowd of people was standing around about ten feet from the action. I walked over and saw Donna, the waitress from Scrappy's Diner. She was going up and down on her toes, trying to get a better look. Both hands were over her mouth and her cheeks were wet.

'Donna, what's going on?'

'My Uncle Frannie's been shot! Somebody shot him in his car.'

I pushed through the crowd and up to the scene. McCabe was lying on his back on the pavement, a wide pool of glistening blood off to his right side. Paramedics were working on him. Two policemen talked to people who'd apparently seen what happened.

Frannie's eyes were closed. When he opened them they were glazed and empty. Fish eyes. At that moment I thought he was going to die. The medics did what they could and then ran for a stretcher. Once he was secured, they snapped it open and had him inside the ambulance in seconds. The doors slammed and they were gone. I ran back to my car and followed them to the town hospital.

The waiting room was empty. I sat and prayed for him. After I explained to a nurse who I was, she said they had to operate at once. McCabe was unconscious. The wound was grave. They had no idea who'd done it.

Half an hour later Magda Ostrova came in looking bewildered. She'd been at the market. She'd just heard. Without another word she came over and we embraced. Sitting next to me in that hospital silence, she squeezed my hand until it hurt.

Hours went by. People came and went. Other cops, many friends. The surgery continued. Magda began to talk about Frannie. What a good man he was. How he'd been like a father to her daughter. How he'd been the man in the Ostrova family after Magda divorced and her father died. She snarled about his ex-wife and how her career in television had been made when he thought up *Man Overboard*. That's right. That ridiculous and successful weekly half hour show was *McCabe's* idea! His wife took all the credit for it, but his snappy suits and expensive goodies had come from a percentage of the show. No wonder he had spent so much time in Los Angeles.

As tactfully as I could, I asked Magda if she and Frannie were together. She laughed and said for a month, years ago. It wasn't good to be involved with him in *that* way.

'What's strange about Frannie is if you're lovers with him, he treats you like dirt. When you're not, he's the greatest guy in the world.'

The surgery was successful but we were not allowed to see him for two days. When I entered his room, his eyes rolled over to me, then back up to the ceiling. I asked how he was and he nodded. I knew they had to operate again.

161

He gestured for me to come over and sit on the side of his bed. He took my hand and held it but didn't speak. We sat there looking out the window. A couple of times he sighed but nothing else.

'Do you know who did it?'

He shook his head.

'Maybe it was Mr Litchfield getting back at you after all these years for burning his car.'

He didn't smile. I asked if he wanted me to go. In a very quiet, un-McCabe voice, he said yes.

It turned out to be the week of the hospital. There was a message on my answering machine to call Edward Durant at Doctor's Hospital in New York. When we spoke, he sounded as quiet and stricken as McCabe. He asked if it would be possible for me to come and see him soon.

He looked much worse than Frannie. I didn't ask what they were doing to him, but there were IV's and electrodes and whatever else they stick into a body when things aren't going well inside. Strangely, he also gestured for me to come and sit next to him on the bed. His lion's voice had disappeared. His sentences frequently stopped midway whenever he ran out of energy.

He had thought he had more time left, but after this examination they weren't hopeful. His once-strong body had been overthrown by a mob of lunatic cells. The situation reminded him of looters in a riot. Running into a store, they take anything they can grab. Anything, so long as it isn't theirs.

There was no self-pity in Durant's voice, only a kind of disgusted wonder. Most of the time he spoke about his son. What was most wrenching to hear was how he referred to Junior in the present tense.

At first I thought he was only reminiscing, but then he got to the point. Out of nowhere, he said he guessed I didn't make that much for a book. I told him it was sufficient. He said he had a great deal of money left. Originally he had planned to leave it all to Swarthmore College with the stipulation they create a scholarship program in his son's name, preferably in the English Department.

He wanted to know if I would consider expanding my book so that it included the life of Edward junior. I said that was no problem – Pauline's husband had to play a very large role in the story.

That wasn't what he meant. 'Don't you see, Sam, the only possible thing I can still do for Edward is vindicate him. I know it sounds crass, but I'd gladly give you any amount of money to do that so people could know what he was really like. Whatever you need that I have – money, connections, anything – I offer to you. My greatest wish is that a real writer tell not only the true story of Pauline's death, but Edward's as well. I know it would mean a longer book, but in the end wouldn't it be a better one? You'd have not only the story of a murder, but the love story of two extraordinary people.'

I knew with his help I would have access to materials normally impossible to obtain. Yet I didn't want to commit myself. I told him to let me think about it and get back to him. He started to speak but stopped.

'What were you going to say?'

His lips trembled and he turned quickly away. He said something I couldn't hear.

'I'm sorry, Edward, I didn't hear you.'

He turned back. 'Who will remember him when I'm dead? Who will remember the little boy spelling God D-O-G? Or how he tried to hypnotize his shoelaces into tying themselves? Sam, *someone* has to tell his story. Not just clear his name.' He grabbed the bed sheet. 'Life is not fair, but it can be just. That's all I want. Help it to be just for my son.'

*

It was raining when I left the hospital. One of those cold unpleasant rains that know how to sneak down the back of your shirt and give a chill before you've gone ten blocks. Hospitals invariably give me the feeling of being coated in an invisible sheen of bloodthirsty germs and lost hope which doesn't disappear until I've walked hard a while and breathed in the healthy world outside, so I kept walking.

I wanted a hamburger. A cheeseburger dripping with grease and a mound of fried onion rings that would clog my arteries and fuck the rest. I knew a nice gross luncheon-ette nearby that had what I needed. I headed in that direction.

Standing on a corner waiting for the light to change, I looked across the street and saw Veronica. My guts did a double salto. I didn't know whether to run away or straight at her.

'Hey, you wanna buy a gold chain?'

A tall black man standing next to me held open a case full of glittering junk.

'No thanks.'

When I looked back across the street, Veronica had metamorphosed into just another lovely New York blond. The light changed and we moved towards each other. Without realizing it, I continued to stare at false Veronica. Seeing me gawk, her face turned to stone.

Later over my cheeseburger, I thought about what it was like to be haunted by a person. What was it like for Edward Durant to think about his son, falsely accused, imprisoned for murder, sexually abused, a suicide?

What was it like to be lying in a hospital bed knowing your time was up? Your soul full of regrets and memories driving the guilt deeper every day.

I put the burger down and asked the counter man for a glass of water. I drank it in one go and asked for another which went down the same way.

Holding the empty glass in my hand, I felt the world around me *increase*. Sounds, smells, the closeness of the people in the room. Some Godly hand had turned up the volume. I knew if I went back outside I would be crushed by the weight. Is that what Durant was feeling? Because for him it could only get worse. Even frozen solid in this jacked up moment, I knew it would pass and I would come through. Drink some water, take a deep breath, rearrange the furniture ... There were a million ways to fix things and go on. But what if all the furniture was gone and the only company you had in that final room were ghosts you'd spawned and fed on a lifetime of mistakes?

There was a phone on the back wall of the place, next to the toilet. I called Durant and said I would write the book he needed.

While in the city there was one more thing I needed to do, thanks to Ms Lake and her hacksaw. I needed a new pen. There was only one place to go – the Fountain Pen Hospital. I liked the store so much that I had taken Veronica there one day. We spent a long time mooning over the thousands of old and new pens. I bought her a vintage Elmo-Montegrappa. More than anything, she loved the name of the company. Said it sounded like a rare tropical disease.

When I walked in this time, one of the owners brightened and said he had a surprise for me. Sotheby's had recently had an auction of objects owned by famous writers. He brought out a worn black leather box and handed it to me. Inside was a plum-colored Parker 51, complete with broad nib. The same model Veronica had cut in half. But the one I was holding had belonged to Isaac Bashevis Singer! I was barely able to keep my tongue in my mouth. With a sinking feeling, I asked how much it cost, knowing full well I'd mortgage the house to own it.

'It's a gift from your friend. The one you were with the

last time you came in? We have the provenance too. There's no question it belonged to Singer.'

'How did this happen?' I couldn't bear to put the pen down. A present from Veronica after everything that had happened made me uneasy but I couldn't let this one leave my hand.

'She came in a few days ago and asked if we had a mustard-colored 51, but you know how rare those are. We told her about this one. She bought it immediately and said to hold it for you.'

'She didn't take it with her?'

'She was sure you'd be in soon.'

'How much did it cost?'

'We're not allowed to tell you.'

It was remarkable, as great a gift as any I had ever received. But did it make up for the chaos and trouble Veronica kept causing? I took the pen but never used it. Mr Singer had owned it, but Ms Lake gave it to me. As far as I was concerned, her juju was a lot more powerful than one of my favorite authors.

Fall arrived like a bully, wasting no time making nice-nice with pretty autumn leaves or crisp cold mornings. It shoved summer in the face and started sleeting in the middle of September.

McCabe and Durant went home from the hospital changed men. Durant knew the big clock was ticking an inch from his head. Like an artist inspired to do one last great work, he threw himself into gathering the details of his son's life and whatever else he could do to help me.

I took to spending whole days with him, going over his research and discussing aspects of the book. His enthusiasm inspired and humbled me. Despite a body full of healthy cells, I had been moping around for such a long time. Being with Edward Durant made me want to go fast again.

Never once did he try to sugar-coat his son or what the boy had done in his short life. 'The only time you need to convince a jury is when your case is weak, or you *know* your client is guilty. Thank God we don't have that problem here. Edward's innocence needs no clever distortion.' He lit one of his atomic bomb French cigarettes and delicately plucked a piece of black tobacco off his tongue.

'You know how you can tell if a woman is genuinely beautiful, Sam? See her when she wakes up in the morning. No makeup or elaborate hairdo – just her. If she's got it, you'll see. Same thing applies here. Tell the truth about Edward and they'll see.'

When he said that, I thought of Veronica in the morning. She liked to sleep in men's pajamas. Opening her eyes, she'd see you and reach out her arms like a child. The only thing she ever said was 'Come.' We'd embrace and when our faces were touching, I could feel her smile against my cheek. *She* was beautiful and those arms held wonders.

Inevitably, as he talked about Edward and Pauline, I found myself telling Durant about Veronica and what had happened between us.

He thought about it a while and then said, 'She sounds like a haunted house. We're all so optimistic and vain when it comes to romance. Convinced *our* love can exorcise their ghosts. But ghosts have forgotten about love. It's not part of their world. The only thing they know is how to make you miserable.

'Veronica probably does love you, Sam. It's unfortunate you didn't meet years ago. You might have been able to save her then. But saving someone is not the same as loving them, is it?'

The doctors said McCabe would recover completely in time, but when he got out of the hospital, he took a leave of absence from his job and spent the time watching television or Hong Kong karate videos. Whenever I was there, he was in his robe and pajamas, watching the tube and rarely talking. We ate whatever I cooked or brought in from outside. When I was gone, Magda Ostrova came by at least once a day with something for him.

He lost interest in my book or investigating what had happened to Pauline and Edward. When I spoke about it, I could see him tune out, his eyes flickering back and forth between me and the TV set.

I knew Frannie was trying to find his way out of the trauma of being shot, but knowing that didn't make it any easier to be around him. A vital part of McCabe had closed down and he didn't seem to be much bothered by the loss.

One day after work at the town library, I pulled up in front of his house and was amazed to see Durant and McCabe sitting together on the porch. It was not particularly cold out, but both were wearing winter overcoats. I had told Edward about Frannie being shot and though he expressed great concern, he seemed so physically weak that I never would have imagined him coming to visit.

'Edward! What are you doing here?'

'Frannie just showed me a Jackie Chan film which held me spellbound. I was tired of sitting around my house, dying. Decided to take a drive.'

I climbed the porch steps, sitting down on the top one. A guy on a motorcycle passed by and for a moment its roar was all the noise in the world.

We spent half an hour shooting the breeze. They were easy and relaxed with each other. Durant was a man who could captivate any audience with no trouble. I was touched to see him, sick as he was, trying to tickle McCabe back to life.

'Did you hear the Cindy Crawford joke? A man's been marooned on a desert island for five years. Alone the whole time, it's finally driving him nuts. He's sitting there on the beach, crying his heart out 'cause he's so sad and lonely.

'Suddenly he looks up and sees someone swimming in towards shore. It's Cindy Crawford, and she's buck naked! She reaches land and they stare at each other. It's love at first sight. They jump into each other's arms and start making love like wild animals. They do it on the beach, in the water, hanging from the coconut trees . . . They're at it seven hours straight.

'Afterwards they're lying there, absolutely exhausted. The guy turns to Cindy and says "Could you do me a favor?"

'She says "*Anything*, darling. I'd do anything for you!"

'"Would you put on my clothes and call yourself Bob?"

'Cindy looks at him like he's crazy, but says okay. So she puts on his running shoes, khakis, T-shirt and baseball cap. She sticks out a hand and says in a very masculine voice "Hi, I'm Bob!"

'The guy says "Bob, you'll never *believe* who I've been fucking!"'

We all laughed. Frannie shook his head. 'That's a Hollywood joke: nothing's real unless there's an audience!'

Durant said, 'And like your friend with the Post-it notes.'

Sitting in a companionable silence with them, watching cars pass by, I thought about the joke and how it applied to most of the people I hung around with those days. Pauline had cheated on her high school English essays so she'd be seen as the best student in class. Durant was obsessed with showing the world who his son really was. Veronica tried so many different ways to make me want her, including becoming one of my fictional creations. And nothing was more important to me than telling this story accurately and with integrity to an unknown bunch of readers. Nothing is real unless there's an audience.

The day began to cool down towards night. I got up and asked if anyone wanted a drink. They put in their orders. As I was walking into the house, I stopped and said, 'I'm really glad I know both of you. I know everything's fucked

169

up these days, but all that aside, I'm very happy to know you.'

While I was in the house fixing our drinks, I heard a car pull up in front and a door slam. Paying it no mind, I finished what I was doing and walked back outside.

There were three boxes from Pizza Hut stacked in the middle of the porch floor. Both men looked at me and smiled.

'When'd you order these, Sam?

I looked at Frannie and shook my head. 'I didn't order pizza.'

'Well, neither did I. Edward and I've been sitting out here the whole time.'

We looked at Durant who shrugged. 'Not me.'

McCabe reached forward and pulled the top box on to his lap. Opening the lid, he peered in and made a face. '*Anchovies*! I hate anchovies. Jesus, I'm not eating this!'

I opened the second. Inside was another topped off with a whole school of those vile-smelling fish.

Durant's arm shook as he reached for the last box. I knew it wasn't fear that caused it. What strength and courage it must have taken him to come to the house today. Now something bizarre was going on and he didn't have any reserves left to deal with it.

He lifted the box top, looked inside, closed it again. 'This one has pineapple. There's a note that says "Hi Boys! Dig in."'

My bowels froze. *He* was here, somewhere near enough to see us. He was here. I looked up and down the street and saw no one. Was he the guy zooming by on the motorcycle, or the thin man driving the red Dodge truck?

I grabbed all of the still-warm boxes and threw them as hard as I could towards the street. Cheese, tomato paste, pineapple and anchovies flew everywhere.

'Fuck you, asshole!' None of the stuff had made it to the street. McCabe's small front yard was a mess of vivid color. I kicked one of the pizza boxes, then anything nearby. I kept kicking and didn't know what I was doing and kicking didn't make me feel any better but I had to do something. Anything.

The fax was humming away when I walked into my office in Connecticut a day later. Sheet after warm sheet dropped into the basket. I looked at one. It was part of a rap sheet on Herman Ranftl. I picked up all the papers and shuffled them into order. The fax was from Ivan and had everything about Herman Ranftl, Bradley Erskine, Francis McCabe, Edward Durant, Senior.

He'd already given me the rundown on Veronica so this completed the cast of characters in my life at that point. I was awed by his thoroughness. Where he got all of his information was a mystery to me, but he was as meticulous as a tax collector. I already knew much of what he had gathered, but Ivan's research filled in important blanks. I started with Ranftl and Erskine.

By the time I finished reading about them, my head was filled with the filthy lives of two very bad men. Bradley Erskine, murderer, was a shit as a kid and went downhill from there. Ranftl was a lot smarter and an even greater monster. McCabe had once given me his argument for capital punishment. 'All the studies say it doesn't stop criminals from killing people and that's probably right. But if you gas these criminals, *they* won't kill anyone again.' Thinking about Ranftl and Erskine, I knew the Chief of Police had a point.

To my dismay, Frannie's biography revealed something new and disturbing. While serving in Vietnam, McCabe had undergone drug rehabilitation twice. When he got out, he'd been treated two more times. Did he still do drugs? Was that why he was so thin and pale? I wanted to talk with him about it, but knew it was none of my business. Especially while he lay around all day in his pajamas,

171

hypnotized by karate kicks on television. The only thing I could do for him now was keep him company and be his friend in whatever ways he needed.

In contrast to the others, Edward Durant's biography read like an Eagle Scout's. Awards, honorary degrees, an advisor to governors ... Success after success, but when you spoke with the man, he saw himself as a failure who had only one hope left – to 'save' his son.

Pete the Postman came up the walk and I opened the door. 'How're you doing, Pete?'

'Fifty-fifty. Not much for you today, Sam. Only one big envelope. Here she is.' A brown manila envelope, my name and address written in her unforgettable script. I noticed at the top left corner she had written only 'Veronica Lake'.

'Austria, huh? Always wanted to go to Vienna and see those white horses. You know, the ones that dance around on their back legs?'

I looked at him questioningly.

'The postmark. Austria?' He pointed to the package in my hands. What the hell was Veronica doing in Austria?

When he left, I continued standing there, looking at the package. I gave it a gingerly squeeze and shake. Felt like a book or a video. The last two videotapes I watched had sent my life into serious fibrillations: the first introduced me to Veronica's porno career, the second documented the end of David Cadmus's life. I wasn't sure I wanted to see what was on this one. But Veronica in Austria was too intriguing and I knew I had to look.

I opened the envelope and took out the tape. There was no label, nothing describing what was on it. Wrapped around it was a handwritten letter in the emerald green ink she liked so much.

Sam,
There are over five hundred people named Bayer in the Vienna phone book, but I found who I was looking

172

for. You'll understand if you watch this. I hope you do. It's only the rough cut, but it'll give you an idea of what I'm trying to do. Working on it made me miss you so much I sometimes couldn't breathe. But I've done so many things wrong that this separation now is the best thing.

I hope your book is going well. I treasure the memory of that sunny morning in Seattle when you told me the idea for the first time. I kept saying to myself 'He is telling me the story of his new book. The one he *hasn't even begun yet!*'

Thank you for making many dreams come true. Thank you for watching this film, if you do find the time. Even if we had never met, it would make me so proud to know Samuel Bayer spent part of a day watching something I did. I mean that with all my heart.

I put her tape straight into the machine.

It began with toast. That familiar scratchy noise of someone buttering a piece of toast. Black screen, scratchy sound. Then a male voice starts to speak and recognizing it even before his face appeared, I hoot with glee.

'Samuel Bayer is a dreadful writer! He was also a dreadful student in class. It surprises me how successful he has become with those tepid little thrillers he writes.' My old high school English teacher (and Pauline's) Mr Tresvant stops buttering. Sighing, he shakes his head. He is in a bathrobe with a pattern on it that looks like 1950s wallpaper. The robe is open at the throat. His scrawny neck and old man's wattles are sad and unattractive. There are a bunch of dark moles across his chest, things we students never saw because Mr Tresvant's shirts were always buttoned right up to the top. He takes a careful bite of toast. Crumbs fall down around him but he pays no attention. How did Veronica convince the uptight fuddy-duddy to go on camera in his robe and pajamas? One of

173

the most controlled people I'd ever known, he looked here like a bum in an eleven-dollar-a-night Utah motel room.

He rambles on, all grumble and gripe. Veronica's brilliant trick was to shoot him in such a way that after a while you don't believe a word he says. This old man is one repellent flop of a human being. Why would you want to hear his opinion on anything, much less trust it?

Off camera, Veronica asks, 'Why aren't you proud that one of your former students went on to become a world-famous writer?'

Tresvant sneers. 'One should never take credit for participating in mediocrity.' He looks away and takes another bite of toast. More crumbs fall. A small piece sticks to the corner of his mouth. He doesn't notice. The camera lingers on him. It is lethal because everything about this man – his pretentious tone, the dingy robe and unshaven face – exudes nothing *but* mediocrity.

'Would you like to hear what Bayer said about you?' Veronica's voice is emotionless.

Which stops the old pedant in mid-chew. His toast goes down and the eyes narrow. You can see he thought she was just going to let him pontificate and throw all the punches. Not so, Iago.

But right there the film blacks out! What the hell *did* Bayer say about Tresvant?

The picture comes back up. I'm in our hotel room in Seattle, pulling on a pair of pink socks. When we traveled together, Veronica carried a small video camera with her everywhere. I never paid attention after the first days because it seemed to be her third eye – she was always filming *something*.

Socks on, I sit back and smile. 'School? The only thing I learned there was what I *didn't* like. That's what school is for – it teaches you what to avoid the rest of your life. Cell

174

mitosis, parabolas, the complete works of George Bernard Shaw . . . things like that.'

Cut to a horse-drawn carriage, clopping down Vienna's Ringstrasse. I knew that beautiful street from one of my many honeymoons – this time with Cassandra's mother.

I had casually mentioned to Veronica that both sides of my family came from Vienna. She remembered. She found great-uncle Klaus and his adorable fat wife, Suzy. They gave her an inspired guided tour of the Bayer family's Vienna. The stories they told, the sights she chose to show, the way she segued from one thing to another – all of it was riveting.

From the top of St Stephen's Church they talked about the Bayer who had helped rebuild the cathedral roof after it was destroyed by Allied bombing at the end of the Second World War. Over dinner of *Tafelspitz* at the King of Hungary Hotel, they described the distant cousin who had been Gustav Mahler's favorite tailor.

Any family memoir is a flock of small stories that periodically collide with history's propellers. The Bayers were no different. Although I was nominally the subject of her film, Veronica chose to paint a much larger, more panoramic picture. By cutting back and forth across time, across continents, from the astonishing to the forgettable, she was able to paint one of those gigantic canvases that portray whole battles, or the building of the Tower of Babel, a day in the life of a great city.

When the story returned to me and my life, she interviewed people and showed events I had forgotten long ago. I kept blinking or saying out loud, 'That's right! God, I forgot all about that.' I was spellbound throughout, and not just because it was my own life on the screen. She chose a narrative line so precise and encompassing that the result was the most thorough and loving biography any person could ever hope for. It saddened me because it brilliantly displayed a side of Veronica Lake I had never seen and could only admire. How I wished things had gone differently between us. What an extraordinary love letter. Tragically, it had been created by a woman who came as close to scaring me as any intimate I had ever known.

Frannie watched as I ferried back and forth from my car to his house, carrying boxes and bags full of mysterious things I hoped would rouse him from his thousand-year sleep.

At a good market in my town I bought a large array of groceries, hoping he'd take one look at the bounty on his kitchen counter and be inspired to help me cook a few fabulous meals.

After my third trip, he followed me out to the car in his green and white striped pajamas.

'What is all this?'

'Resurrection Soup.'

'What do you mean?' He put both arms behind his back. Standing there shrunken in wrinkled pajamas and flyaway hair he looked like an alumnus from *One Flew Over the Cuckoo's Nest*.

I hoisted a jumbo bag of groceries out of the trunk. 'Frannie, have you noticed me busting my ass here lugging these groceries? How 'bout joining the process?'

Once we'd gotten everything into the kitchen, I pushed him out and said he could come back when I was ready. It took a while because the look and presentation of the meal had to be both dramatic and inspiring. I did my best. When it was done, I thought what I had cooked looked pretty damned spiffy.

A few minutes before, the telephone rang but I barely heard it. Coming out of the kitchen, I heard him laughing very loudly. I was thrilled to hear him answer anything with a full sentence. What person these days could make him laugh like that?

He was alone talking on his portable phone, wearing a genuinely happy smile. He waved and held up a finger for me to wait a sec. 'Here's your man, fresh out of the kitchen. He's cooking something mysterious in there and won't let me see. You wanna talk to him?' He put his hand over the mouthpiece and said, 'It's Veronica.'

My eyebrows went up as far as they could go. The only contact I'd had with her in weeks was the videotape from Vienna. When had she gotten back? Why was she calling him? He pulled the phone away from his ear, as if she was shouting at him.

'All right, all right, take it easy, Veronica! You don't *have* to talk to him. What? Yeah, okay. Bye.' He pressed the disconnect button and dropped the phone into his robe pocket. 'Whoa! What did you do to the girl? She freaked out.'

I tried to speak calmly. 'Frannie, Veronica called you?'

'Sure she has, every day. She's been as nice as you since I've been sick, Sam. She comes by, cooks, calls ... She's a good woman. I'm sorry things haven't been working out between you two.'

'She comes here and *cooks* for you? Why didn't you tell me this?'

'Because she asked me not to. That's her right. I gotta respect it. Besides she's been so *kind* to me, you can't believe—'

I put up a denying hand. 'How did she know you were shot?'

'She was going to interview me for your movie, but then it happened. She's been watching over me ever since. I got all these guardian angels around me these days. I'm a lucky guy.'

'McCabe, if you knew some of the things about Veronica that *I* know, you'd arrest her.'

'What, the thing about cutting your pen in two? She told me! I laughed my ass off. Sam, the woman's a hundred thousand volts. She knows that and that's probably why you like her, if you'll just admit it to yourself. You can't have everything safe and predictable when you're with her. That's part of her attraction.'

I looked at the floor and told myself several times this was a sick man who needed gentle treatment. 'I don't want to talk about it. Come in the kitchen and take a look.'

'At what?' He walked over and bumped me with his hip. 'We're not having an affair, Sam. She's nice to me. That's all. You gotta be grateful to people who are nice to you.' For the first time in weeks, he had the old glint in his eye. 'You know what I've been thinking about today? I was telling Veronica: high school. I've been thinking how we used to walk down those halls so fuckin' sure of ourselves. A hundred and fifty pounds of sperm. Remember that bulletproof feeling? We were King Kong, teflon, hard-on, radioactive, and free as a dollar you find in the street. Everything was *imminent*, you know what I mean? Everything was right around the corner, due to arrive any minute. And we had no doubt it would arrive because it *had* to. Because we were *us*! That's what's great about being a kid: you know things will work out and you can beat every guy in the house.'

Although I cooked dinner that night, for the first time in ages Frannie pitched in by chopping leeks and dicing potatoes. I had to order him to stop turning the new Cuisinart I'd bought on and off, but he didn't suggest TV when we were done. We spent the rest of the evening talking about the good old days. My hopes were up.

The next morning there was something on the windshield of my car. It had snowed the night before and this early in the morning, everything was silent and still, covered in white. The air smelled cold and clear with a hint of wood smoke in there somewhere. I stood on the porch looking around, enjoying being outside while things were still wearing their white hats, untouched. A bird flew off a tree branch causing snow to drift lightly down. The sky was full of dark clouds whizzing by. I heard a car coming, its tires hissing on the wet pavement. A black Lexus rolled slowly by, the color contrasting starkly with the white world around it. A good-looking brunette was driving and to my great delight, gave a big wave. I understood. Here we were, just the two of us out in this picture postcard morning, all ours for a little while longer. Hello there, isn't this great? I waved back with two hands just as the car went around the corner, adding glowing red tail lights and gray exhaust smoke to the picture.

Smith, McCabe's cat, stood on the other side of the street looking at me. The color of orange marmalade, he stood out vividly against the snow. It surprised me Frannie kept any pet. The tough guy I knew years ago would have owned a psychotic pit bull or a Komodo dragon. But adult McCabe got real pleasure out of owning a *cat*.

It leapt up on to the hood of my car and froze, only his tail curled back and forth in the air. Another car passed. Then I noticed my windshield had been cleared of snow and a piece of paper was under the wiper. Had I gotten a ticket? Parked in front of the Chief of Police's house?

Approaching the car, I listened to the snow crunching beneath the soles of my sneakers. My shoes were much too thin for the weather and I felt the cold through them in no time. Smith stayed on my car, impassively watching as I walked towards him.

'What's under the windshield?'

He looked at me with nary a flicker in his indifferent gold eyes. I reached over and lifted the wiper. Beneath it was a standard-size envelope wrapped inside a plastic baggy. I took my pocketknife and slit through the plastic, then the envelope itself. Inside was a Polaroid photograph of my daughter and Ivan walking down a street, smiling at each other. The photographer could not have been more than three feet away from them. On the back of the picture was a green Post-it note with this typed on it:

'Hi Sam! I want to read what you have written so far. Put it on a disk (MS-DOS, please) and send it to Veronica Lake. I will tell her what to do with it.

Don't tell anyone about this. Cassandra is pretty. Act fast.

I tried to swallow but couldn't. Suddenly there wasn't enough oxygen on the planet to fill my lungs. My daughter? This scumbag had been killing people for thirty years. Now he knew who Cassandra was and had gotten close enough to photograph her? I realized I was talking out loud. Of course he'd gotten close to her. This was the same man who left the videotape on Cadmus's doorstep, a taunting note on my papers after the lecture in New Jersey, pizza on McCabe's porch.

But why send my book to Veronica? How did she fit into this? Was she in contact with the killer, or was she being used by him for some unknown purpose?

My daughter! He had stood a few feet away from her. She and Ivan walked by, oblivious to everything but their shared happiness.

I looked at the photograph again and realized it had been taken from directly in front of the couple. They'd probably seen him, but would they remember? Kids don't see anything but themselves, especially when they're in love.

My manuscript was already on computer disk. There would be no trouble copying it and sending it to Veronica, but then what?

The thought was unbearable. He said I shouldn't talk to anyone, but I had to ask Frannie – the cop, my friend, the person who had been as close to this story as anyone.

'Do what he wants, Sam. Make a copy and send it to

him. What else *can* you do? Why are you even asking? He said don't tell a soul. Well, I'm a soul.'

'Frannie, for God's sake! You're the only one I know who knows about this kind of crap. What do you think I should do? I'm lost here, man! This is my *daughter*! Do you understand? Cassandra! The dirty son of a bitch was *this* far away from her! Have a fucking heart, willya? Help me!'

We stood in the kitchen. For the first time in weeks he was dressed in normal clothes – a pullover, jeans, boots. At another time, I would have rejoiced at the change in him. But a blade was an inch from my neck now and maybe Cassandra's.

Before I showed him the note he had been full of good cheer and wisecracks. Now he had his hand on the button of the Cuisinart and kept switching it on and off as he had the night before. Only now it was every second and so annoying I wanted to throw the thing out the window. I didn't have to.

When I finished accusing him, my chin was stuck out so far I could feel the chords of my neck stretching. He did nothing but look at his hand on the machine. On off on off on ... Then without any warning, he scooped the gadget up and heaved it like a fastball against the refrigerator. KA-BAM! Parts exploded in every direction. It had been so long since I'd seen how strong Frannie was. When we were young, he did things in fights that amazed everyone. You never ever, not even in your dreams, messed with Frannie McCabe.

Yanking his sweater up, he pointed at the thick white bandage across his stomach. 'I was *shot*! The guy put a hole here 'cause he wanted me dead. Understand? I can't help you with your kid, Sam. Sorry, but my tank's empty at the moment because I'm scared too. They're after me, you, Cass, *everybody*! And we're not gonna win this time.

'You can be good or moral ... So what? Fuck you! You still die, because some nobody don't like the way you *breathe*. Now you're beginning to understand it. I saw it in 'Nam, I saw it here, and now they shot me. Look what happened to Pauline! Makes absolutely no sense, and that was thirty years ago. Compared to today, things were safe then! She fights with her boyfriend while some mass murderer's watching. Guy doesn't even know her but kills her anyway! Hey, why not, she's pretty. So her poor husband goes to jail, gets the shit beat out of him, goes nuts . . . Come on!

'I give up, Sam. I admit it. I give up. I'm gonna sit in my house, watch videos and listen to *The Pirates of Penzance*. What should you do? Show the guy your book. Save your daughter. Save *your* ass. Forget the rest.'

To my immense relief and dismay, Veronica acted like an angel. With great reluctance, I called and told her about the killer's demand. She was aghast to hear about the photograph of Cassandra and said she would do whatever she could to help.

Neither of us mentioned what had happened between us recently. Hearing her voice on the phone again, part of me melted, another part stiffened and wanted to shout 'Why did you lie to me? I need to trust you now, but how can I?' But I kept my mouth shut because I desperately needed her and Cass needed her. Plus what she had to do to help us might be extremely dangerous.

How would the killer contact her once she had the disk? I despised him for putting me in this spot. Why couldn't I just have sent it to him at an untraceable address, or drop it off someplace—

'Because he wants you to know how much he knows about your life,' she said gently. 'Maybe he shot Frannie, maybe he sent the envelope to Durant with the old clippings, took the picture of Cassandra . . . Think about it. It's intimidation, Sam. He wants you to feel him breathing in your face.'

'So what happens if he reads what I wrote and doesn't like it?'

'If he was someone else, I'd say you were in trouble. But he's different. He wants you to do this. It's his only chance of immortality. I don't think he'll do anything other than give you suggestions.'

'*Suggestions*? Jesus Christ! I've already got an editor I hate. Now a second one? Who kills people?'

'Stop fretting, Sam. There's nothing you can do about it except go along with what he wants. Let's figure out—'

'Veronica?'

Her breath hitched as if she was sure I was about to say something she didn't want to hear. Her 'Yes?' was a whisper.

'Thank you for your help. Thank you very much.'

She exhaled loudly. 'You're welcome. It's the least I can do after the trouble I've caused. Listen, I had lunch with Cassandra. Please don't be mad. I know *you* don't want to see me now but I thought it would be all right if she and I met and I told her everything. I asked her not to tell you till I did. We had a good time, Sam. She said she'd like to introduce me to her boyfriend. She's so smart. She's a great girl.'

I sent her the disk. Two days after it arrived, the monster called and said to meet him at noon at Hawthorne's bar. The choice wasn't surprising, given all the other things he knew about us. Still, I hated the irony as he probably guessed I would. That place had only lovely memories for me. Now it was off my map forever.

Not knowing what to expect, Veronica took only a small purse that contained the disk and her wallet. She said she was tempted to bring a small pocket tape recorder and turn it on before entering the bar. I shuddered hearing that because who knows what he would have done if he'd discovered she had it.

She took a subway downtown. Almost as soon as she got out of the train, she was grabbed from behind and slammed against a wall face first. It cut her forehead badly. She saw the thief for only a moment when he took out a small knife and cut the strap of her purse. When she cried out and tried to stop him, he pushed her into the wall again, snatched the bag and ran away.

'It was a *boy*, Sam. Very dark-skinned. I think he was Indian or Pakistani. But a boy, fifteen or sixteen. He must have followed me all the way from my apartment and been on the train. It was so smart! Hire a kid to steal it.'

Because it was New York, no one helped her. After it was over and her head was bleeding, one woman – *one* – came up and gave her a handkerchief to cover the cut. Veronica managed to get to her doctor and then the police. They made out a report but shrugged when she asked if there was anything more they could do.

I waited the whole time in her apartment. When she had been gone two hours, I called Hawthorne's but they hadn't seen her. It was dreadful to sit there helpless, thinking of the bad things that might have happened.

When she returned, the first thing I saw was the bandage across half her forehead. I ran across the room and we embraced. I wasn't thinking of anything but she's okay! After the hug, she took my head in her hands and pulled me into a long, deep kiss. Great relief carries its own surprises and this was no exception. The kiss became plural and soon we were on the floor making love. Thank God it was crude, fast and over quickly because slow sex with Veronica was as addictive as any drug. This was hard touch and relief, are you there? Yes, feel me, I'm right here.

When it was over, both of us were shy and completely out of synch with each other. Immediately I wished it hadn't happened, but it had been necessary and that made it okay. Despite all the things that had happened between us recently, there was a large part of me that wanted her back in my life.

We got up off the floor without looking at each other and dressed. I went into the kitchen to make tea. She came in a few minutes later. Blood had soaked through her white bandage, staining it. The red was so bright and alarming.

She came over and reached out to touch my arm. At the last second she stopped and her hand fell to her side. 'I'm sorry. That was my fault.'

'It was no one's *fault*, Veronica. Don't think that. Sometimes you've got to touch someone to ground yourself. We both needed it.'

'I dream so often about sleeping with you again. But that was only fucking.'

'Fucking is great. Especially after something like this.'

She sat down and gently lowered her cheek on to the kitchen table. 'I was so scared. After it was over, I was angry. But when he hit me I was so scared, Sam.'

I arranged the tea things on the table and waited for the water to boil. It was hard to look at her, the wide spotted bandage, the pain on her face. Knowing that the sex had already turned into a mistake, a place neither of us wanted to be. All because of me. All my fault.

Outside it was snowing again. The sky was a mysterious plum-gray. In contrast, the white flakes were huge and fell slowly.

'What are you going to do now?'

The snow was so full of mischievous life that it was an effort to turn away from the window. When I did, she looked sad and defeated.

'There's nothing I *can* do but wait to hear what he says. Wait to hear what *grade* he gives me on my term paper.'

Closing her eyes, she touched the bandage with one finger. 'I couldn't *do* anything, Sam. I wish—'

I walked over and got very close. 'I missed you, Veronica.

I thought about you all the time. There was nothing you could do! You were attacked.'

Her voice was a plea. 'But I thought if I met him, I might be able to . . . I don't know. I feel very dizzy. I'm going to lie down. You can go home if you want. I'll be all right.'

'Don't be silly! I'm staying. You go lie down.'

She sighed and stood up slowly. 'The only thing I ever wanted was to be your friend. But when everything else happened and we got so close, I ruined it.

'Now I can see in your face it won't come back. It's over and it's all my fault. Everything that's gone wrong has been my fault. I hate it! I *hate* what I've done and what's worse, I still love you so much. But looking at your face now, I see it's gone. All my love has done is made you afraid of me and the sex is fucking and there's nothing more I can do!' Her lips trembled. She closed her eyes and squeezed them tightly shut. Then she walked into the bedroom and closed the door.

I have heard women say if they were able to remember the pain of childbirth they would never go through it again. I think that is true with anything traumatic. I know it is for me. I cannot objectively describe what happened to me later that day. Like a faulty nuclear reactor, some safe-guarding system in my soul closed down that part of my memory. And I am grateful because what I do remember of it, however diminished by passing time, is still appalling.

I waited for Veronica to reappear but she didn't. I sat on her couch and read *The Utne Review* magazine cover to cover. Then I stared out the window at the snow and darkening afternoon, walked several circles around her living room, turned on the television . . . Whatever there was to do while she hid herself from me and the truth she had spoken earlier. As the afternoon died the room lost all of its dim light. I lay down on the couch and quickly fell asleep.

I don't know how long I was out, but it must have been some time. It was that fathoms-deep, bottom of the ocean sleep where you don't even remember closing your eyes, much less any dreams. On waking, gravity has increased tenfold. You can barely raise a hand.

I think what woke me was the flickering, but that may only be my selective memory. Something flickering back and forth across my closed eyelids. I'm not sure, because it might have been her voice. A soft, urgent susurration inches from my ear. Lots of S's. Did they start the unconscious alarm going inside my sleeping skull? Impossible to say and ridiculous to try. This is what happened.

I awoke to her voice whispering nearby. The room was pitch-black except for the flickering somewhere. And noises. There were more noises, voices, other voices besides hers. But hers was the closest. I could almost feel the hair inside my ear moving from the force of her breath.

Veronica was saying, 'Stealing. It was always stealing. Something of yours. Sex, sacred things. It was so close, Sam. Sometimes it was so close it was *inside* me—'

I had been so deeply asleep that despite the distinct flickering in front of my open eyes, it didn't register above her voice. I blinked a few times but didn't move, like an animal caught in the headlights of its doom. She kept talking. Low, sexy, as intimate as a lover's fingers stroking your neck.

My eyes finally focused on what they were seeing across the room. The television was on and playing a video of us in her bed, making love. I had never known she filmed us doing it, never seen a camera in her bedroom. Nevertheless there we were, rolling and tumbling, making the secret sounds you think about afterward and love to remember. All of it on tape, Veronica's secret home movie.

How long had she been talking to me? How long had she been sitting on the floor next to the couch, a foot away, talking and running this film while I slept? What kind of person would do this?

She said something I didn't understand and laughed. A lewd, joyous laugh that might have come in the middle of terrific sex. An electric zap of fear shot through my body. This was madness, velvety-soft but complete.

For however long, although it could not have been more than a few seconds, I lay there thinking as fast as I could about what to do. But there was no good answer because demons lived here, serpents and ogres, creatures from deep inside this woman's disturbed consciousness that lived in their own world and had no space or time for anything else.

Because I could think of nothing to say, I uneasily watched the television. The picture cut from her bedroom to a busy New York street. I come walking along and enter Hans Lachner's bookstore, the place where Veronica and I first met. This part of her film meant nothing to me until I saw the suit I was wearing. Then I shuddered. It was a blue and white seersucker I had bought a long time ago at Brooks Brothers. Two years before, Cassandra had accidentally knocked a bottle of permanent black ink across both the jacket and pants. The dry cleaner said it would be impossible to save the suit, so I gave it to charity. Two years before. Veronica was filming me *then*? How long had she been following me? How long had she been circling my life before we ever met?

I moved to get up, but she put a hand on my thigh and gently held me there.

'A few seconds more, please! I was going to give this tape to you for Christmas. You have to see this next part before you go. I want to watch it together. It's a big surprise.' Her beautiful face was turned to the television and she was smiling. A child's smile, full of excitement and impatience. Slowly I eased back on to the couch. There was enough adrenaline in my body to bring three cadavers back to life.

The film abruptly cut to some kind of formal dance. The women all wore long white dresses, the men tuxedoes. Hairdos announce the time period. Almost all of the younger men had too-long hair, mustaches or beards, whether it looks good on them or not. The young women wear their hair very long and ironed straight, as if they're all trying to look like soulful folk singers like Joan Baez or Joni Mitchell. It's the sixties.

Pauline Ostrova and Edward Durant Junior dance up to the camera and stop. Without thinking, I pointed at the screen. It's them! That's them! Grainy and awkward as the film is, I remembered her face. That wide mouth, the small eyes. I *remembered* her. Thirty years had passed. I was a man well into middle age, pushing a heavy wheelbarrow full of life and experiences in front me. Yet on seeing her, I do exactly the same thing I did whenever I saw her, any time, any place: I gulp. Guuulp. Seeing Pauline Ostrova always made me gulp. In excitement, raw fear, adoration. Just like a fool, like any boy chocked full of hopeless dreams and jumbled love, his heart fireworking over the most interesting girl he had ever seen.

It was the first time I had seen Durant junior outside of the photographs his father showed me. It added a dimension to the son I had never sensed. For he was a big man although he moved with great lightness and grace. If I hadn't already known, I would have guessed he was either an athlete or a dancer in Broadway musicals. The handsome one in the second row of the chorus of *Oklahoma!*, wearing blue overalls and a smile that makes you think he's having a hell of a time up there.

The couple mug for the camera. Edward dips his head in front of Pauline's. She pulls his ear to get him out of the way. Both of their faces are so animated! They go on like

189

that, young and attractive, hamming it up and having such a good time together.

Seeing them on that summer night years ago made me long to freeze the film. Keep that frame of them smiling forever, holding each other. I was barely able to ask, 'Where did you get it?'

'There are other clips of her on the tape. I went around Crane's View asking people who knew her if they had home movies from that time. Everything I found is here. I spliced it all together. You'll see.

'This came from Edward Durant. When I told him what I wanted to do, he handed it right over. It was a summer dance at their country club.' She stood up and turned the television off. Ejecting the tape from the video machine, she slid it out and brought it to me. 'I want you to go now. Merry Christmas, Sam.'

Her mood had changed so quickly that I wasn't sure how to react. Then I remembered a few minutes ago she was making me watch a secret fuck film and whispering weird things in my ear. That was enough to get me going again. I stood up.

'Will you be all right?'

'Do you care, Sam? Really, what do you *care* about me?'

Leaving her building, I walked out into a snow storm. Luckily I'd taken the train into the city. After dinner with Cass, I planned on spending the night at a hotel.

Standing at the curb looking for a taxi, I thought I heard something over the street noise from way above, someone calling me. Looking up through the swirling snow, I saw a head sticking out a window halfway up the side of her building. It was hard to tell, but I thought it was Veronica. Wasn't that a patch of white on the face? Her bandage? She was shouting down at the street. I couldn't hear what she was saying. Then she started waving an arm as if she needed even more emphasis. What could it be? What more could she want after all that had already happened that afternoon? Moments went by. I thought about turning around and going back to see but right then a taxi hissed up in front of me. I opened the door and looked up at her, or whoever it was, shouting down through the snow. What she said before was right – I didn't care about her anymore. After the friendship and intimacy, the travel and talk, the wonderful hours in her arms. After her tricks and deceptions, lies and flat-out frightening acts. What *did* I care? Not enough to stop me from getting into that bright yellow New York taxicab and riding off into the snowy night.

I checked into the Inn at Irving Place and sat down for half an hour in a fat comfortable chair before meeting with Cassandra. There was a video machine in the room. I was tempted to sneak a peek at the rest of Veronica's tape, but there wasn't enough time. It could wait till later.

The afternoon had left me in a bizarre mood – half despair, half exhilaration. I had no desire to make small talk with my daughter. At the same time, I was glad to be with someone that night while my mind sorted and sifted through all the new information. Sitting there with eyes closed, so many different images and memories of Veronica floated through my head. Like an aquarium full of exotic, beautiful and dangerous fish they swam leisurely by, one after the other.

There was a knock at the door. Surprised, I jerked out of my trance and got up to open it. Cass stood there in her spotless white down jacket which emphasized the red of her cheeks and eyes. Like her mother, hers was one of those faces where, whenever she cried, everything went royal red to the point of near-incandescence. I pulled her in and closed the door. She stood there stiffly with hands jammed into her pockets and a grief on her face that made her look a hundred years old. Her voice was enraged when she spoke.

'They wouldn't let me come up! I *told* them I was your daughter, but they didn't care. Did they think I was a prostitute? I had to show them my stupid ID card. God! I said call you but they wouldn't. They were so stupid. I—' Boom. Her tears came without warning and they just about knocked her flat. She refused to come any further into the room although I kept pulling on her sleeve. Almost as if she was afraid that if she moved an inch, she would break in a million pieces on the spot. Her hands stayed in her pockets.

'I don't wanna come in! I didn't even wanna come here tonight, but what was I supposed to do, go home and be with *Mom*? She doesn't understand anything!

'Daddy, Ivan and I broke up. We had a ridiculous fight about something so absurd you wouldn't believe and then we broke up. I don't know what I'm gonna do!'

'Sit down, honey. Will you do that? Right here is good, right here on the floor. Tell me what happened.'

It was odd to be sitting on the floor a foot away from the door. But that was as far as she would come.

A friend of Ivan's had had a bunch of people over that afternoon. The friend was a very handsome painter studying at Cooper Union. He was interesting and clearly interested in Cassandra. They talked and talked, sometimes with Ivan around, sometimes not.

'But nothing happened, Dad, he was just nice. Nothing *would* have happened, because I don't do that! It's not me. But Ivan! Oh, Ivan acted like I was going to elope with the guy. So immature! What was I supposed to do, put on a veil and lower my eyes? It was a party. You talk to people at parties. You *socialize*.'

'Sounds like he was a jerk.'

'He was! God!'

'You had every reason to be angry, Cass.'

'Damned right I did! I'm good, Dad. I'm true to someone

if I love them. Even if I were interested in Joel, I would never do anything as long as I was with Ivan. Never. You know me.'

'I do, and jealousy always has a bad odor. But honey, he loves you. You're his woman. He was scared and unfortunately he showed it in an ugly way. That's *not* an excuse. You have every right to be angry. But I'm going to tell you something, and you must think about it carefully.

'I've made a mess of just about every relationship I ever had with women. You name it, I did it wrong. I wrote the textbook for marital failure. I just spent the afternoon with Veronica and it's probably the last I'll see of *her* because there are just too many problems. It breaks my heart because there are great things there, but not enough.

'But you know what I *have* learned? The single lesson that's penetrated my cement brain? There are very few people you can hang around with and be content with most of the time. If you find someone who is your pal that way, fight for them. Fight hard for the relationship.

'If Ivan fucked up today, tell him what upset you and try to work it out. You two go together well. It's so obvious. The problem is everyone gives up so quickly now. Including me. It's too easy to turn around and walk away. Bye-bye. That was nice but who's next?

'I don't know what'll happen with you two in the future, but it's worth trying to work out because you've really found the person you were meant to be with now. And that's worth a lot of work.'

Her eyes were so young and full of confusion. I saw six-year-old Cass in them, but also the woman she was quickly becoming.

The head and the heart are always racing each other to some finish line. They never cross it at the same time. She slid across the floor and put out her arms. We held each other like two hands wrapped in prayer. My magnificent

193

daughter. The only long-time pal I had ever had. She would be gone so soon.

Three days later a postcard with a bent corner sat alone in my mailbox. On the front was a photograph of me that had been taken for an article in *Vogue* magazine. I frowned and turned it over. On the other side was one typed line.

'The book's good. Keep going.'

Nothing else.

Jitka Ostrova died laughing. She and Magda were watching the *David Letterman Show* and Robin Williams was on. Both women were laughing so hard at what Williams said that Magda had to run to the toilet before she burst. While in there, she still heard her mother's laughter. By the time she returned to the living room, the old woman was dead. We could only hope one minute it was laughter, the next eternity. Not a bad way to go. It reminded me of a Muslim friend whose father died after a long and terrible illness. I was curious to hear where he thought his father was after passing on. My friend said, 'Oh, in heaven. He did all his suffering while he was alive.'

I didn't know Mrs Ostrova well but her death shook me. Such a good soul forced to live a hard and ultimately crushing life. All that mattered to her was her family but two-thirds of them died years before she did. What was most impressive was how she had still somehow managed to keep alive her kindness and good humor in the midst of so much misfortune.

The day of her funeral was one of those sharp blue and white winter treats when sky and sun blind you every time you look up. The air smelled of wet stone and the many chestnut trees that surrounded the cemetery. Once in a while a strong cold breeze blew up and the trees shuddered. Because of the intense sunlight, most of the people at the ceremony wore sunglasses. One might have mistaken the group for a bunch of the famous or infamous gathered one last time to say good-bye to someone who was probably wearing sunglasses too inside their wooden box.

And it *was* wooden. Jitka didn't like funerals, ceremony or extravagance. 'What would I do in a fancy coffin? Dance? Show off for the bugs?'

So she was buried in the same kind of simple coffin she had chosen for Pauline years ago. The two lay next to each other in the Crane's View cemetery. Mr Ostrova was on the other side.

There was a large turnout which wasn't surprising. Frannie stood next to Magda and her daughter. I hadn't seen him since our last showdown and was surprised at how hearty he looked.

I was also surprised to see Edward Durant there. *He* was not looking well. We stood side by side during the service. He carried a metal cane which he incessantly shifted from hand to hand as if it were too hot to hold. He told me he had remained in touch with the Ostrovas over the years and was frequently invited to their house for dinner.

A Czech priest from Yonkers performed the ceremony. I kept looking at Magda and her daughter, wondering what was going through their minds. Sometimes Magda rested her head on Frannie's shoulder and sometimes the two women embraced, but there were few tears. I think Jitka would have liked that because she overflowed with good nature and common sense. I imagined her watching over us with arms crossed and a satisfied smile on her face.

When the ceremony was finished, Frannie separated from Magda and came over. Putting an arm around my shoulder, he said, 'How you doin', stranger? You finish your book, or what? We don't see you much these days.' His voice was light and playful.

'To tell you the truth, Fran, I kind of got the feeling you'd rather be left alone.'

'You've got a point there, but you coulda called and asked how I was doing.'

'You're right.'

He poked a finger into my chest. 'I've been cooking, you know?'

'Really? Oh, that's good news, Frannie! I'm so glad to hear that.'

'Yeah, well there's more. After you left, Magda started coming over a lot. She's the one got me cooking, cleaning up the house, going out again ... We talked, you know, did things together. And ... I don't know. We hit it off really well.' He stopped and gave a kind of all-over shiver. He had something big to say and needed a lot of air for it. 'We're going to get married, Sam.'

Before I could reply, Magda came over. Earlier she had been standing so far away that I hadn't really seen how pretty she looked. She had lost weight, and the high Slavic cheekbones of her face stood out prominently. She had always been attractive, but now she looked much younger and almost beautiful. For some reason I looked at her hands and saw that her fingernails were painted a sassy Chinese red.

'How are you, Sam?'

'I'm okay. Congratulations! Frannie just told me you're getting married!'

She frowned, glanced at him, then quickly smiled. 'Frannie wants to get married. I haven't decided yet. I think he's just grateful to me for pulling him out of his space walk and back into the mother ship. I told you before, he's got a lotta kinks to work out before I agree to sign *that* contract!'

He pinched her cheek. 'You know you love me.'

'Loving's not the question – *living* is. Love builds the house, but then you got to furnish it. Sam, listen, we're all going down to Dick's Cabin for a meal. That was Ma's favorite place so we thought it was a good idea. Will you come? And would you ask Mr Durant too? She always had a crush on him.'

'Of course. But are you going to get married?'

They looked at each other and a shyness passed between them that was delightful. After all they had been through together, they were back to courting. Nothing had been decided. Frannie was eager, Magda honestly hadn't made up her mind.

Frannie slipped his arm through hers. 'She didn't say no.'

'True, I didn't say no. You go ahead now. I've got to say good-bye to the people. Remember, Frannie, you promised to tell him. Now's a good time.'

We watched her walk away. 'She was so great to me, Sam. Did everything to take care of me. But those kinks she was talking about? I've got to tell you some stuff. I promised her I would and I've wanted to for a long time anyway. Let's take a ride before we eat. Drive around a little bit.'

Durant was very pleased to be invited to the restaurant. When I told him about Jitka's crush on him, his face went blank and his mouth tightened. Only after a while did it relax into a small smile. 'Funny. I had a crush on her too. Ostrova women have magical powers over Durants.'

'Drive up to the Tyndall place.'

I looked at McCabe and raised an eyebrow. In all the time I spent in Crane's View recently, I had avoided going back there. By accident I drove past once but looked away because it brought back bad memories.

Lionel Tyndall made a fortune in oil in the 1920s. He owned houses all over the country but preferred Crane's View because it was so close to New York. His was one of the largest houses in town. One of those Colonial behemoths you passed out on Livingston Avenue as you were entering the town limits. Oddly, despite the size of the house, there wasn't much land around his place.

Tyndall died in the early fifties. His greedy family went to war with each other over his vast holdings. The legal suits and counter suits continued for years. During that time, the house stood empty. Town kids started breaking into it almost immediately after Tyndall's death. What they found became legend.

Lionel Tyndall was a collector. Books, magazines, furniture so large it could only have lived in a house of twenty-five rooms. He loved magic and was an amateur magician and ventriloquist. I never saw them, but as a boy heard marvelous apocryphal tales of kids entering rooms full of elaborate decaying theatre sets and puzzling objects with names like The Madagascar Mystery and The Heart of God. These things were long gone by the time we began snooping in there, but the stories only enhanced the sense of danger and mystery attached to the house.

What I remember was the smoky, dusty smell of the place. Light came in through the floor to ceiling windows and played across the impossible number of objects still in there. Boxes of children's toys, a desk top covered with playbills from Broadway shows, an orange velvet chair that had been stabbed full of kitchen utensils. Spatulas, carving knives, soup ladles stuck in backwards. Who would think of doing something like that?

Kids would. Bums would. Part of the danger of the Tyndall house was you never knew who would be there when you snuck in through the broken basement door. Vagrants loved the place because there was a roof over their heads, grand furniture to sleep on, a boundless array of things to steal.

Once when we were there two miserable, evil-looking men, both wearing porkpie hats, suddenly came around a corner and scared the shit out of us.

'What are you kids doing here?'

'Same thing you are, mister,' said dangerous twelve-year-old Frannie McCabe.

The two men looked at each other and, as one, disappeared back into the house's shadows. We continued our scouting party. Soon though we began hearing strange sounds coming from rooms not far away – high laughter, furniture being struck, fragile things breaking. We figured where it was coming from and snuck up to the door.

Racing through the dappled, split light of a cavernous room, the two men chased each other, playing a kind of ghostly tag. They were like children, laughing, scrambling, screeching, jumping over furniture, sliding on the wooden floors, tripping over rolled-up rugs.

The bliss was that when anything fell down or smashed, *it didn't matter*! When kids play tag and something breaks, run for your life. Heaven turns to Hell in one second. Mom's favorite vase in shattered pieces, a table punted across the floor, the silver frame a hundred years old until this minute . . . Game over.

But in Tyndall's living room that afternoon, full of stopped time and long shadows, no one cared about these objects, no matter how valuable they might have been. I'm sure they *were* valuable – the rugs were Oriental, and one glass that hit the floor shattered into beautiful colors. It didn't matter. The room was Tag Heaven that day.

That is only one of my memories of the Tyndall house. There were many others, some equally queer or memorable. We were there often. It was our castle and forbidden land in one. It rarely failed to captivate us.

The summer before I was sent away to private school, a bunch of us went back to the house. We knew we were too old for it by then. Having used it so often for our games and schemes, we'd squeezed out all of its juice long before. But this day, August boredom prevailed and we were desperate for anything different to do.

McCabe had heard one could make a fortune selling old copper wiring and pipe to a junkyard in Rye. His plan was to check out the Tyndall place, then come back with the right tools and strip it bare. The idea of ripping wire out of old decaying walls in ninety-degree heat didn't excite us, but what else was there to do that day? Part of the reason Frannie was such a good ringleader was his ability to get fired up about things. Projects excited him; he was the one who could imagine money in our pockets after a job was done, whereas the rest of us had to be pulled along behind him like broken toys. Normally we just wanted something to do; he wanted to turn our days upside down.

Other than being hot as the inside of a kiln, there was nothing different about the house that afternoon. I knew it was pointless being there. Dumb too – like riding around on a bicycle so small that your knees keep hitting the handlebars.

We went in through the basement and worked our way up the back stairs to the kitchen. McCabe kept pointing to pipes running parallel to the floorboards. He'd say only 'copper' in a firm professional voice, as if he was giving us a guided tour of untold treasure. We were unimpressed. We wanted girls in orange bikinis, free tickets to the Yankees game, a great party to look forward to that night. Copper tubing did *not* do it.

'Green Light' Al Salvato was there. After Frannie said 'copper' for the hundredth annoying time, Salvato picked up on it. Pointing to everything (his shoes, the floor, Frannie's ass . . .), he said 'copper' in the same serious, informed tone of voice. McCabe pretended not to hear and continued to lead the way.

Through the kitchen into a large pantry the color of burnt toast. We climbed a servants' staircase to the first floor because our boss wanted to have a look at the bathrooms. We scouted one out and sure enough, a copper bonanza was in there. But by then Frannie knew we didn't give a shit, the house was *hot*, and none of this was going to come to anything in the end.

His way of admitting defeat was, on catching Salvato mimicking him, to shoot 'Green Light' a savage knee in the balls that put him on the ground in the shape of a comma.

'You guys don't like my plan, fuuuuuck you!' He stomped out of the room, leaving us with guilty smiles and our hands in our pockets. We were too old for this foolishness. Too old to be traipsing around empty houses looking for anything to do. Too old to be hanging around, too old to be biding time when we knew out there in the real world every other teenager on earth was having parties, getting laid. *They* were living lives that didn't depend on copper tubing, the whims of Frannie McCabe, or luck. Of course we were wrong and in the intervening years we learned every kid believes life is happening where he ain't. But that knowledge wouldn't have helped back then because we wouldn't have believed it.

I was glad my parents had had enough of my bad behavior and sullenness to be sending me away to a school where there would be new faces and experiences. Looking for copper pipe in a dilapidated house couldn't have been a better reminder that anywhere *had* to be better than this nowhere.

We helped Salvato off the floor and left the bathroom. Right outside the door, McCabe came rushing back up. He put a finger to his lips and beckoned us to follow.

He moved along in a semi-crouch, the way Groucho Marx walked in his films. Salvato copied him, but only because he was afraid McCabe would give him another nut-knocker if he didn't follow the leader step for step.

'What're you doin', Fran? Practicing deep knee bends?' Ron Levao asked. McCabe shook his head and waved us to follow. He duck-walked down the hall till he came to the top of the main staircase. We caught up and saw for the first time what was on his mind.

Down below in the strewn chaos of the living room, Club Soda Johnny Petangles was sitting on a decrepit once-white couch, singing to himself. Lying across his lap was my dog, Jack the Wonder Boy. The two sat there unmoving, completely at peace.

I had never heard Johnny sing and was surprised at his sweet, frail voice. My dog lay panting from the heat, eyes closed. His small red tongue hung out one side of his mouth. From his long daily walks I assumed Jack knew every inch of the town, but since when had he and Petangles become buddies? Had the dog been lured into the Tyndall house, or did the two of them roam around together while the rest of Crane's View went about its business?

Someone behind me snickered, 'That's your dog, hah, Bayer?'

I nodded but didn't turn around.

McCabe looked at me and hissed, 'What's that retard doing with your little dog, Sam?'

'Singing, looks like.'

He slapped my head. 'I see that! But I wouldn't let no fuckin' retard touch *my* dog! How do you know he's not feeling him up or something?'

'You're *sick*, McCabe! People don't feel up dogs.'

'Maybe retards do.'

We squatted there and watched the simple man sing to the dog. The two looked contented together. Johnny was crooning the Four Seasons' 'Sherry' in a falsetto voice that was a decent imitation of lead singer Frankie Valli. Jack was panting so hard it looked like he was smiling. Maybe he was.

'You gonna let him get away with that?'

'Get away with *what*, Salvato? The guy's singing!'

Green Light looked eagerly at Frannie. 'I think Petangles is a Mo. I think he's a dog fag.'

I shook my head.

But McCabe thought it over, then nodded sagely. 'Could be. You never know with retards.'

'Fuckin' A right, Frannie! I think he's doing something to that dog. We just can't see it from up here.'

I hissed, 'Salvato, you're full of shit! Come on, let's get outta here. It's hot.'

McCabe called the shots – all of them. Maybe it was the heat. Or maybe I'd come to the end of the line with these guys and this life. Maybe McCabe sensed that and wanted to throw one last rabbit punch. Whatever it was, just being there with him and those other knotheads made me want to go home and wait for Fall when I would leave Crane's View.

I started to stand but Frannie shoved me hard in the chest with both hands. I fell backward. We looked at each other and I felt sure he knew everything I had been thinking about him and the situation. It frightened me.

Everyone tensed. In a second, it felt like the temperature had risen ten degrees. At a moment like this, McCabe was friends with no one; he'd bash whoever he felt like. No one was exempt. All of us had been his target at one time or another. If you wanted to hang around the guy, the unspoken rule was do whatever you can to stay on his good side – or else. We always knew when someone had crossed his line, but not what Frannie would do about it and *that* made it even more alarming. Sometimes he would laugh, pat you on the back or offer you a cigarette. Sometimes he'd beat you until you bled.

Joe O'Brien had brought a six-pack of beer. Frannie snapped his fingers for one. Joe quickly opened a bottle and handed it over. McCabe threw his head back and drank it down in one go. When he was finished he dropped it on the floor and walked over to the staircase. He looked down, then back at us, at me. He smirked and unzipped his fly. 'Come on, guys. I think Johnny's hot down there. It's time for a little shower.'

Salvato was first up, the ass-kisser. Then my supposed best friend Joe O'Brien, Levao ... they all rose and undid their zippers. I stayed seated and stared at McCabe. I hated him, hated what he was about to do for no reason in the world except boredom and pure meanness.

'Don't do it, Frannie. It's not right. They're not bothering you.'

He had both hands in front of his jeans. He looked at me over his shoulder. Suddenly his expression changed – something new had come to him. 'Okay! Hold your fire, boys! I'll tell you what, Sam. If *you* piss on them, we won't. How's that? Fair?' Delighted, the other guys looked back and forth between us. No matter how this one turned out, they were off the hook. Now they could relish Frannie's threats and not worry about him destroying their day.

'You want me to piss on my own dog? You're a fucking psycho, McCabe!' If I'd had an inch of courage, I would have punched him in the face. But this was *Frannie*. He knew I wouldn't make a move but wanted to make sure everyone saw my cowardice.

'Rather be a psycho than a pussy, Bayer. So I guess it's time to give Johnny and your doggy a golden bath.' Staring straight at me, he reached down and pulled out his dick. I quickly looked away. Next came the metallic hiss of the others unzipping, then their embarrassed giggling.

Then, 'Pssssss . . .'

I jumped up and ran back the way we had come. As I reached the other end of the hall, I heard Johnny Petangles shouting down below, 'Heyyy! What are you doing? Heyyy!' Then the dog barked.

Because I had avoided looking at the house, I hadn't seen that the ground all around was torn up and everywhere were signs of construction.

'What're they doing here?'

Frannie put up a hand. 'Stop here. Let's get out and walk a little. The Tyndalls are so greedy that they held on to the place way too long. They thought it'd sell for a fortune. But they ended up taking a bath when the bottom fell out of the real estate market up here. They couldn't find a buyer for four years. A think tank in New York finally bought it for next to nothin', I heard. They're making it into one of those weekend conference centers.'

From a distance, the building looked as shabby as it had years before. But as we got closer, I saw a great deal of renovation had already been done. There were new doors and windows with the labels still on the glass. Sections of the porch had been completely restored. There were highly polished brass ornaments on the porch banister and front door.

We climbed the steps and looked in the windows. Inside, the wooden floors glowed, their lush dark color contrasted perfectly with the fresh white on all the walls.

'Man! It's a little different from the last time I was here. Looks like a monastery.'

'You wanna go in?' Frannie was already opening the front door with a large key.

'How'd you get a key?'

'Sam, you keep forgetting I'm a cop.'

'*Were* a cop. Aren't you on a leave of absence?' I followed him into the house and was immediately assailed with the acrid chemical smells of wood sealant and new paint.

'I'm going back to work next month. That was part of my deal with Magda.'

'Good! Know what I was thinking about as we drove up here? The day you guys pissed on Johnny Petangles and my dog. I wanted to knock you out so badly that day. Now I can ask Magda to do it.'

He shook his head. 'Don't be so sure. She might piss on 'em with me. That's what I like about her. Come on, I want to show you something.' He walked across the entrance hall, his leather heels clicking loudly on the shiny wooden floors.

It was such a contrast to the last time I'd been *chez* Tyndall. That day, the house was roasting and smelled like old ashes mixed with wet wool. Strewn everywhere were filthy, stained, broken objects you didn't want to touch. Today the rooms were white as a cloud, clean and empty. The smell completely different but just as strong. It marched proudly into your nose and proclaimed everything here is brand new, sanded fine, freshly painted, ready to go. New life is about to begin.

'Remember my cousin Leslie DeMichael? He's foreman on this job. Knows I'm interested in the Ostrova case, so a couple of weeks ago he called and told me to come over. They'd found something when they were about to paint this room. Said I had to see. It's right over here. I asked them to leave it like it was for a while. That's why they haven't finished in here.' He pointed to one of the few unpainted walls. Crudely carved there was a cock and balls, looking like something a ten-year-old doofus would hastily draw on the wall of a public bathroom. Beneath it were carved the words 'Beehive and Bone – forever.' I ran a finger into the deeply gouged letters of the words.

'Who did this?'

'*Pauline*, dummy! That's why I wanted you to see. You know Durant called her Beehive. "Bone" was her nickname for him. Very few people knew that. He was supposed to have had a dick like a Sequoia tree.'

'How do you know about Durant's *penis*, Frannie?'

'Jitka. Pauline told her. She used to come up here all the time to have sex. Something about a haunted house that made her horny.'

'Pauline used to *fuck* in this house? Get outta here!'

'It's true. And not just Eddie Durant either. Before him there were others. Remember though, back in those days you didn't have so many places to go. You did it on the back seat of a car, out in the woods, or ... the Tyndall house. At least here you had a roof over your head.'

I shuddered in disgust. 'Phooey! You remember what this place was like! What it *smelled* like? How could anyone be turned on by that?'

'Oh, excuse me, Mr Best Seller, but weren't you recently together with a woman who made porno films and was in the Malda Vale? No offense but some people would find *that* a little weird.'

'True. But why are we here, Fran? Not just to see this.'

'No, but guess who was the first to tell me about Pauline coming up here? Veronica Lake! Last time she was here she knew all about it. Jitka only filled in the details. Your ex-girlfriend may be flaky, but she knows how to find out things. If she were normal, she'd make a good cop.

'Anyway, we're here today because I see this house like our relationship, Sam. We had a history before, but now the whole thing's changed. New paint, walls, everything.

'The other day Magda asked me who my real friends were. I said you.' His eyes narrowed and he licked his lips, as if he were afraid of what my reaction would be. 'You and two other guys. That's it – three people on earth. I don't know if that's great or pathetic, but that's how it is. What do you think?' He did a nervous two-step, like a boxer standing in his corner waiting for the bell to ring.

'I'm very touched. And I agree – I think of you as a good friend, Frannie.'

'Good! That's a relief. But if we're going to be real friends, then there's things you gotta know. The main one being I'm a junkie. I've been one on and off for years. It started when I was in Vietnam, but then it got nuts in California. Nobody knew it but Magda and now this psychiatrist I got, Dr Dudzinska. Magda made me go. Said she wasn't going to live the rest of her life with a fuckin' junkie and she's a hundred percent right.

'The guy who shot me was a dealer. I owed him a thousand dollars and didn't feel like paying. So he comes up to me that day and says real friendly, "Fran, what about my thousand?" I say, "Hey Loopy, I don't have it right now." So lovely Loopy shoots me in the stomach. Simple and to the point. No hard feelings – just business.

'It got out of control in California when my marriage went bad. I was going to parties and hanging out with sludge. I got this bad habit of thinking I'm bulletproof. I thought, hey, what the hell, these clowns are doing it and they seem okay. Plus I did a lot of grass and acid in Vietnam and I always stayed on top of it. The dirty trick is you *can* handle it for a while. Then one day it swoops down and gobbles you up.

'But I'm hoping it's over now. Or it's *beginning* to be over. I'm in this group therapy thing and go to the analyst. It hurts, Sam. All that stuff hurts because it makes you admit how weak you really are, but it's good.

'Know where I went the first time I left my house after I got shot? Over to Loopy to give him his money. No hard feelings, Loop, even though you *did* try to air condition my stomach. You fuckin' skivvy rat!'

The only thing I wanted to do was hug Frannie, so I did. I put my arms around this curious man and hugged him with all I had. He started to say something, but shut up and hugged back. When we separated, both of us had tears in our eyes.

Embarrassed, he chuckled and then sniffed. 'In the old days, I woulda just killed Loopy.'

We walked through the empty house talking about being young there. I said, 'Maybe this is what happens to us after we die. They bring you back to a place where you spent a lot of time in your life; like Crane's View or the Tyndall house. But now it's empty and only *white*. All your memories are there, but the furniture and everything is gone. So it's just you and empty rooms full of ghosts.'

'What are you, Conway Twitty? You sound like a country and western song. Forget it! Come on, Bayer, let's get out of here and eat some steak. You make me depressed. I brought you here to start a new chapter in our relationship, but instead you're—'

'Waxing poetic?' I suggested.

'More like ear wax. Come on.'

Walking toward the door, I did a detour to Pauline's wall art. Putting my hand over the deeply carved letters of her nickname, I said, 'I wish I'd known her. The more I work on this book, the more I miss her.' I took my hand away and spontaneously kissed my fingertips.

Frannie took a Polaroid photograph out of his pocket. It was a close-up of the carving. 'I thought you'd want this. So let's do her a favor and find the guy who killed her.'

When we walked in, Dick's Cabin was full of familiar faces. The restaurant looked exactly the same as it had when my family went there for Sunday dinner. Full log cabin motif, it was all 1950s when steaks and chops were king, pass the salt and you want extra butter on that baked potato? If you had asked for Perrier water there they would have kicked your ass. I loved it.

I sat at a table with Edward Durant, Al Salvato (still nervous and shifty-eyed, full of himself and his mediocre small-time success), Don Murphy, fart master of our high school class, Martina Darnell, my one-time dream girl ... If Durant hadn't been there to catch me, I would have fallen into a full nostalgia swoon.

The first half of the meal was spent talking to the old gang and catching up on the years in between. It was lively and diverting and there were moments when first I felt a hundred years old, then thirteen again an instant later. Martina told a story about teaching Patricia Powell how to French kiss in sixth grade by demonstrating tongue technique on a flowing water faucet. Salvato tried to interest me in investing in a shoe factory in Bangladesh. Murphy asked if I remembered how he used to fart in history class. As these people talked and laughed, a line from a novel Veronica had given me kept going through my head: 'Once upon a time there was a time that some people say is still going on.'

Frannie moved from table to table, still master of ceremonies after all these years. Checking on the guests, he made sure everyone had enough to eat and was cared for. Later Magda told me he paid for everything to do with the funeral, which must have set him back thousands.

Some time during the meal I looked up and was surprised to see that Johnny Petangles had come in and was devouring a giant T-bone steak. McCabe sat next to him with an arm around the big man's shoulder, talking seriously to him. Johnny ate and nodded, his eyes never lifting from his plate. I wondered what was going on, but just then Durant touched my sleeve.

'How is the book going?'

The others at our table were deep in conversation about the Crane's View basketball team, so I had time to tell Edward what had happened since we last spoke.

He was shocked at the story of Veronica being hit and robbed in the subway. He asked a number of detailed questions about how the killer had contacted her, what he'd said, how he could have possibly known about her in the first place. I could hear the old prosecuting attorney in him coming back to life and it made me grin. I answered as best I could but it was clear he was unsatisfied. I finally admitted I couldn't tell him anymore because Veronica and I were no longer speaking. His eyes widened around that tidbit, but he didn't pursue it which I appreciated.

He became very quiet and withdrawn. When I asked if he was feeling all right, he patted my hand and said, 'I'm fine. I'm just thinking about Veronica. She sounds like a strange woman but very devoted to you. I'm sorry it didn't work out. It took great courage for her to go to that meeting.'

I started to answer but someone tapped on a glass and the room went quiet. Frannie stood with a fork in one hand, a wine glass in the other. Next to him Johnny Petangles was still working on his steak. Everyone else was looking at McCabe.

'I'm just going to say a few words and then let you get back to your meals. We're here in Jitka's favorite restaurant to say good-bye. I know she'd be happy because all of you were her friends and she loved a good party. At a time like this, it'd be easy to wax poetic – ' he looked at me ' – about losing such a good woman—'

'Go ahead and wax, Frannie!' Salvato shouted out. The room chuckled.

'Yeah well, some other time. Right now I'd just like to do two things. First, I'd like to propose a toast to Jitka Ostrova, wherever she is. I hope she's near, but even if she isn't, maybe she can still hear us. Here's to you, Jitka. We love you. We miss you, and Crane's View won't be the same town without you.' He lifted his glass and held it high. We did the same and drank. How wonderful to be loved by so many people. What an amazing accomplishment.

'And the second thing is, as you all know, Jitka loved the operetta *The Pirates of Penzance*. She used to sing it all the time, and if you ever heard her, you know what a terrible voice she had. But she didn't care. Those songs were hers and she had the whole thing memorized.

'As a tribute, I've asked Johnny to sing us her favorite song. She taught him this one, just like Pauline taught him to read thirty years ago. So he's the best guy to do it. Johnny, are you ready?'

Petangles dropped his knife and fork on the plate, sending a loud clatter into the middle of the hush that held us. Standing quickly, he wiped a hand across his mouth.

Then for the second time in my life, I heard Club Soda Johnny sing. His voice was exactly as I remembered from the day he sang 'Sherry' in the Tyndall house with Jack on his lap; soft and sweetly high.

'I am the very model of a modern major general;
I've information vegetable, animal and mineral;
I know the kings of England and I quote the fights
    historical,
From Marathon to Waterloo, in order categorical . . .'

There was no intonation in his voice. The words must have meant nothing to him. He was simply singing a song Jitka taught him and he wanted to do it correctly. He only stumbled on one line but that didn't stop him. He closed his eyes and nodded as if to reassure himself, then pressed on and finished without a hitch. Most of the people in the restaurant started out smiling at this unique event, but by the time Johnny reached the end of that funny, complicated song, we were in tears. All of us wished we could take a photograph of him singing and send it to Jitka, wherever she was. To show her how well he had done, how well she'd taught him.

PART THREE

When I got back to my house in Connecticut, there were nine messages on the answering machine, all from Cassandra's mother. Woe is me. I do not want to talk about the woman because to this day she is a never-ending toothache in my soul. Normally she called when she was out of money or boyfriends to support her insanely lavish lifestyle. Chump that I am, too often I'd grind my teeth and reach for the checkbook, if only to keep peace with the mother of my daughter.

Next to dying, talking to her was the last thing I wanted to do after that emotional day, but nine phone calls was a record even for her and there was always the chance something bad had happened to Cass. Standing in my overcoat, the dog staring accusingly at me from across the room, I called.

'Is she with you?' Her voice was as loud as it could go without creating a sonic boom.

'Is *who* with me?' The woman had the most maddening habit of beginning a conversation in the middle of some private context and then expecting *you* to locate where she was on the map.

'*Cassandra*, Sam! Is Cassandra there?'

My mouth twitched involuntarily. I'm sure my voice echoed that instant alarm. 'No. Why? Why would she be with me?'

'Because she's not here! She went out last night and

hasn't come home. Ivan's here and doesn't know where she is either. Where were you? I've been trying to reach you all day. Why wasn't the phone in your car working?'

'Because I turned it off. I went to a funeral today and didn't want to talk to anyone afterwards. Is that okay with you? Let me talk to Ivan.'

Her voice flew up into a mad, birdy falsetto that made the situation worse. 'Don't you be an asshole! Our daughter's missing, Sam! Don't talk to me like that.'

'I'm sorry, you're right. Would you please let me talk to Ivan?'

She said his name and there was a rustling on the other end as she handed over the phone.

'Mr Bayer?'

'Hi, Ivan. What's going on?' Even before he spoke I thanked God he was there.

'I don't know. Cassandra and I were supposed to go out today. I came over and we've been waiting ever since. It's not like her. She's never late. She stayed out all night and we don't know why. She always lets me know if something's changed.'

'What do *you* think happened? Did you two have a fight?'

'No, not at all! Actually, we've been very close lately. She said you two talked and since then she's been really sweet to me. No, there's nothing wrong with us. That's what's so *strange* about this. She's just gone.'

We spoke for a few minutes and then he handed the phone back to my ex-wife. I tried to reassure her but the hitch in my own voice said I didn't have any faith in what I was saying.

Cass was gone. She was the most dependable, trust-worthy person I knew. She kept not one but two pocket calendars with her day's business printed in careful block letters in both. She promptly wrote thank you notes for

216

everything. You could always set your watch by hers because it was never off.

The moment I hung up, I called McCabe and then Durant to ask their advice. Frannie said to sit tight because even the police didn't start looking into a disappearance until twenty-four hours had passed.

'I don't give a shit what *procedure* is, Frannie! It's my daughter. She's disappeared. The girl doesn't *do* things like this. Don't say sit tight. Tell me what I can do.'

'Take it easy, Sam. You want me to come over and sit with you?'

I almost lost it. I had to swallow repeatedly, or else I would have reached through the phone and torn his head off. 'You're a cop, *help* me on this. Will you, Frannie? Just do whatever you can.'

'Hold on and I'll get to work on it, Sam. Give me some time. I'll get back to you soon as I can.'

I hung up and rubbed my hands over my face. I had to calm down if I was going to accomplish anything. It was so hard. A ghastly picture grabbed hold of my quaking mind and refused to let go. An anchorman on the six o'clock TV news. Projected behind him is a huge photograph of Cassandra. He is solemnly describing what terrible thing has happened to her. Only later did I realize part of that vision came from having spent so much time thinking about the life of Pauline Ostrova, another young woman who went out one night and never came back. I have always hated those news photographs. Invariably TV chooses pictures that portray the victims as either beautiful, or doing something festive or domestic – decorating the Christmas tree or eating a chicken wing at a picnic.

In contrast to McCabe, Edward Durant reacted like a guardian angel. When I described what had happened, he got off the phone quickly, saying he had to talk to certain people. He called back half an hour later, having mobilized every troop he knew and, reading between his lines, calling in many favors from professional people who could help. I could imagine how imposing he must have been in court. His voice was so calm and authoritative. You felt he was a man who would take care of everything. Here was the man who knew exactly what to do.

Later Cassandra's mother called, indignantly asking who was this Edward Durant, and who the hell did he think he was, giving *her* the third degree? I tried to explain, but she was so tied in knots that only some of what I said seeped through. Once again, I had to ask for Ivan. I told him to tell her about Durant and that he was one of the few people who could actually help us in this predicament. While we spoke, she kept shouting in the background.

'Why are you *talking*? Ask him why he's not out there looking for her? *Why aren't you doing something, Sam?*'

When my mother was in the hospital for the last time in her futile battle against cancer, she developed a certain pattern of behavior that is common among seriously ill people. I cannot remember the formal name of it now but that isn't important. In essence what happens is because the patient's world has narrowed down to only that room and their daily schedule, the few things left take on tremendous importance. Where is my orange juice? The nurse promised me a glass of orange juice half an hour ago but it still isn't here! Fury, frustration, real bitterness. Did you move my *Time* magazine? I put it on that table but now it's gone! Frequently I saw that good-hearted, forgiving woman fly into a tearful rage at the lateness of a doctor, or the fact they had had green Jell-O for dessert two days in a row.

It makes complete sense because they know their world is evaporating and the *only* thing they can do about it is to hold fast to their few remaining objects and events with the tenacity of a person clutching a life preserver a thousand miles out to sea. That doesn't make it any less searing to witness, however.

In the two days we waited for news of Cass, I found myself acting exactly the same way my mother had. The house became my hospital room, the smallest detail my largest concern.

At the beginning I was able to do some work. Writing has always been both my shelter and escape. When things went wrong in the past, I would scurry to my room, close the door and hide behind whatever novel was in progress. The great thing about writing is it enables you to cast aside your own world for a while and live in the one you are creating. Raise the drawbridge against the outside world, pick up a pen and go to work.

But not when your child is missing. Not when you know outside your safe little study, inches beyond the glow of the green lamp and the drying ink on the half-filled page, the worst thing in the world might be happening and you are powerless to do anything about it. There was no way on earth I could either write my way through this night-mare or ignore the growing stillness around my heart.

On that first day, I tried to cling to the writing. As long as words came out sounding right, as long as something familiar stayed logical and fixed, I was still in control; life still made some sense. But writing Pauline's tragic story only made matters worse. Not very surprising.

I desperately needed something concrete to do while waiting for the telephone to ring. I decided to clean the house. I think I vacuumed the large living room rug in forty-five seconds. But I mean *thoroughly*, not just a couple of quick shoves into the curled corners. I was the Road Runner moving through the house at such speed that if it had been a cartoon, smoke clouds would have been waft-ing up behind me. I sprinted from room to room wiping, mopping, polishing, scrubbing. I stepped on the fleeing dog twice in my crazed assault on the house. For once, his bad temper didn't put me off or shame me. His resentment was nothing compared to my frenzy, the maniacal need to keep moving, working, busy hands, not thinking. Trying so hard not to think. I was crazed, scared and enraged in equal measure, but helpless above all. Jesus God, I felt helpless.

The first time I finished cleaning, the house shone. The *second* time I finished it was in shock. I had taken a toothbrush to the cracks in the wooden floors, a steel brush to the stones in the fireplace. The blades on the exhaust fan above the stove shone, the dog's food bowls exorcised with liquid bleach. I realized things were on the verge of going too far when I decided to wash all my hats.

I took a shower and two hours later a long bath, the telephone always within arm's reach. I watched television until there was nothing left but midnight-hour evangelists. I wept at what they said. I prayed whenever they told me to. Please God, let my daughter be safe. That first night I fell asleep on the floor, the TV remote still in my hand.

The next day I would have taken the dog for a walk around the United States but was petrified to leave the house in case *the* call came. One moment the silent telephone was the monster ready to strike; the next, the only angel that could bring deliverance.

For all her seriousness and good habits, Cass's secret vice was playing video games. Nintendo, Play Station, Sega ... brand names didn't matter. She loved them all – chest-pounding monkeys jumping over barrels, Ninja fighters throwing death punches, or knights weaving their way through mazes. I couldn't stand them. To make things worse, the noises they made were as annoying as anything ever heard on planet Earth. I had bought Cass these games, but begged her to wear earphones whenever she played because half an hour of listening to the saccharine music from, say, 'Final Fantasy 3' drove me close to the border of dangerously unhinged.

The second day, I had been playing 'Final Fantasy 3' since five in the morning when the telephone rang. I was so upset both by the ring and what the call might mean that suddenly I couldn't put down the controls for the game. For some seconds while the phone rang, I kept pressing the buttons to keep my creature alive. I was terrified, frozen in place.

'Sam? It's Edward Durant. Veronica Lake has your daughter. That's for certain.'

'*Veronica*? Why? What is she doing with Cass? Is she all right?'

As always, Durant's voice was composed and even. 'We don't know yet. She picked her up outside your ex-wife's apartment in New York. Two witnesses saw it happen. Veronica got out of a yellow cab just as Cassandra was about to enter the building. I assume she had a convincing story to lure her into the car. Didn't you say they don't like each other?'

I was about to say no, but then remembered with icy clarity Veronica mentioning how they'd spent an afternoon together and that Cass wanted her to meet Ivan. I told him that.

'Yes well, then she convinced Cass to go with her. That's all I know, Sam. But it's a beginning and it's concrete. The police know who to look for now. They've already checked Veronica's apartment but didn't find anything that could help. One last thing, and it's a difficult but necessary question: Do you think Veronica would hurt her?'

'Normally I'd say no, Edward. This doesn't have anything to do with Cass. But now? I don't know. It's another way for Veronica to get to me.'

'Then we must assume she will be in touch with you about it. All right, I'll call as soon as anything new comes up. And you do the same.'

I called McCabe and told him. He sounded both surprised and irritated. 'How the fuck did *he* find that out? I pulled every string I know, but nobody came up with squat.'

'Frannie, Durant was a federal prosecutor for thirty years. He must know a lot of people who could help. And you said yourself, the police always wait a day before they go into action. Durant started as soon as I talked to him.'

'So did I! I'm just being a cop, Sam. Anything that makes me wonder, I ask about. Try to understand that. If I come across as a jerk it's only 'cause I care. That's all, nothin' more.'

My brain and soul were spinning in a centrifuge, getting the full flap and flop. The worst part was I didn't know if it would ever end.

The doorbell rang. I hoped when I opened it there would be Cass, smiling, already assuring me all was okay. She was back, the nightmare was over. Instead, a boy in a Mohawk haircut wearing a brilliant lilac parka stood on the porch holding a showy bouquet of flowers. 'Mr Bayer?'

'Yes.'

'Flowers for you.'

'Who are they from?'

'Dunno.'

Back inside, I unwrapped the paper and searched inside the arrangement until I found the card.

'Hi Sam! Don't worry about Cassandra. I know where they are and will take care of everything. Just keep working on my book.'

I called the store in my town and asked where the flowers had come from. I was given the number of a New York florist. After much hemming and hawing, New York admitted the sender (a young, nice-looking Indian man) had paid in cash, given his name as David Cadmus, and used Veronica's address.

When I called and told McCabe, he gave a long whistle. 'I would not want to be Veronica Lake today. The killer's probably been watching her a long time. Now she pissed him off! Taking Cass keeps you from concentrating on his book. Notice how he called it "my"? We gotta find them fast.'

Durant went ballistic. I'd never heard him so angry. 'She should have *known* he'd have her watched! Didn't she understand that after he had her beaten up?'

'How does it change things, Edward?'

'I don't know. Maybe it's good. But I don't like unpredictables and now we've got two of them to deal with.'

Because there was nothing else to do while waiting, I paced the house. I wanted to leave so badly. Get up and walk out into the world where I might be able to *do* something. Not stay stuck and helpless in a stale house that exuded only tension and fear. But the damned phone was there and I didn't dare stray from it.

I ended up back in the study, staring at the manuscript. I didn't touch it; I didn't *want* to touch it.

If I had never begun the book, David Cadmus would still be alive. Cassandra would not be in danger now. The trouble between Veronica and me began when she decided we should collaborate on the story. From that point on, everything went bad.

While I was zoned out thinking about all this, the phone rang again. I picked it up but wasn't really clear-headed when I said hello.

'Hi, Sam!'

'Where is my daughter?'

'She's with me. She's safe.'

'Where *is* she, Veronica? God damn it! Don't tell me she's safe. You kidnapped her. If you have problems with me, okay, but let *her* go. Tell me right now where she is and don't fuck around any more.' I was horrified at my demanding voice and wished to God I could have taken it all back the moment I said it.

'I will, I promise you I will. But there are things I have to tell you first. They're so important! I know you don't believe me, but just even for a few minutes . . . Sam, this is *so* important for you.'

'I don't want to hear it! Just tell me where Cass is and then get away from us.'

There was a silence followed by a scraping sound. Cassandra came on the line. 'Dad?'

My body froze with joy and relief. 'Cass! Honey, are you all right?'

'Yes, I'm fine. Dad, don't worry. Everything is okay. Please do what Veronica asks. She won't tell me what it is, but I know it's important. She says there was no other way you'd talk to her and that's why she took me. But I'm okay. I'm fine. Really!

'Dad, we've been talking and talking. I was so wrong about her! She's led the most *incredible* life! I've been sitting here the whole time listening with my jaw hanging down. She's made documentaries, she lived all over the world, she was in the Malda Vale . . . She's done so much. She *knows* so much. It's amazing.

'I was really mad at her at first, but not anymore. And she loves you, she loves you *so* much. You've got to do this one thing for her. If not for her, then do it for me. She wasn't going to call you because she's so afraid, but I made her. Please meet her and then everything will be all right. I know it. I'm sure of it.'

'Cass? One, two, three?'

'Yes, absolutely. One, two, three.'

It was our secret code. We had worked it out when she was a child. It was our way of asking if everything was all right without having to say it, in case the wrong ears were listening.

'I'll meet her. But don't you know what she wants to talk about?'

She giggled. It was the most extraordinary thing. In the

middle of all that anxiety and dread came the holy sound of my daughter's silly laugh. I knew then for sure she really was okay.

'Veronica won't tell me! You still won't tell, will you?' From somewhere nearby, I heard Veronica say 'Nope' and *both* of them laughed. Like two girls jammed together into a phonebooth sharing the phone while talking to some boys.

'All right, put her back on. But Cass, for God's sake be careful. No matter how much you like her, she gets unbalanced sometimes. I love you. More than life. I'm so glad you're all right.'

'I'm fine, Dad. I swear! One, two, three.'

The phone changed hands again on their side, wherever the hell that was. 'Sam?'

'Where do you want to meet?'

'At the Tyndall house in Crane's View. Can you make it in two hours?'

'Yes. Veronica, don't do anything to her. I swear to God—'

'Never. She's a special girl. But don't bring anyone, Sam. *Don't* tell anyone.' Abruptly the phone went dead. That was all right though, because I couldn't catch my breath.

Snow began to fall ten minutes after I got on the road. Luckily most of the drive to Crane's View was on the turnpike because the stuff was beginning to stick with a vengeance.

Clutching the steering wheel as tightly as I could, my head locked in one position, I glared through the wind-shield and tried not to crash into everything. A mighty sixteen-wheel trailer truck bombed by in the fast lane, the jolt from its airstream slamming my car. I wanted to be that truck driver then. Oblivious to the weather, sure that my tons of truck and cargo would keep me glued to any road. The guy probably had country and western music howling from ten cranked-up speakers in his cab. He was probably singing 'Goodnight Irene' and steering with only one hand.

I hated Veronica for seducing a young, trusting woman into believing her love, that foul black soup, was really ambrosia she would willingly fill my cup with until she died. I pictured the two of them sitting in a grimy roadside diner somewhere, working on their fourth cups of thin coffee while Veronica hung her head and spun magnificent lies about what went wrong with our love. Cass, the great listener, would sit very still, but there would be tears in her eyes. When Veronica finished on some triumphantly tragic note, my converted daughter would reach over and tightly squeeze the other's hand.

Luckily my car hit a patch of ice and for a few blood-freezing seconds slid left, right, back to center. My mind burned clean of all Veronica thoughts. First get there. Concentrate on the road. Get there.

Snow was flying wildly all around when I drove into Crane's View. The scene would have been beautiful, worth a stop and a long look round, if the day had been different. As it was, I barely kept control of the car. Every few minutes it decided to ice skate so I had to keep the speed down to a crawl.

The day was already full of too many highs and lows but looking back now, one of the images that stays most firmly in my mind was driving down Elizabeth Street. A mile or so from the Tyndall house, I saw a lone figure trudging through the flying snow like a soldier on winter maneuvers. Hup. Hup. Hup. There was nothing else around – no cars, no people, the only sign of life a traffic light forlornly blinking its yellow warning to no one. Just this one person. What the hell were they doing, out walking in this blizzard? I couldn't help slowing even further to have a look at the hearty goof. Johnny Petangles. Wearing only a white dress shirt and trousers, bare hands and a Boston Red Sox baseball cap pulled down low. I loved him. Thank God for something normal today. Loony Johnny out on his daily rounds in the middle of a Yukon blow. His mouth was moving. I wondered what television advertisement he was repeating, what song he was singing to the wind and snow and arctic emptiness around us. Just Johnny and me out in the swirl. If I stopped to offer him a ride he would only look at me blankly and shake his head.

There were no cars on the street when I pulled up in front of the Tyndall house. The driveway went up at a slight angle and I didn't want to risk getting stuck so I parked directly in front.

When I got out the wind gusted snow into my face and made me close my eyes. I locked the car door and turned toward the house. Lights were on in the ground-floor rooms. I stood there, hoping to see something inside. Hoping to see my daughter standing at the window.

A scraping down the street announced a snow plow was on the way. It was so quiet otherwise that the sound of the blade on the pavement was remarkably loud and reassuring. Like Johnny Petangles out on his march, the snow plow doing its job said when this is all over, beyond this hour's fear is your every day and soon you can have it back again. I waited until the truck had passed and was ridiculously happy when the driver gave me a wave as he rumbled by.

I took a deep breath, made fists and started for the house. The fresh snow crunched beneath my boots. I was so hot from worry I could feel myself sweating beneath the heavy coat. I said to myself, Be calm. Hold your temper. Just go in there and get her back. Just get her back. Just get her back.

The brass doorknob turned smoothly in my hand.

I walked into the house and closed the door gently behind me. The hall floors shone with wax, the house was so cold my breath feathered out in plumes.

'Veronica?'

'In here.'

Her voice came from the living room. The room where they'd pissed on Johnny Petangles, the room where Pauline had carved on the wall. I walked in.

Sitting on the floor in the middle of the room was Pauline Ostrova.

Same red hair, same face, same clothes I had seen her wearing in an old photograph I kept framed on the wall in front of my desk. For a few seconds a hundred years long, everything I had known, lived, thought about for the last months dissolved. Everything I had believed was true wasn't. *She was alive!*

I was so overwhelmed by the apparition that it took more seconds to realize it wasn't Pauline, but Veronica made up so perfectly that she could have fooled anyone into believing it – for a short while.

She clapped her hands like a child and giggled. 'It worked! I can't wait to tell Cass! She said you'd never fall for it but you did. You thought I was her!'

I wanted to strangle her. 'Where is my daughter, Veronica?'

'Come on, Sam, give me some credit. For two seconds I had you. Did you see this?' She jumped up and ran to the wall where Pauline had carved the names. 'Look! Pauline did it—'

'Yes, Veronica. I saw it. Is that what this is about? Is that why I'm here, so you can show me some names cut into a goddamned *wall*?'

She turned away from me and touched the words. Her hand slid slowly down the white wall and dropped to her side. It was the most defeated gesture I had ever seen. She stood motionless. 'No, that's not why. But I didn't know you'd already seen it. It was going to be an extra surprise for you.' She walked back to where she had been sitting and dropped to the floor again. 'I have to tell you what I discovered. It's going to change your whole book, Sam. Do you know about John LePoint?'

I could barely contain myself and was just able to ask, 'No. Who is he?'

'Edward Durant Junior's cellmate at Sing Sing. He's still alive. I found him for you. He lives in Power, Maine. You have to talk to him. You *have* to.'

'I don't give a shit about the book, Veronica! I want my daughter. Just tell me where she is. Tell me and I won't say anything to anyone. No cops, nothing. Where–is–she?'

Her head dropped to her chest so I could only see the lush red hair spilling down, covering everything. Another wig, another trick. 'Why can't you ever just be yourself, Veronica? Why do you always have to lie or pretend you're other people?' Looking at her bent over like that, repentant again for yet another awful act, my anger took precedence over everything else.

Her head rose slowly and she looked at me with a crooked smile that gave away nothing. When she spoke, her voice was cool and far away. 'Because you were *the* one. The person I have loved and admired most. It began a long time ago and then for a little while, it was happening. We got so close I could smell it, I could feel it in the palm of my hand! God, God, God!' She shuddered and closed her eyes.

'When I realized I'd done it all wrong, *again*, I thought maybe I could transform myself into someone you would love. But I kept getting that wrong too, didn't I?' She touched her cheek and shrugged, defeated. 'I met Cass's mother. I followed her around one day and struck up a conversation in Bloomingdale's. About lip blush. About *mascara!* Jesus Christ, what a loser, Sam. What a stupid, vacuous loser she is! All Armani and half a brain. But you married *her*, didn't you?' She slammed her open hands on the floor. The slap echoed throughout the cavernous room.

The jolt to her body caused a small revolver to jump out of a dress pocket and fall on to the floor.

I stepped backward. Mustering my courage, I managed to whisper, 'Where is my daughter? Please.'

She picked up the pistol and put it in her lap. Then she took a deep breath and letting it out, her cheeks ballooned. 'At the Holiday Inn in Amerling. Room 113. I would never hurt her, Sam. *Never*.

'But it was the only way you'd talk to me. I saw it in your eyes the last time we were together. I thought, okay, I'll leave him alone now. But maybe I can still help him with his book. So I kept researching. Then I found out about LePoint and knew we had to talk again, just once. So I—' She tried to say something more, but the words died on the cold air.

Amerling was only two miles away. I could be there in ten minutes. I took a step towards the door. She stood up so quickly that I didn't have a chance to move. The gun was in her hand, pointed at my head.

'Stop there! You *have* to listen to this! I've been looking and looking. I wanted to help you so much that I stopped everything else. All I've been doing is research. And I found it! I found everything, Sam! Everything you need for your book. Talk to John LePoint. That's all I'm asking. I swear to God I'll leave you alone. Just promise you'll go talk to him—'

'I don't *care* about the book, Veronica. Burn it right now, right here on the floor, I don't give a damn. Let me go. Let me get my daughter and take her home.'

'The only people you love are your daughter and Pauline. The only ones. You can't love anyone else. Except yourself.

'But you know what? Your daughter likes me! She likes me a lot. That's what she said before I came over here. "I pray you and Dad work this out." I don't care if you believe that, but it's true. That's exactly what she said!'

I stabbed a finger at her. 'Oh, I believe you, but which *one* does she like? Huh? The real Veronica Lake, whoever *that* is, or one of those masks you carry around in your pocket like breath mints? Yeah! Breath mints, to cover up the smell—'

'Shut up! Stop it, Sam!' She turned the gun from me and put it under her chin. The dark metal against her pink skin. The dent it made. 'You can't love me? Fine. But I can haunt *you*. That's good. Second best. Good enough! You're going to watch this and I'll live in you forever!'

'Veronica! Don't do it! Please!'

Her face softened and she seemed to relax all over. But then she lurched violently forward. At first I thought she was throwing herself at me. I heard shattering glass and saw a great jet of blood shoot out the middle of her chest. As she staggered, she was hit again. Only then did I know she'd shot herself! She did it, she shot herself!

But that couldn't be because she had the gun under her chin and would have gone backward, not *forward*, like someone had given her a hard push from behind and the blood would have gone the other way and her pistol was so small so how could there be so much blood and why was it coming from the wrong way and . . .

After the second shot, her arms flew up. The pistol sailed out of her hand and hit me in the face. I twisted away as she pitched forward and slid a long way across the floor.

I went down and grabbed her. Her blood was everywhere, smears, gobs. It continued to pump out, still alive, deep red and shiny.

'Veronica!'

Her eyes fluttered and closed.

Deep and distant in my mind I knew someone outside had shot her but I could not move. I could not give up her body even if it meant a good chance of seeing who had done it.

I held her and looked at her face – half Pauline, half

Veronica. Then my mind cleared and I put my hand on her chest and felt soft ooze. No skin anymore. I was touching only warm slippery things and sharp snapped bones. I pulled my hand out and looked at the blood and viscera covering it.

I don't know how long I sat with Veronica's body in my arms. I spoke to her for a long time. I don't remember what I said.

When I was able, I lowered her gently to the floor and stood up. At the door, I turned and looked back. She lay in the middle of the room. The only thing keeping her company was Pauline's old love lines on the opposite wall. The two dead women in there together.

I walked down the hall and went outside. On the porch directly in front of the door was a bouquet of flowers exactly like the ones I had received earlier in Connecticut. They were colorful and fragile against the cold whiteness of the snow. I should have been frightened but wasn't. Could the murderer stand and watch me after having shot her? No, He was smarter than that. He would be driving out of town, slowly so as not to have an accident or chance trouble. I picked up the flowers and looked for the note. It said, 'Hi Sam! Now she won't bother you anymore. Your daughter is at the Amerling Holiday Inn, room 113. Go home and finish the book.'

I crumpled the note and dropped it on the porch. I didn't want to touch it again. He had shot her twice in the back and left me flowers. I knelt to pick the note up but stayed hunched down, the full effect of what had happened washing over and making me sick to my stomach.

The street was empty and silent. Darkness had come and the streetlamps lit small patches through the blowing snow. Lights were on in all the neighboring houses: people were watching television, talking, drinking scotch and enjoying the coziness of being at home on a snowy night.

232

I walked to my car and opening the door, switched the telephone on and called Frannie McCabe. I told him what had happened and that I was going to the motel to get Cass. He asked me to stay where I was until he got there. I said no, I had to get my daughter. I would return when I knew she was safe. He said he'd send someone to the hotel for her immediately but please stay where you are. I hung up.

The Holiday Inn glowed welcomingly. If I had been a traveler I would have been so happy to see its familiar sign.

When I found the room, fear squeezed my chest. I put my head against the door and knocked.

'Yes? Who is it?'

'Your dad.'

A very different kind of horror followed that day. Cassandra was traumatized by Veronica's death. She could not get over it, and despite being told the facts innumerable times, she still felt that my behavior towards Veronica forced her to be in that house, on that day, waiting for those bullets.

My daughter refused even to speak to me for three weeks and when she did was hostile and rude. When she finally agreed to meet, she insisted Ivan be in the room. The girl I had for so long thought was strong and perfect was no more and no less than a very smart and fragile teenager from a broken family who for years had been holding too many things inside. No longer. Veronica's death brought them all out.

Most of what Cass said to me was the absolute truth, which is always the hardest to bear. I had thought our love for each other was the only good, true thing in my life. The only relationship I had worked desperately hard to nourish and protect. That was only partly true. I had made big mistakes with her, many of them, and now my daughter did not hesitate describing them to me.

Today things are much better between us, but often when we are sitting together and I risk a peek at her when she isn't looking, I wonder about so much.

It turned out Veronica Lake had no family and her affairs were chaotic. When I discovered how few people knew her well I was deeply saddened. I willingly took on the job of setting everything straight – paying her debts, arranging the funeral, closing up the very peculiar shop that had been her life.

For a time I considered burying her in Crane's View but realized how much misery the town had caused her. It seemed she had never had peace in her life. Couldn't I do that for her now? Veronica often mentioned how much she loved the ocean and the towns far out on Long Island. After some inquiries and negotiating, I was able to find a small, rural cemetery for her not far from Bridgehampton.

Only Rocky Zaroka, Frannie, Magda and I attended her funeral on a bitter cold and colorless day. Cassandra wanted to come but her mother absolutely forbade it. The minister wore a pair of blue gloves with white reindeer on them when he said the final prayer. Watching him, I realized it was the kind of detail Veronica would have enjoyed.

Afterwards, Zaroka came over. 'Did she ever show you her photo album?'

Surprised, I shook my head.

'She only had one. It was photos of the view from her lovers' windows. Interesting, huh? The only pictures in there – no people, or landscapes. And you know she'd met so many people and been around the world so many times . . . But she only kept those photos.'

'Did she have a lot of lovers?'

'No. Not at all. There were a lot of pictures in the album, but only because she kept taking pictures as long as she was with the man. When she told me about you, I asked if

234

she had taken one from your window yet. She said no and that she hoped she never had to.'

'What does that mean?'

The expression on his face remained the same but his eyes filled with hatred.

Riding back up the Long Island Expressway towards Manhattan in McCabe's car, I asked if he remembered catching fireflies when we were young.

'Of course I remember – every kid does it.'

'But remember how easy it was to catch them? How *tame* they were?'

I was sitting in the backseat. Magda was in front but turned around, smiling. 'That's right. They really *were* tame. You just had to reach up and you could catch as many as you wanted.'

'But you never knew what to do with them once you had them. You'd hold them in your hand a while, or else put them in a bottle with wax paper over the top. But you knew they'd be dead by the next morning if you kept them in there.' I looked out the window. 'But we still went out every summer and caught them, didn't we?

'That's what it was like with Veronica. In the beginning, she glowed – like a firefly and I really *wanted* to hold her. But when I had her, I didn't know what to do. I've *never* known what to do with women. Three marriages? How can you be married three times and not learn something?'

'Sam, don't get all nostalgic about Veronica, huh? The woman kidnapped your daughter!'

'I know. But no matter what happened, it was my fault too. I knew the minute we met she was going to be a handful. Why didn't I just leave her alone? How long does it take to learn to keep our hands in our pockets? Learn to just *watch* things fly around, out there in the world where they belong?'

Snow had begun to fall again. I watched it. My heart felt like it weighed a million tons. 'I blew it, Frannie. I'm not even talking about Veronica. I'm talking about her *and* Cass *and* three wives . . . Yoo hoo – how come none of this is working? How come everyone is saying pretty much the same thing? None of it nice, all of it true. How come everyone I know is on the other side of this glass?'

Edward Durant collapsed the afternoon of Veronica's death. On coming to, he was barely able to call an ambulance. In the hospital they discovered there were new things wrong with his body, all of them working in concert to kill him as quickly as possible.

I visited him in his hospital room where we talked for hours and hours about Cass and what I could do to reconcile us. I realized his intense interest in my situation was due to his own failure with his son. With so little energy in his body, he would still grab my hand, look at me with feverish eyes and say, 'Fix it! Use whatever you have. It's the only thing that matters, Sam.'

The investigation into Veronica's death was long and useless. All they found was two spent shells from a deer rifle. Nothing else. But I was questioned until I thought I would go mad and, good cop that he was, McCabe didn't cut any corners for me. He wanted to know everything that happened that afternoon, but whatever I remembered didn't seem to help at all. God knows I *wanted* to help, but certain memories stuck while others fled. How had Veronica gotten into the house? I didn't know. I remembered the way she fell, but not the sound of the two shots. Or if I saw anyone at the window behind her. I was not a good witness. More than once I saw both derision and disgust in my friend's face. I could understand why and that made me feel worse.

I had dinner one night with Frannie and Magda after

Veronica's funeral. It was awkward and much too quiet to do any of us any good. I left early feeling failed and alone.

The end of this story is full of ironies, but the greatest for me was that my estranged daughter saved me. Naturally after Veronica's death I thought almost nothing of the book. I knew *he* was out there waiting, but I heard nothing from him after the murder. Which was good because despite the unspoken ultimatum he had given, I could not work.

But once during a particularly difficult meeting with Cass, she asked me how the book was going. It was the first time she had mentioned it and it took me offguard. I stared at her as if I didn't know what she was talking about, then admitted I hadn't done any writing since that day.

'So it was for nothing? Veronica did all that work for your book and found out whatever her big secret was but now you're not going to finish it? You *have* to, Dad! You can't stop.'

I would like to say I went back to work with renewed purpose. But the truth is I went back to work because of the threatening look in my daughter's eye and nothing more.

I re-read the manuscript and all the notes I had taken. I listened to the tapes and stared out the window and watched as spring arrived in Connecticut. Somewhere along the line the professional writer in me took over and told me what to do. Without telling anyone, I began working day and night. One rainy afternoon I contacted the man Veronica had told me was Edward Durant's cellmate at Sing Sing prison and arranged a meeting.

John LePoint lived in a town in Maine very much like Crane's View. I arrived early for our meeting and spent an hour sitting in a run-down coffee shop wondering what was the name of this town's Pauline Ostrova – its wild girl with too many brains for her own good and consequently, a fifty-fifty chance her life would be tragic.

LePoint turned out to be a jolly old man in size 14 shoes who spoke about his life of crime as if it were one big joke. He regaled me with stories about break-ins and assaults, great meals and women paid for with stolen money, prison life and some of the oddballs he had known along the way. But he was 'retired' now. He had a pregnant cat and a skinny son who sent him money. There was a pain in the ass neighbor who he wouldn't mind seeing dead, but he was too old for that kind of shit now and besides, in jail they didn't let you choose which channel you wanted to watch on TV.

I asked him repeatedly about Edward Durant, but he only waved his hand dismissively as if the subject wasn't worth discussing. I persisted and after getting up for the sixth time for more beer, he told me the story.

They were together only two weeks. Durant's former cellmate was moved for an unknown reason and LePoint arrived in time to witness Edward's end.

I stayed in Maine for two days and ended up paying LePoint five hundred dollars to answer all of my questions. His story never varied. He said when you spend most of your life behind bars, you develop a hell of a good memory because about all you *can* do there is keep running a soft cloth over your memories so they stay shiny.

On the drive back from Maine, I stopped in Freeport and wandered around the L. L. Bean store until a salesman came up and gently asked if he could help. Coming out of my deep daze, I looked at a tent that was immediately to my right and said I needed that. It sits in my garage now, the box never opened. I have never owned a tent but I will keep it to remind me.

When I could no longer contain it, I pulled off the road and called Frannie McCabe. I told him LePoint's story.

When I was finished, his only response was 'Saying the word "fire" won't burn your mouth.'

'What do you mean?'

'If that's the truth, then that's what it is. I'll come visit you as soon as I can. I got some things to tell you. But what LePoint said makes sense. Oh, and Sam? We set the date. Gonna be a June wedding. Whaddya think?'

I wrote throughout the spring and into the early summer. Always vigilant, always alert towards what was going on around me. More than ever before. I had to finish the book fast and turn it in. Frannie explained why and he was right. He said there was probably more danger now that before, despite what we knew.

So much of what I had learned I could use, but it all needed turning. Sometimes 180 degrees. McCabe helped the whole way. Following his instructions, I never spoke to him on the phone in my house.

Cass and I didn't see much of each other. I knew I had to leave her alone until she was ready but I ached for her. Every time the telephone rang, my hope jumped.

All that spring Durant was in and out of the hospital. He was in the last stages of his illness, but despite that he held on like a terrier. When the doctors admitted there was nothing more they could do for him, he said he wanted to go home and die there. They could not stop him.

He refused to let me visit because he said he looked too dead for his own good. We spoke often on the phone and despite his description, at least his voice sounded as robust as ever. Two days after I finished the book, expressed copies to my agent and editor, and verified they had received them, I called to tell Edward.

'That is *spectacular*, Sam! What a surprise! I had no idea ... You have to give me a copy so I can at least *start* to read it before I die. I can't tell you ... Oh, that's the best news I've had.

'Look, how about coming over for dinner tomorrow night? Bring the manuscript and we'll eat like French kings. Fuck what my doctors say! We'll drink every bottle of wine I've got left. This is a great occasion!'

The three of them were waiting in the driveway when I arrived. His two dogs wore small top hats held in place with rubber bands under their chins. Edward had on a normal-sized one which contrasted comically with the anthracite blue robe and pajamas he was wearing. He leaned heavily on an aluminum walker. His face was sunken and wan but his eyes were huge and lit like a child's on Christmas morning. He reached down slowly and picked up a bottle of champagne he had at his feet. He held it straight out in the air.

'Hail the conquering hero! The Germans would call you a *Dichter*. The greatest praise for a man of letters. Welcome!'

'This is quite a greeting.'

'And well deserved! I wanted to hire the Grambling marching band but they were already booked. Come on, come into the house. Is that it?'

I had the manuscript in a gray cardboard box under my arm. It was four hundred and seventeen pages long. Not so long. Not as long as I had once thought it would be.

'Yes.'

'Fantastic!' He handed me the bottle and slowly led the way into the house, the dogs waddling eagerly behind him.

There were flowers everywhere. It looked like a greenhouse of the most exotic, colorful flowers I had ever seen. All of the rooms smelled like paradise.

'All I need in here is Rima the Bird Girl to make it complete. Don't mind the flowers. It's just nice to have them to look at these days. They remind me of better things. Sit down. Do you want some champagne or a drink?'

'Champagne would be fine.'

He started to open the bottle but stopped and, faltering, closed his eyes tightly in pain. I got to him just in time and helped him over to the couch.

'Damn it! I swore I wasn't going to let that happen. I asked my body for just one night and then it could do whatever the hell it wanted. We have to celebrate!'

I opened the bottle and poured into two beautiful crystal glasses on the coffee table. The same table where he had shown me the murderer's news clippings so many months ago. I handed him a glass.

'I'm sorry I can't stand right now, but here's to you, Sam Bayer. Here's to you and your book and a life that I hope brings you great surprises and much love.' He took a sip and licked his bottom lip. 'Ahh! Almost perfect. My tongue is off these days, but who can blame it? All these pills and medicines they have me swallowing ... May I?' He gestured with his glass towards the gray box now sitting on the table.

'Sure.' I drank. The sweet bubbles burned the back of my throat and made me want to burp. I watched as he took the box on to his lap and smiled.

'My God, it's really done. This is *it!* Do you mind if I take a quick look? I can hardly wait.'

'Go ahead.'

He pulled off the top of the box and gently lifted out the manuscript. 'It's big! Heavy! How many pages is it?'

'A little over four hundred.'

'That'll be, what, about three hundred and fifty pages when it's printed?'

'Something like that.'

'A good size. And that title! A great title, Sam. Provocative, mysterious. It really catches you.'

'Thanks.'

He lifted off the title page and saw the dedication page. His eyes widened and he looked at me, perplexed. 'Veronica? You dedicated it to *Veronica*?'

I leaned forward. 'Yes. Don't you think it's appropriate? She died for the book, Edward. Who did you think I would dedicate it to?'

'No, you're right! It's entirely appropriate. Don't forget, I'm a father, my friend. This *is* Edward's story and I only thought . . . Oh, it doesn't matter. We've got the *book*, right? That's what's important. The whole book is here and it's finished! And *you* did it.'

Lifting off the dedication page to the first page of text, he began to read. As his eyes moved across my words, his smile fell slowly. I don't know how far he got. It didn't matter because everything was in the first sentence. Everything that mattered.

The day after Edward Durant Junior murdered Pauline Ostrova, Club Soda Johnny Petangles went around Crane's View writing "Hi Pauline!" in two-foot tall letters on everything he could find.

'What is this, Sam?'

'It's the story of your son and Pauline. Just not the story you wanted anyone to *know*. But it's the truth, Edward, and both of us know it.'

'How can you say that? After everything—'

'I'll say it too so you can hear it in stereo, Counselor.' McCabe came in from the kitchen, eating an olive. 'You should see what he's got in there for dinner, Sam. You're going to leave this house a fat man tonight.'

Durant looked stonily at McCabe but didn't ask how he had gotten in.

Frannie sat down next to me and slapped my knee. 'Do you want to hear the short version or the long, Mr Durant? Let me give mine first.

'I started thinking real hard when Cassandra disappeared and you suddenly knew a lot more things about what was happening to her than me. I'm a competitive man. Competitors are suspicious. If they lose, they want to know *why*.

'Then one day I heard this heavy metal song on the radio. You know heavy metal music? The group's called Rage Against the Machine. There was this line in one of their songs: "Rally round the family with a pocket full of shells." That got me thinking even more, and I decided to start looking around. One of the places I looked was here, *very* thoroughly, while you were in the hospital.'

'You went through my *house*? Did you have a search warrant?'

'No, but I had a flashlight.'

Durant snorted. 'Then whatever you found is inadmissible.'

'I know that, but I still found it.'

'What? What did you find?' Durant shifted in his seat, his eyes crinkling in pain.

'Bills mostly. Phone bills with calls to hotels where it just so happened Veronica Lake was staying, even one to Vienna! A monthly bill from your trap and skeet club where they go on and on about what a *marvelous* marksman you are. What else? Master Charge receipts for a round trip plane ticket to LA the day before a certain movie producer got shot there. Little things mostly, but you know how they add up. Especially when you're suspicious.

'Then I found a big one which pretty much clinched it for me. A bill from the Silent Running Services in New York. Famous place. Especially if you're a cop and know about businesses like that who cater to the paranoia of the rich and famous. Among other things, the company sells machinery for illegal phone tapping. So I got a guy to take a look at Sam's phones and Bingo! Guess what I found? Why would you of all people tap Sam's phone? I thought you guys were working together.'

Before Durant had a chance to reply, I said, 'John LePoint. Do you know who that is?'

He looked at me but did not move or speak.

'He was your son's cellmate at Sing Sing.'

'No he wasn't. A rapist named Bobo Cleff was.'

'Until two weeks before Edward died. Then Cleff was transferred and they moved LePoint in. I spoke with him. He said Edward confessed to Pauline's murder two days before he died.

'He said they'd had a fight about *you*. Pauline told him that you had tried to seduce her and ... he hit her. He killed her.

'But you knew, didn't you? *Didn't you, Edward*? All these years you knew that because you tried to *screw* your son's wife, he ended up killing her. Plain and simple. He kills Pauline, and you kill Veronica and David Cadmus thirty years later for no reason other than to make him look innocent. But he *wasn't* innocent! Oh no, Edward killed her! He beat her up, threw her in the river to drown and then ran away. That's the real story, you bastard! That's what my book says. You wanted his story? Well, you got it. The whole, despicable truth—' I tried to say more, but my throat closed and I had begun to cry. For all of them and for my own exhaustion. For all the dead.

'Did you kill those other people too? The one in Missouri, the one in—' I threw a hand in the air. I couldn't finish the sentence.

Durant looked offended. 'I killed no one else! You mean those newspaper clippings I showed you that day? I researched similar murders over the years. Sifted through and chose those. There were so many similarities between the three that of course it looked like there was a pattern. Good hard evidence. I needed to convince you, Sam. And I did.' He tried to keep his face blank but I could see, I could tell he was resisting a smile.

Frannie elbowed me. 'Tell him what else LePoint said.'

Durant ignored McCabe and stared at me. There was nothing in the room then but eyes.

Annoyed by the standoff, McCabe blurted, 'Then *I* will. LePoint said your son didn't hang himself. He was murdered by one of Gordon Cadmus's people.'

Durant let out a howl that, even today, freezes me to think of it. A canine cry thirty years long of remorse, absolution, unimaginable pain and gratitude. The room could not hold the sound. When he stopped, there was a silence – total, absolute silence. He began to cough and when he put his hands to his mouth, a trickle of blood spilled up over them and down the front of his robe. None of us moved.

When he was able to speak again, Durant's voice was a skate scratching across ice. 'I knew it! I knew it the whole time! I knew you would find it, Sam.'

'Why did you kill Veronica, Edward?'

Again, his voice became indignant. 'Because she was a threat! She threatened everything. Every time she came into your life again she stopped everything. Nothing was getting done! When she lied about having contact with the killer I knew that was the end. She was becoming dangerous and who knew what she'd do *next*?'

'And David Cadmus?' Frannie's voice was low and quiet. He held the champagne cork against his chin.

Durant looked only at me. 'At first, killing him was only part of my plan to get you moving on the book. But after what you've just said? It was correct. An eye for an eye, Sam. The sins of the father. "*Cave ignoscas*." Beware of forgiving. I always knew Gordon Cadmus was involved. That's why I was a good lawyer. *Instinct*.' His face was triumphant. 'Are we ready to eat? There's so much food.'

'That's it? That's all you have to *say*? You killed two people, just so I'd write a *fucking book*?'

He looked at me pityingly. 'It's not a book, Sam. It's my saving grace. It *isn't* the book I hoped for, but just knowing after all these years that Edward didn't kill himself . . . It's a miracle.' He stood up, took hold of the walker and slowly shuffled toward the kitchen. For the first time, beside the scent of the flowers, I could smell the delicious aromas of food. Over his shoulder, Durant called out, 'Have a glass of champagne, Frannie. I'll be back in a minute.'

I looked at my shoes. I heard one of the dogs' ragged breath. I heard Durant shuffling pots in the kitchen.

'Did you hear that scream, Sam? I told you that old man would have killed you too if he'd known what you were writing. That's why I said finish the book and turn it in before you show him. Now there's nothing he can do.' Frannie filled the glass and took a sip. 'I hate champagne. It always reminds me of the feeling in my foot when it falls asleep.'

Almost whispering I said, 'Why did you lie to him? LePoint never said Gordon Cadmus had Edward killed! He said he committed suicide.'

Frannie rolled the empty glass between his palms. 'That's true, but it worked. We got our confession. Nothing else we can do with him. He's too dead to arrest. Plus I'd love to see the look on his face when he reads your book and finds out the truth. Sur-prise!'

'*Cave ignoscas*.'

McCabe snorted. 'Yeah, right. *Cave ignoscas*, mother-fucker.'

Durant re-appeared at the kitchen door wearing two bright red and yellow oven mitts. He was beaming. Not a maniac's smile either. It was the smile of a man who believed no matter what, nothing could touch him because the truth had set him free.

'So what happens now, Frannie? Are you going to arrest me? I'll probably be dead before they indict.'

'I know that. What happens now, Edward? You're going to die and go to hell.'

'True. But let's eat dinner first.'

EPILOGUE

For almost two years I have had trouble sleeping. It has nothing to do with bad dreams because usually I don't dream at all. Since Veronica died, some part of my body or psyche or something else mine and unknown is constantly *on*. I don't know what to make of it and I suppose if I went to an analyst they would have an answer. Maybe it would help but I haven't gone for that help because there's also the very real possibility they would only confuse me more which would be disastrous.

So I wake five times a night and stare into the off. It's all right. I've gotten used to it. Until recently I've been working so hard and so late that I'm exhausted by the time I get into bed. I manage to snatch a few hours of real sleep before the gremlins start to shake me awake.

But I was finished now and for the past week I had done little but walk around the house and stare out various windows for long times. That night I had gone to bed early and was a hundred fathoms deep when I heard the voice. Soft but insistent, it tore through the fabric of sleep, reached a large hand in and pulled me back to the surface. Once there, I slowly realized someone was in bed with me, gently tugging on my shoulder. The voice was a woman's but in those seconds of confusion before really waking I fought with it, thinking 'Woman? What woman? There hasn't been a woman here, in this bed since—' *That* did it. Since anything is possible in that no man's land between sleep and coherence, my eyes shot open when I abruptly thought, '*Veronica? Veronica's here in bed with me?*'

I whipped my head to the side and saw a familiar face, but it wasn't hers and for a moment my soul sank when it remembered everything.

'Dad, wake up! Get up!'

Cass was so close to me that I felt her body's warmth. I smelled her cologne, the intimate aroma of *her*. It was all bewildering because she hadn't gotten into bed with me in years.

'Cass? Yes? What's the matter?'

'I read it, Dad. I just finished the whole book!'

'I didn't even know you were here.'

'I let myself in. Oh Dad, why didn't you tell me what you were writing? I saw it on your desk and couldn't believe it. I couldn't *believe* it.'

'No one knows. I finished a couple of days ago. I wanted to let it sit a while before I went back to have a look.' I reached over to the night table for a cigarette.

Cass frowned. 'You told me you were going to stop.'

I dropped the cig on the floor. 'Now I have to stop. I made a deal with myself that I could smoke until I was finished. Now I don't have that excuse.' I turned over so I could see her better. I needed to see the first expression on her face after I asked. 'What did you think? Did you like it?'

'I loved it! It's the best book you've ever written. No question about it. But it's so different. It's not like anything you've ever done. It's ... It's *simple*, do you know what I mean? There's nothing wasted, nothing showy. It just a story of this woman's life and you move so fluidly from chapter to chapter that it's just one beautifully rounded ... ball. No showy stuff. Just this vivid and strange life. You caught it, Dad. You really caught the whole thing.'

'I thought that was enough.'

'I have to read it again. I have to read it slowly because I was rushing through and I know I missed a lot. But—'

'But what?'

'But I wanted to know what happened. That's a stupid thing to say, isn't it?'

'That's where I was when I'd go out of town all those times. I was doing research. I've never done so much in my whole life. I am now the world's leading authority on the life of Veronica Lake.'

'She loved your work so much. She would have been so proud to know this. You wrote her biography. It's your best book, Dad. The absolute best.'

She slid closer to me and I put my arms around her. We lay together in silence. I'm sure both of us were thinking our separate thoughts about Veronica.

Morning and the rest of life were far away. For now it was good to lie awake and dream of a life that, like a flare shot into the night, had glittered and fled on its own singular arc into the sky and then was gone.

Also available in Indigo paperback

The Marriage of Sticks

JONATHAN CARROLL

'Just the smallest twist of the dial away from normal – one click – and everything we know for certain vanishes.'

Returning to her class reunion after fifteen years, Miranda Romanac has her heart set on meeting James Stillman once again. Her first boyfriend, her life's never quite measured up to the ideal he represented for her. She is devastated, therefore, to learn of his death three years before, in a car crash.

Her life settles back into its routine in New York, but things start to change when she meets the fabulous Frances Hatch, mistress of many of the great artists in Paris in the twenties. At the same time, Miranda starts an affair with Hugh, a married man. Then she sees James Stillman again, waving to her across the street. Is it possible? Oh yes, and things are just beginning for her . . . .

£6.99   ISBN 0 575 40249 0